PATHOLOGICAL SINNER

RYKOV SINNERS

BOOK ONE

JACLIN MARIE

Line Editing done by Britney Waldrop Edits
Copy Editing and Proof Reading done by Antonia Salazar from AMS Editing
Physical Cover and E-Book Cover done by Ama from After Dark Cover Designs

ISBN: 979-8-9916373-6-7

This story contains mentions of abuse (physical, mental, sexual), graphic sex with scenes that contain gun play, primal play, and dubiously consensual sex, forced marriage, child abuse, torture, blood, organized crime, etc.

If any of these topics are triggering for you then I suggest not to move forward with this book. Slade Russo is not the hero or the good guy. He is very much the bad guy in this book and he makes that very clear. He isn't just a red flag, he is the blackest flag there is!

But if you guys love a good morally gray character then I can't wait for you to meet Slade!

PLAYLIST

TELESCOPE	**TWXN, LL CLAWZ**
LIKE HIM	**TYLER, THE CREATOR**
NUN ID CHANGE	**YEAT**
FLOKI X THE LOST SOUL	**LAJNO**
DO I WANNA KNOW?	**ARCTIC MONKEYS**
EVIL JORDAN	**PLAYBOI CARTI**
MARCELINE	**LIL GOD DAN**
SOUTHBOUND	**ARTEMAS**
ANGEL	**MASSIVE ATTACK**
LAUGH NOW CRY LATER	**MAREUX**
UNFAIR	**THE NEIGHBORHOOD**
U.N.E.N.O.	**ROCKO**

Isabella

He was just suppose to be my roommate. I never thought
that accepting his offer was going to have me questioned
by the police and on the next flight to Russia.
Slade was a quiet and introverted individual like myself
but in reality he was just hiding his true colors.
He's a pathological sinner who will doing anything to get
what he wants.
And his eyes are set on me.

Slade

I was on a mission when I first saw her. I knew that she
was going to be perfect for my plan.
An obedient little book worm who's going to help me win
the crown.
I shouldn't have acted on impulse but I never knew how
to control myself.
Living in a world full of darkness and blood made me
different from the rest.
Isabella will soon learn that.

To the girls who love a Russian man with a filthy mouth,
Slade's waiting for you.

PROLOGUE
SLADE

I knew when I first saw her walk through the busy streets of New York, her head in a book, that she was going to play an important role in my plan to get the crown.

Some might say my task is easy, but I prefer the missions where I can shut off my mind and not think. The ones where I can take a line and blackout before shooting up an entire office building.

This one, this one is a little bit tricky.

It's a Friday night in Manhattan.

The city is alive per usual.

College students are out partying, friends are watching the game, couples are out on a date night, and tourists are in Times Square getting lost.

I've always liked watching, it's been my thing since I

was a kid. Being the quiet one in my family had its benefits.

I'd learn as I watched and that always gave me an advantage.

Tonight, I have to kill a club owner near Times Square. I'm getting paid $200K for this, which honestly means nothing to me since I've had more than that to my name since I was a baby.

I just like killing for the rush. The need to feel something when I don't.

I could kill for my family, but I try to avoid them as much as possible.

Currently, I'm sitting on top of a building, waiting for the owner of the club to arrive. It's pretty early in the night, around 10 p.m. so nothing much is happening.

The club is called 2nd Floor and the owner's name is Mitch Heck. He runs a women's trafficking organization under the club so I'm excited to have a little bit of fun killing him.

Most of the people I eliminate are bad but every once in a while, I do have to kill an innocent. They either get in the way, or they just frustrate me so I end up acting on impulse and going for the kill.

While waiting for Mitch to show up, I'm watching the streets, looking at the city line, and also keeping my eyes on who enters the club.

My phone starts buzzing in my pocket. I take it out and roll my eyes at the caller ID.

"Yea?" My ski mask muffles my voice.

"What are you doing, *mladshiy brat*?" my older brother Landon asks.

He doesn't call me as much as my other older brother, Ryker.

But Landon gets off on annoying me.

"What do you think I'm doing? It's a Friday night. I'm working," I say while staring at the door.

"Same shit, different day with you. Don't you ever get bored?"

"I don't know. Don't you get bored stalking your ex on Instagram?"

Landon Rykov has been obsessed with his ex from high school for more than six years. He doesn't know when to give up. He hasn't even touched a girl since her because he's that fucking dedicated to her.

He's more pussy whipped than he was when he was in high school dating her.

"Don't talk about her," Landon says in a low, almost threatening tone, but none of my family scares me.

There's only one person who did and he's dead now.

"Yea, whatever," I say as I notice a guy following a girl on the street as she walks past the club.

The guy is wearing a baseball cap and a hood to cover his features so I can't see his face. The girl has long brown wavy hair. She is wearing a leather jacket and blue jeans, her eyes stuck on a page in the book she's reading.

How stupid can someone be, walking around the streets of New York with their head in a book while a man is following them?

"Did you hear a single thing I said?" Landon asks in an annoyed tone.

"Got to go, Lan. My target just arrived." I hang up and stuff the phone in my pocket before throwing my hood up.

I jog across the top of the building, stalking the guy who's following the idiot with her nose stuck in a book. She has no fucking clue that's she's about to become someone's target.

The guy pushes the girl into the alleyway, and she screams. He cuts her off with a palm to her mouth as he pulls her deeper into the alleyway.

Her book drops while she tries her best to push him off and fight but it's no use.

She is very slim and he has muscle packed onto him. I search for a way down. There's a ladder at the very end of the alleyway.

I can hear her struggling against him, begging him to let her go but he just laughs.

After I get down the ladder, I take my gun out while walking towards them in unhurried steps. When I stand behind the guy, the girl's eyes widen as she stares at me.

She stares at me as if I'm the one who's the real danger instead of her tormentor.

Maybe because she can only see my eyes.

My mom always said that my eyes were the scariest thing about me.

They are like a dark void with nothing in them and the scar I have doesn't help either.

I strike the gun against the guy's head. He winces, letting go of the girl before turning around.

He raises a hand to fight but I slam my gun against the side of his face. He falls limp to the floor.

He lies unconscious while the girl has a petrified look in her eyes and breathes heavily.

I tower over her as she stares up at me with those innocent doe eyes. She's probably around 5'6 while I'm 6'2. Her face is dotted with freckles and she has long eyelashes along with plump lips.

I step closer to her, and she flinches before pressing her back against the wall. I'm towering over her, tilting my chin down as I keep eye contact with her.

She's pretty.

Really fucking pretty.

She's the kind of pretty that makes you want to stop in your tracks and worship her.

She opens her mouth slightly and takes a deep breath again before saying, "Please don't hurt me." Her voice is soft and she sounds younger than I expected.

I lean in closer to breathe in her scent.

She smells sweet like vanilla, and all of a sudden, I want to get on my knees in front of her and find out what she tastes like.

My dick twitches and I refrain from groaning.

"I'll give you money or anything you want. I don't want any issues, please just let me go," she begs with tears forming in her eyes and now I'm starting to think about ways to make her beg for other things. "I'll give you anything please just let me go." A tear falls and I can't help but reach out and wipe her cheek.

She flinches and keeps her eyes on me as I tilt her head up, inspecting every little freckle on her face.

They are like stars decorating her skin.

An alarm sounds on my phone, letting me know that there's movement in Mitch's office.

I need to go.

I almost forgot about the main objective of tonight when her eyes catch mine.

I hold back a groan before backing away from her.

I grab her book from the ground.

Unrecognizable is the title and there is a vine wrapped about a broken concrete heart. If I had to guess, I would assume it is some sort of fiction book.

Thriller? Romance? Historical? Mystery?

I wish I could just say fuck it to this mission and follow her to find out more about her.

I hand her the book, and her fingers graze mine, shocks denoting beneath my skin as she clenches onto the book and pulls away.

She watches me as I back away from her. I motion my head for her to leave, and she takes it as her cue to run like her life depends on it.

Doesn't matter though because I'll get to her again.

I'll find out who she is and all her likes and dislikes.

I'll figure out who her family is and what they do.

I will know everything there is to know about the little book worm before making her the perfect role in my plan.

1

ISABELLA

When I moved to New York, I knew how busy and crowded it was going to be. I wasn't worried unless I had to be near Times Square, the busiest area in New York in my opinion.

So, I do my best to steer clear of that area, even if it means taking the long way home to avoid going through the crowds of people there.

When I told Grams that I was going to be moving to New York, she started freaking out even though the drive between us wouldn't be that far away.

She lives in New Jersey. It's maybe a two-hour drive from Manhattan to her house.

I remember when I first moved here she was so worried I'd get lost in the city despite how many times I've visited New York when I still lived with my grandparents and parents.

I'm on the phone with her now and she's making a big deal about how I just got kicked out of my apartment.

The manager of the building I live in told me he's evicting everyone since they are rebuilding. So for the past week I've just been trying to find a new place or at least a new person to room with.

"You should sue, Bella. They cannot just kick you out of your home," Gram says, but she doesn't understand how renting works.

She's only ever owned since her first ever big purchase was her house. "I wish I could, Gram, but it doesn't work like that. What am I going to sue him for? He is giving me a month before I have to find a new place."

"See this is why you should live here with me and find a job nearby. You wouldn't even have to worry about rent, Bella," she lectures. "And from what you told me last week it sounds like New York isn't safe at all. What if someone killed you in that alleyway?"

Grams brings up me moving in with her all the time, but this week, she has brought it up to me at least once a day.

I knew I shouldn't have told her about the alleyway incident. I don't want her to worry about me.

Just thinking about what happened, the way the masked man stared at me, with death in his eyes, makes me have nightmares. It's all I've been dreaming about.

"I'm fine. I keep telling you. Right now I'm going to

look at an apartment. It's way nicer than mine and closer to my job so I think this will be better for me."

"Would you have a roommate?"

"Yes. I'm going to meet him right now. I'm actually almost at the apartment, so I'll call you after to let you know how it goes, okay?"

"We aren't done with this conversation, Bella. Call me as soon as you're done," Gram says.

We say our goodbyes as I walk towards the entrance of the building.

The lobby is nice with black accents and dimmed lights. There is a coffee machine and a doorman along with other small amenities.

It's hard to believe that this place is cheaper than the building I'm about to get kicked out of.

I walk up to the front desk and the receptionist greets me with a smile. "Hi, I'm meeting with Slade Rykov. He's on floor seven and apartment number sixteen."

"Oh yes, Mr. Rykov. He told me he was expecting someone today. What's your name, honey?" she asks as she holds the desk phone to her ear.

"Isabella Rossi."

She nods and dials numbers on the phone. "Hello, Mr. Rykov, I have a guest here to see you. Her name is Isabella Rossi." She nods. "Perfect, I will be sending her up." She puts the phone back on the cradle. "You can go to the elevator. Press the seventh button and you'll find his apartment number on that floor."

I thank her before leaving her desk. My nerves start to set in as I wait in the elevator, the numbers slowly going up.

I clench my hands and take a deep breath when the elevator stops. I walk out and look at the apartment numbers as I pass by them. When I get to apartment sixteen, I knock and hold my breath as I wait for him.

It's quiet on the other side of the door and I wonder if anyone is in there but then the door opens.

The first thing I notice about him is his eyes.

They give me deja vu as if I've seen his eyes somewhere before. They are like a black void with nothing in them. No emotion, no reaction, nothing.

And then I notice the long scar that starts from his eyebrow and goes down to his cheek.

I don't stare at his scar for too long because I don't want to be rude so instead I put on a small smile. "Slade?"

He nods and opens his door wider.

I walk in, my heart beating so hard and fast I feel like it's going to burst out of my chest. He closes the door behind me as I glance around the apartment. For a guy's apartment, it's pretty clean.

"Feel free to walk around. If you have any questions let me know," Slade says, his voice deep and calm with a hint of an accent that I can't place.

Slade goes to the kitchen and I'm assuming continues what he was doing. He has a black hoodie sitting on the kitchen island, and it seems like he's trying to get a stain out. He has a bottle of bleach near the sink with paper towels, stained with red.

I admire the kitchen. It has white cabinets and countertops, a stainless steel fridge and high top chairs around the island. In the living room, there is a big white cloud couch with a black blanket laying on the side. On the coffee table, he has a few books, some of them have bookmarks in them which makes me assume he reads.

He has a bookshelf next to the window and a couch in the center of the living room. There is a TV mounted to the wall in front of the couch.

Just from seeing the kitchen and the living room, I'd assume that this apartment was more than just two grand to rent out one bedroom. I feel like I should be paying more than five grand.

Slade is still scrubbing and washing his hoodie, and red liquid drips into the sink.

"Hard to get that out?" I ask, and his eyes meet mine.

Slade is a guy that every girl wishes would kidnap her. He has very short hair, close to a buzz cut, long muscular arms that are covered in tattoos, and a sharp jaw that looks like it would cut your finger.

You can tell he goes to the gym and takes care of his body.

"No. Do you need something?" He raises an eyebrow, and I feel butterflies in my stomach.

I shake my head. "No. Everything looks really nice here. Where's the bedroom?"

He rests the hoodie on the sink and shuts off the tap. I follow him down the hallway, and he opens one of the doors. The empty bedroom has its own closet and enough space for me to fit my books.

"The bathroom, washer and dryer are across the way. But this would be your room."

This all seems too good to be true.

"How much did you say it was again?"

"About $2500," he says, crossing his arms, making his arms appear bigger than before.

I try my best to keep eye contact, but it seems like that's even worse.

Butterflies fill my stomach and chills run down my arms as he stares down at me with those dark intense eyes.

"That's perfect. Would I have to give you a deposit and how soon could I move in?"

"Just next month's rent since this month is already paid for. You can move in whenever." He shrugs.

I nod and lick my bottom lip. His eyes go down to my lips before meeting my eyes again. "Okay, I'll take it," I say, giving him a small smile.

"Good, then I'll just get your information and few signatures from you," he says before walking out of the room. I follow after him. He goes through a drawer in the kitchen and hands a form to me. "While you fill that out, I do want to say there are a few rules and things you should know."

"Okay."

"I don't usually allow people over. I like my privacy. So if you want to invite someone over just ask me first."

Understandable since it's not my place. He's just letting me live here for super cheap.

"I usually come home pretty late. You can order in food or eat anything I bring home. You can grocery shop but I usually do that so if you want me to get anything let me know. I'm not usually strict with anything else. Just make sure to clean up after yourself, do your dishes, laundry, and keep the place clean." His list all seems pretty reasonable to me. "And lastly, no going in the room down the hall. That's my room and it's off limits. If you need something from me, just knock on my door or text me. Don't go in there."

I gulp and nod.

He made it seem like a threat or like he's hiding something but maybe I'm just being paranoid. I mean I've never shared an apartment with a guy. All of my past roommates have been girls.

"Okay that doesn't sound like a problem. I'll probably start packing my stuff tonight and hopefully move in by next week."

He nods. "Do you have my number saved?"

"Yea, I got it."

"Text me when you're going to come over again and I'll give you a key."

I just hope that having a cheap apartment this nice doesn't bite me in the ass.

2

ISABELLA

"I don't know. He seems sketchy. I'd be careful with him," Becky, my friend and coworker says as we walk towards my office.

I've known Becky since I first started here, which was less than a year ago. I got signed with this publishing house after I got attention for my books online. This publishing house is known for taking in a lot of indie authors and somehow I got noticed for my mystery thriller books.

If it wasn't for them, I probably wouldn't have been able to move to New York or survive here.

I make a pretty okay income here as a top writer but not enough for me to drive a nice car or be super rich.

Becky is also a writer and she loves writing romance books, mostly dark romance since that's her thing. I've read a few of her books and they are pretty good.

"He is just super quiet. That's really the only sketchy thing about him. Along with the price I'm paying for such a nice sky rise apartment."

"Do you have a picture of him?"

"Yea, I did my digging before I met up with him. I wanted to make sure that he's not a serial killer or a drug dealer."

"Ooo, let me see," Becky says as we walk into my office.

I pull up the picture I found of Slade and turn the phone to show her.

She grabs it. "He looks like he will kill you in your sleep. Don't know if I'm jealous of you or scared for you."

"He's quiet but I mean I don't mind. At least I'll get a lot of work done." I take the phone back from her and set it on my desk.

"Well, call me if you ever need to escape. We can have a girls night and I can kick my boyfriend out."

I smile at her. "I'll take you up on that one of these days. He doesn't like people coming over, so I guess no more sleepovers."

"It's fine." Becky shrugs

"But I can't believe I got so lucky with this place."

"Have you slept over yet or officially moved in?" Becky asks.

"Yesterday was my first night. He wasn't there when I was moving in, only when he gave me a key. That's the last time I saw him. I didn't hear him come in last night, and when I left this morning, I didn't see his keys or any sign that he'd come home."

"Maybe he is a serial killer. Watch out, Isabella."

"I'm sure I'll be fine. He just keeps to himself is all." I turn my computer on. "I would love to continue chatting with you but I have a book to write and our lunch ended like ten minutes ago. I know Bentley will be wondering why we're here talking rather than typing."

"Okay, I'll leave you alone." She stands up with her bag. "Drinks after work?" she asks, as if I'm twenty-one.

I have less than a month until I turn twenty-on, but she is getting impatient.

"I wish, but I still have to unpack. Next time."

Becky smiles at me before leaving, and I look at my computer, at the last words I typed.

This current book I'm working on is about a serial killer who is targeting a human trafficking organization, and the traffickers end up kidnapping the love of his life.

I don't usually write romances, but Bentley, the head of Bentley Publishing House, decided he wanted me to challenge myself and have me try something I don't usually write, which is romance. He favors romance books over all other genres.

I mean who doesn't?

I love reading romance, but writing it is hard since I've never experienced my own romance before.

I don't know what it's like to fall in love or be in a relationship. The closest thing I had to a relationship was a talking stage over Snapchat that lasted two weeks.

I usually stick to myself and focus on my work because relationships make you think too much.

I spend the next four hours just writing, taking some breaks to either talk to other people on the floor, chat with Becky, or go on Instagram.

The day passes pretty quickly, and when it hits five-thirty, I start packing up my things and leave.

It's only a fifteen-minute walk to the apartment, which is very convenient. The last place I was living was an hour walk so I usually had to take the subway to make it to work on time.

I never liked taking the subway.

A lot of weird people coming and going in the subways.

When I walk inside, the apartment is empty, not that I'm really surprised.

I lock the door behind me and go to my room.

I still have some boxes of clothes that I need to unpack. My bed and dresser are here. I got some professional movers to help me. I would have asked Slade, but he wasn't around. I also have my bookshelf with all of my books and other people's books. My big bookshelf is at Grams' house since she let me turn one of her spare rooms into an office/library. I love writing at Grams' house. It's where I feel most comfortable writing and I enjoy being surrounded by books.

I change out of my work clothes and get into sweatpants and a tank top.

Slade showed me how to use the TV, but I don't feel comfortable enough to sit in the living room. He just has everything so neat and clean.

Even the couch is perfectly made with the blanket folded and the pillows fluffed.

After unpacking my clothes, I go into the living room and look at what he has on his bookshelf.

He has a lot of books from authors I know. Most of them are thrillers, dystopias, and biographies, or about criminal psychology.

He has an interesting selection of books, and it makes me wonder what he does for work.

Especially with how he can afford an apartment like this.

It's around 11 p.m. when a yawn comes out and Slade still isn't home. I mean I don't think I should complain, but I wish I was able to at least see Slade once and a while since he does live here. I don't want him to think just because he has a roommate, he can't be comfortable in his own home anymore.

Maybe he doesn't like me.

I try to not think much about it as I fall asleep.

3

SLADE

The best part about my day is always showering.

A rapist's blood fills the drain of the shower as I'm left alone with my thoughts and feelings. This is the time when the line of coke I took before the kill wears off.

I get to calm down and relax while also processing everything.

But lately it feels like my shower time has been consumed by Isabella Rossi.

It was pretty easy to find my little bookworm.

Since the night I first met her in the alleyway, I can't stop thinking about her. All I can smell is her fucking vanilla and rose scent. All I can see is her big brown eyes and those stars that decorate her cheeks.

After she ran for her life, I went into Mitch's office

and did the kill. Once he saw me, he knew his life was over.

There are rumors all around the city of people going missing and about how it might be the shadow of New York.

But even if I were to ever get caught, nothing would happen because of who my family is. Being in the Bratva makes my life so easy, but people assume I was born with a silver spoon in my mouth even though it was the complete opposite.

Compared to my brothers, I got treated like shit. There were so many times I could have died and none of them even knew.

No one other than my mom knows the truth, but we swore never to speak about anything that happened.

I wash my hair and body to get rid of the blood and crimes I've committed. When my hands run down my chest, I can't help but think about Isabella's soft hands going closer and closer to my dick.

It's weird wanting a girl, especially a girl like Isabella.

I've never liked relationships, boys or girls. They've never interested me because I never understood the point of them.

Even the sex.

If anything, sex repulses me. It has since I was a kid, but it got worse after my eighteenth birthday.

He ruined everything for me.

Maybe if it wasn't for him, I would enjoy sex and be normal, but he made me into a monster.

Maybe that's why he gave me the task he did, because he knows it'll be hard for me and not my brothers.

He knows exactly what he fucking did to me.

But from the moment I saw Isabella and she let out that scream for help and begged me to let her go, I became obsessed.

I haven't figured her out as a person yet, but I want to know everything about her—learn what her favorite color is, what her family's like, what foods she likes, what books she likes reading, and most of all, how she'll feel against me.

I squeeze my dick and let out a soft groan. She's in the room down the hall sleeping, but I wonder if she'll hear me if I start masturbating.

I take a deep breath and let go of my dick and turn the shower off.

Not tonight.

I need to calm down.

I've only known her for about two weeks and I've had one real conversation with her.

I step out and grab my towel, wrapping it around my waist.

I stand in front of he mirror and my eyes go to my scar.

I remember the screams my mom let out when she saw the blood dripping from my eyebrow.

And my brothers begged me to tell them who hurt me.

My little sister Angela was scared of me for a month because of this scar, but she grew out of it.

Even now, people can't stop staring at it. They seem curious about it.

After shaving my face and putting cream on the scar, I throw the towel in my laundry and go into my room where I put sweatpants on.

A book is on my side table next to my bed, but I need to do one thing first.

I make my way to Isabella's room and slowly open the door.

There are two unpacked boxes, probably full of clothes, but she stacked all of her books on one side of the room and placed some stuff like makeup and jewelry on the top of her dresser. She has the window open and blankets wrapped around her.

I quietly move towards her and brush a strand of her hair from her face, making her stir.

She has no makeup on, and I swear she is one of the most beautiful and captivating people I've ever seen. I feel the need to lock her in my room so that no one but me can see or have her.

I want to hurt her, break her, and make her mine.

My finger grazes her cheek, but I move it away when she stirs again.

I stay in her room, watching her for god knows how long. I'm trapped—how can someone make me feel things like this?

I've never experienced this before, like something is bursting in my chest. Or the need to hurt anyone if they looked at her the wrong way or touched her.

The guy in the alleyway, I fucking slit every inch of his body and made him slowly bleed out while he was still conscious, just because he tried to kill her. I would have done worse but I was on a time crunch since I only allow myself time for one kill a night.

If I did more than one kill, I would need another line or just something to calm me down and level myself.

It's not that I don't like killing, because I do, I love the rush and adrenaline, but after all that wears off, guilt and disgust consume me since this is what he wanted me to be.

My eyes go to the journal on her side table, next to her charging phone.

I grab the notebook and flip through the pages, scanning everything she's written down.

It's mostly book ideas.

It wasn't hard to find her. All I had to do was look through the street cameras. First, I found out where she worked, then I figure out what she did at her job, and from there, it was easy to find her picture on the back of a thriller book.

She writes psychological thriller books.

The fucking coincidence.

I read every single page of every single book she has ever written.

Even though I know what happens in her books I still read all of what's in her journal so that I can get to know her and her mind a little more.

It takes me about thirty minutes, and I'm surprised she doesn't wake up.

I'm sure she has more notebooks somewhere with more ideas or stories because this journal isn't even halfway filled.

"What goes on in your head, *avtor*?" I look down at her and twirl a strand of her hair just so I can touch her.

I'd rather feel every inch of her body against mine but I know it's too early. I need to play this smart and not rush.

All good things take time.

4

ISABELLA

The smell of bacon fills my nose as I slowly start to wake up.

My room is dark since I don't keep the curtains open. I reach over to my desk, knocking down my journal, to grab my phone. I click the side button, turning it on, and see it's 7:30 a.m.

My eyes widen and I throw the blankets off me and jump out of bed.

I run out of my room and into the bathroom to start getting ready, ignoring the grease crackling in the kitchen. I'm surprised that Slade is even up or out of his room since I haven't seen him since I got the keys.

I brush my hair and teeth and put some makeup on so I at least look alive.

Luckily I don't have to think too much about what I'm going to wear since in the office everyone wears casual, business casual, or business professional. There isn't really a dress code, as long as you get your work done.

I decided on blue jeans and a black t-shirt that's so tight it basically sticks to my chest.

By the time I'm done getting ready I have five minutes until I have to leave and get to the office.

"Don't you usually leave around seven forty-five?" I hear Slade say.

I look up at him and my eyes can't help but go to his chest. He is shirtless in the kitchen while preparing two plates of breakfast. He has tattoos on his chest. One is of a statue wrapped in a red rose vine with thorns on it. That tattoo catches my eyes because he always seems like a statue, wrapped in barbed wire instead of a rose vine. I notice one on his collarbone that says something but it's in another language.

Maybe Russian?

I wonder if he's Russian.

He looks like he is, with the sharp jaw and hooded eyes.

The way he stares at me feels so familiar, like I've seen his eyes or that scar before.

"Isabella?" My name rolls off his tongue sensually with his hint of an accent.

My eyes meet his. "Sorry. Yea, I'm running late. If I don't leave now, I'll have to run to work."

"Sit. I can take you to work if you'd like. I made breakfast."

Hesitantly, I sit. "Thank you."

He watches me for a few minutes as I gulp down my food before he leaves, probably to put clothes on. By the time I'm finished, he comes out of his room with a motorcycle helmet. I furrow my eyebrows.

"Woah, I'm not getting on any type of motorcycle."

Slade's lips twitch as if he's going to smile or laugh at me. "Relax. It's safe. Plus you'll get to work in less than five minutes."

We leave the apartment and go down to the garage level.

I've never been on a motorcycle before so my nerves are going through the roof and my heart can't stop pounding.

We walk up to a black sports bike that has some carbon fiber touches on it. When he turns the bike on, I feel my insides flip.

"As long as you hold onto me, you should be fine." Slade comes up to me, the helmet in his hands. "Who knows maybe you'll end up enjoying it and begging me to take you on another ride." He smirks, like he's suggesting something else.

He puts the helmet over my head and straps it tightly on me. "I've only talked to you twice and now you're making me go on a motorcycle with you?"

"I'm not making you do anything, *avtor*."

"*Av*-huh?" I furrow my eyebrows at him.

Slade chuckles lightly. "Means author in Russian."

"So you are Russian?" I raise an eyebrow at him, even though he probably can't see.

He tightens the strap before letting me go. "How'd you know?"

"The tattoo on your collarbone is in Russian. I connected the dots."

"Does that mean you were checking me out this morning?" Slade raises an eyebrow at me, a soft smirk appearing on his lips.

He can't see the way my cheeks heat up, thank god.

"I can't admire your tattoos?"

Slade smiles for a second before he covers his face with the helmet, leaving the visor up. "Admire me all you want, Isabella. I won't lie and say I haven't been doing the same thing since you walked into my apartment last week."

He looks at me and deja vu hits me again but ten times harder.

How do I know him?

"You've never ridden a bike before, right?"

I shake my head.

"Okay well it's pretty simple. You move with me. It'll only be a short ride so I'm not even going to bother telling you everything." He swings his legs over the bike, closes the visor and holds his hand out for me.

"If I die, I'm going to haunt you."

"I wouldn't mind, trust me," he says, his voice muffled from the helmet. I place my hand in his and he pulls me closer to him. "Hold onto my hand or shoulder and pull yourself up. Put your foot here and your other one in the same place on the other side of the bike."

When I put my foot on the little pedal, I push myself up and hold onto him tightly. I swing my leg over the bike and then sit down.

The bike rumbles loudly underneath me and it sends a sensation to my core, especially when Slade lightly touches my thigh. "Remember to move with me. I won't be able to hear you while I'm riding so if you need something tap my shoulder."

I nod against him.

He closes my visor for me and turns around, putting his hands on the gears. "Hold tight."

The bike moves, making me squeeze his abdomen. I yelp as he takes off and speeds towards the exit of the garage.

When we come out of the garage, he looks left and right before heading onto the street. He moves swiftly in between cars, and I feel like I'm about to shit myself.

I keep mumbling to myself, telling him to be careful even though he's probably done this a bunch of times and I'm over here freaking out and distracting him.

I rest my head on his back and try to relax as he races through the busy streets of New York.

The drive really isn't that long.

He starts to slow the bike down and I see my office building come into view. When we come to a full stop, my heart slows down and I thank God for getting me here safely.

Slade kicks the stand down and holds his hand out for me.

I take it and get off the bike, stumbling a little when my feet touch the ground. He grabs onto my waist to steady me, his hand sending sparks through my entire body.

"Come here," he says, motioning me to come closer to him.

I approach with hesitant steps. He unbuckles the strap and pulls off the helmet making my hair go all over the place. Slade opens his visor and watches me fix my hair. His intense eyes cause goosebumps to erupt on my skin.

"Thank you," I say with a small smile. He nods and now I don't know what to say or do. I should say more, but I'm close to being late for work. Slade keeps staring at me, almost like he is mesmerized. "I should get going before I'm extra late."

"Right." He breaks eye contact and looks at his bike. "I'll see you later."

"Will you? You're never at the apartment." I don't

know why I said that or made it such a big deal when it shouldn't be.

We aren't even friends.

He can do whatever he wants.

"Why, you're expecting me?" He raises an eyebrow.

I blush and smile softly. "I'll see you later, Slade."

He pulls his visor down, starts his bike and gives me one last look before pulling onto the street, his bike echoing so that all of New York can hear him.

And when I enter the office building, I realize I never gave him the address of where I work.

5

ISABELLA

I walk through the front door of the apartment at the same time I see Slade coming out of the hallway that leads to our rooms.

His hair is wet and he has no shirt on, only sweatpants, showing off his strong arms and tattoos.

It's been a week since he gave me a ride to work on the motorcycle. I've seen him a total of two times. Once was this morning when he was coming out of his room with wet hair, from his shower I'm assuming, and the other time was last night when I got home from work and he was walking out of the shower again.

We've exchanged a few words but nothing like how we did when he dropped me off that morning.

Every time I see him, I get all giddy and excited. I can't stop thinking about the ride to work with him. I will admit, it was fun and exhilarating. I wouldn't mind going on another ride but I'm not going to ask and he hasn't offered.

"I feel like you take more showers than me," I comment while locking the door behind me. "I always see you with wet hair."

"I just like being clean and having everything in perfect condition I guess you can say." He shrugs before moving to the kitchen. "I was going to make some food if you want to go take a shower and change before we eat."

"Oh you're staying tonight?" I raise my eyebrows.

"Yes, I don't have work today or anything going on."

"What do you do for work?"

"We can talk about it over dinner. Go shower," he says, motioning for me to go to the bathroom.

I smile at him and leave the kitchen.

It doesn't take me long to get cleaned up. By the time I finish showering and get in comfortable clothes, the food is finished and Slade is setting the island for two.

It's weird seeing him here, in his own apartment.

I can count on one hand how many times I've seen him. I feel like I'm here more than him but at the same time, we have different schedules.

"What did you make?" I walk out of the hallway.

"Grilled chicken, mashed potatoes, and brussels sprouts."

"Smells good." I sit down.

Slade places two plates on the island. I'm not surprised

that Slade made something pretty healthy because I can tell he takes care of his body.

He is sculpted like a god, each muscle carefully carved to perfection. Tattoos like Russian quotes, a statue with a vine wrapping around it, and a snake litter his skin. He looks like a work of art that God took his time creating.

"You're staring again," he says before walking down the hallway only to come back with a shirt on.

"You have cool tattoos," I say, trying to ignore the heat growing on my cheeks.

"Are you going to keep going with that lie?" He raises a perfect eyebrow.

I smile.

Instead of admitting the truth, I say, "Your tattoo in Russian, what does it mean?"

"Eye for an eye," he says before he starts eating.

"Why that?"

He stays silent, ignoring the question.

"So what do you do for work?" I ask instead.

"I bartend at night sometimes and I'm a contractor as well."

"You could be a chef with the food you make. This and the breakfast you made are really good."

"I learned how to cook at a very young age. My mom taught my brothers and I the simple basics of living."

"Are you originally from here or Russia?"

"Russia."

I assumed he was from Russia because of the light accent. It's subtle enough that he probably moved to the U.S. at a young age.

"Now you. Do you just write books or is there anything else you do?" he asks.

"No I'm just a writer."

"What kind of books do you write?"

"Mostly psychological thrillers."

"Why that genre?" His eyebrows furrow as he listens to me instead of eating his food.

"I find a psychopath's mind interesting. I think if I wasn't an author I would have been a criminal psychologist or a forensics scientist."

"What makes you find them interesting?"

"That their mind isn't like ours. We were all born in the same world, none of us have the same genetics but we all get a chance at life. I want to know what makes a criminal, a criminal," I explain, enjoying the conversation.

I love how he is listening while I'm talking, as if he is trying to grasp onto every single word I'm saying and hold onto it.

"What are you currently writing?" Slade asks as I take another bite of my food.

"A book about a psychopath slash serial killer who is trying to take down a human trafficking organization. His girlfriend got kidnapped so his ultimate goal is to save her."

"Do you usually include romance in your books?"

"No, but my boss wants me to challenge myself so I'm including light romance in this book."

He looks down at his food, as if he's thinking before looking back at me. "Do you have any drafts or notes on your book? I'd love to read some of it."

I can't help but smile as I nod. "Let me grab my notebook. I jot down all of my thoughts there." I leave to get it from my room and come back to Slade sitting in the same spot, waiting for me. I hand him the notebook and our fingers graze one another, sending shock waves down my body.

He opens it and starts reading. I take bites of my food and watch him read. He is really reading every single word, trying to memorize every detail, every part of my soul I've put into my notes and writing.

When I finish eating, I clean up my area and put the dirty dish in the sink. He's still reading, his food forgotten.

I'm washing my dish when he closes the notebook and sets it to the side. "Can I add one thing?" he asks. My eyes meet his, waiting for him to start. "If you have him kill one of the rapists, make sure he tortures him before killing him. If he's a psychopath, they usually like to play with their food before they actually kill it."

"Yea, I would include some torture scenes but I have no idea how to write a good one or what types of torture to include."

Slade shrugs and tilts his head lightly. "Cutting off his dick and shoving it up the ass is a creative one."

I laugh and shake my head lightly.

Slade smiles softly. "How about slitting his entire body, not enough to make him bleed out but enough to hurt him. After, cut off his tongue and keep it to the side for later. Then take his vision, shove a needle in his eye. Find out his fear and make his worst fear happen. Grand finale would be to shove that same tongue down his throat and make him choke on it." By the time he's finished, his eyes are filled with darkness, not the regular kind but the kind that makes him look deadly or like he's capable of anything.

Capable of torturing someone.

Slade snaps out of it and stands up from the island, taking his plate and walking towards me. "If you need more ideas, I've got plenty."

Can't tell if that's a bad thing or a good thing.

6

SLADE

"When are you going to come back, Slade?" my little sister, Angel, asks in Russian. "Mama misses you and can't stop worrying about you."

Angel and I have always been pretty close, mainly because we are three years apart. Ryker and Landon are close because they are not that far apart in age.

"I don't know, I'll see. I've been busy, Angel," I tell her in a soft tone.

Really, what I've been busy with is killing someone new every day, slowly decreasing the population of New York. If I'm not doing that, I'm at the apartment giving Isabella advice for her books.

Sometimes when I give her ideas, she'll look at me like she should be scared of me but I can also tell she is fascinated.

The past week with her has been nice.

I've been at the apartment a lot more, mostly seeing her in the morning unless she stays up super late. Before I would just wait until she left the apartment to come out of my room but we're slowly becoming more comfortable with each other.

"Busy doing what? Probably forgetting about me," Angel says and I can tell she is pouting on the other end of the phone.

My eyes go to the bastard in front of me that I'm meant to kill today.

He's sweating and mumbling through the piece of cloth over his mouth.

His name is Thomas Templeman and he is a forty-two year old pedophile who has been sexually abusing some-one's daughter. I got paid good for this job but the money isn't why I'm doing it.

It's mostly to get out everything I'm feeling.

"My job, Angel. Tell mom I said 'hi' and that I love her. I need to go, but keep doing good in school. I'll still be coming to your graduation, I promise."

"Okay, Slade, I love you. Talk to you later."

I hang up and pocket my phone.

My eyes connect with Thomas'. "So, Thomas?" I rip the piece of cloth off his mouth and he takes a deep breath.

Right now we are in a warehouse that was bought

under my mother's name since no one knows about her. This is the place where I'm able to take my time with the kills. After I kill them I usually dump their body somewhere with a note saying why they deserve to be dead, just so that they will have died with the world knowing how much of a pig they were when they were breathing.

"Please, man. I swear I don't know who you are or what I did wrong. If you want money, I have it. Tons of it. Let me go-"

"Shut the fuck up." I groan and roll my eyes. "You think I need your money?" I raise an eyebrow. "I don't mean to sound like a douche but I probably had more money than you when I was a baby. I have more money than the President. Trust me the last thing I need is money."

The line I took thirty minutes ago is starting to really take effect, getting me excited and my blood pumping.

"Then what do you want?" He winces.

He's going to beg and plead for mercy or for someone to save him but he has no clue that he's fucked.

No one will hear his cries or screams.

"Tell me what you did to her first." I grab his hair and pull his head back.

"What?! Stop! Dude, what are you even saying?! Let me go!"

"Tell me what you did first to the 12 year old girl that

you sexually abused," I say in his ear and he goes silent and tenses. "All quiet now, Thomas?"

I let go of him and smack him across the face with my gun.

"Ahh! I didn't do anything to that bitch."

"Then why did I get a message from an unknown source, begging me to make you pay for what you did to that little girl?" I ask. He shakes his head, pleading for me to let him go. I nod, realizing he isn't going to talk unless I make him. I grab my blade from the table and walk towards him. "You asked for this."

I grab ahold of his head and start making small slits in his neck, not going too deep but deep enough to make it painful. "Still don't wanna talk, Thomas?"

He screams instead of answering me.

I nod again and grab a mallet off the table that's filled with torture tools. "I'm assuming you used your hands first, right? Did you grab her by the waist first or use your voice to lure her?"

"I didn't do anything! I swear!"

I bring the mallet down on his hands. His screams fill the warehouse.

"Thomas, no one can hear you in here," I say before bringing the mallet down on his hand again, harder. He screams but gives up nothing. "Still not hearing any answers. Let's bring out my knife and go for your throat since it's basically useless if you aren't saying anything." I drop the mallet and pull out my blade. "Any last words before you can't say anything?"

"I'm sorry, I didn't mean to! I tried to stop myself, I swear." He cries, tears falling down his cheeks.

I dig my gloved fingers into the wounds on his neck. "How did you approach her, Thomas?"

"I told her she had a pretty dress on."

"And? What else? I know there's something else. I saw the footage of you and her."

He cries and shakes his head. "And I asked if I could take it off."

I nod before using my knife to start cutting off his clothes, making him bare.

I grab his neck and tighten my grip so that he is starting to suffocate, gasping for air. "You're going to wish you were dead, Thomas."

Then I get to work.

I start with his dick, making cuts in it and all over his body. He screams but I'm just smiling through the pleasure it's bringing me.

The way he's begging me to just kill him already.

I cut his dick off and leave it to the side, similar to what I told Isabella about the tongue.

She has no clue that I used the exact torture method I told her about on the person I killed the day before.

My sweet innocent little bookworm has no clue she's living with a murderer.

She'll find out soon.

"Before I kill you, I want you to think about what it felt like for that girl. How scared she was thinking she wasn't going to survive, that she was going to die,"

He begs and pleads as I shove my knife in his chest, thighs, and hands. I bring the mallet down on his body too many times to count.

He's sweating and not screaming anymore.

Instead he looks exhausted.

I cut off the ropes on his hands and point to him with my blade. "You are about to feel exactly what she felt."

I throw him on the floor so he's on his knees, barely able to hold himself up. I grab his dick, spread his hole before shoving his dick inside. His screams and cries fill the air again.

I start fucking him in the ass with his own dick and his body falls to the floor. "What's wrong, Thomas? You don't like your own dick? You can't take it? Is it too much? Keep fucking crying, *ublyudok!*"

After what feels like an hour of torturing him, I throw him on the floor.

After decapitating his body, I'm covered in his blood. The clock on the wall tells me it's been three hours since I started.

The high from the coke is starting to wear off but I'm still pumped with adrenaline.

I clean up my knives and send a picture of the body

and the mess to Niko, my second in command. He takes car of all of the things I don't feel like taking care of.

I would clean it all up myself but I hate having the feeling of someone's blood and organs on me. I need a shower and then to take a nap since I've been up for the past forty-eight hours.

I leave the warehouse and it's a forty minute drive back to the apartment. No one is in the elevator, thank god, since I probably smell and have Thomas all over me.

I unlock the door and get inside, sighing as I close my eyes, wanting to just fall asleep already. My eyes are blurry when I open them. I stumble towards the hallway, slowly making my way to my room.

The sound of a door unlocking makes me feel wide awake. I stumble in the hallway as I hurry to my room.

"Slade?" Isabella says as I unlock my door. Before she can walk towards the hallway, I get in my room, slam the door, and fall on my side.

7

ISABELLA

I'm sitting on the couch when I see Slade walk in.

His hair is wet from his shower and he's wearing a white T-shirt and black shorts. He looks so fresh and clean.

I didn't even know he was home.

I have my laptop in front of me, trying to figure out how to start writing this new chapter, which is supposed to have another torture scene.

I would have gone in my room but I wanted some background noise so I put the TV on.

"Are you writing?"

"Yea, another torture chapter. Kind of having trouble with it."

"Let me see what you got," he says as he sits down next to me, his thigh brushing my bare one.

I'm wearing cotton shorts and a tank top. Feeling his

bare skin touching mine makes goosebumps appear on my skin.

I hand him my laptop and pull the blanket over my lap to cover my legs. I watch him, the light from my computer reflecting on his face.

I heard him come home a few days ago but right when I called out to him he shut his bedroom door. I usually get home after him and he has just been staying in his room, probably showering and doing god knows what else in there.

His room is the one place in the house I haven't been to and I'm so curious about what's in there or what it looks like.

I'm sure it's clean because like he said, he likes everything spotless.

I glance down at his biceps and see the way they flex and unflex, his muscles straining through his shirt.

I still cannot understand how perfect he is.

"This is pretty good but I would add a few more things," he tells me while giving me my laptop back.

"Like what?" I ask.

"You should show more of what's going on in his mind to prepare for the torture. Who is the person he's killing?" he asks, resting his hands over his strong thighs.

"It's a pedophile."

He nods. "Okay, what did he do to the girl?"

I think for a minute, still not really sure. "He took her from school first."

"Okay, so what you wanna incorporate, for the torture part of the chapter, destroying his hands first since he obviously used his hands to take her right?" He raises an eyebrow at me and I nod. "Alright so maybe a mallet to destroy his hands or a knife to cut his hands open to the point where you can see his bone."

I chuckle softly. "Wow, you are not holding back, are you?"

Slade shrugs. "I mean I read criminal psychology books, so I guess it fucks with my mind a bit."

"Why do you read them?"

"Because I find them interesting. I like learning about new things as well."

I write the first part of the chapter as Slade watches me silently. I can't help but feel nervous under his gaze.

It's like he's trying to capture every word I type, and I just hope that it makes sense by the time I'm done. I always check my writing after I finish a section.

Slade shifts while I'm writing and part of the blanket falls from my thigh. I watch his reflection in my computer screen. He glances down. I turn my head slightly to see what he's looking at and his gaze is on my thigh.

I stop typing and try to relax.

It's not anything serious. It's just when he stares at me,

I get nervous and suddenly I forget what I'm even supposed to be doing in that moment.

Slade looks up and his eyes catch mine. They go down to my lips, making me lick them. His pupils darken and he looks like he's going to ravish me and make me scream his name.

My body feels hot and the spot between my legs is sensitive. "Where have you been the past two days?"

"Don't worry about it."

I furrow my eyebrows. "You can't just pop in and not expect me to wonder what you're doing."

"You don't even know me, Isabella. We've had what? Five conversations?" He raises an eyebrow. "There's a reason I don't come here."

"And what is it?" I tilt my head, wondering what he could mean.

His eyes go to my lips again before locking with mine. "I'm trying to hold myself back, but if you keep tempting me, Isabella, I'll take that as my sign to release the tight leash I have on myself and fucking take you."

My eyes go to his lips this time and he groans faintly.

He sighs and then looks at my computer. "Show me what you have."

I'm still trying to calm my racing heart as I give him my computer.

Now my core is pulsing and all I want is for him to

take off that leash and grab me like he is telling himself not to.

I want him, he wants me.

The tension is there.

We're just both denying it and holding back as best as we can.

Slade reads what I wrote and types a few more things before he nods and hands me my computer back. "I'm going to sleep. What you have is good so keep working on it."

He gets up from the couch and walks towards his room.

I let out a breath I've been holding and try to calm down, replaying every word he said and every look he gave me.

8

ISABELLA

My boss called me into his office to talk about how the book is going.

I sent him part of my draft the other day and I'm assuming he just finished it since he wants to talk to me about it.

All I'm hoping for is that he likes it.

I feel like I have been doing a good job with this story and how it's progressing.

Slade's advice and ideas are helping me a lot.

He has dark, twisted thoughts and ideas and I don't know why I feel so drawn to that or him.

I haven't seen him in two days which is becoming normal now. Sometimes he'll be gone for two to three days and then magically appear again before disappearing.

Just thinking about the small moment we had together makes me excited and eager to see him. How he looked down at my lips and he how close his body was to mine. I can't get that moment with him out of my head.

We're both scared of the possibilities and making the first move but there is undeniable tension.

I have no clue why he would be scared since he looks like he'd be a confident person especially when it comes to women, but I guess everyone has their insecurities that others wouldn't understand.

Bentley is scrolling through his notes as I wait for him to say something. He usually does this before every meeting he has. He told me it's so he can get his thoughts in order.

He looks away from his computer and smiles at me. "Isabella, my favorite writer."

I laugh softly. "You say that to everyone."

"Yes, but right now you are killing it with this new book. All of the marketing ideas you've given us are making me excited. I couldn't wait anymore, and I had to read some of it." He smiles at me. "I feel like you should write more romance. The way the main character seems so devoted and obsessed with the female main character makes me want a romance book about them and how they met."

I smile at him. "Thank you, that means a lot."

"I mean the tension between them in the flashbacks and the way he cares about her, and tortures people for her, really showcases that love. Your dialogue is amazingly done. I can't wait to see what you do with the rest of this book," Bentley compliments. "When do you think you'll be done? I'm excited to send it over to editing and get this book published."

"I should be done hopefully by the end of next month. It's going to be a very long book and from what I'm hearing you want a second book."

"Keep writing what you're writing kid, and I will be begging for one." He laughs and I join him. "One question. How do you come up with such creative torture scenes? I mean, only a serial killer could think of doing these things without grimacing."

I smile and nod, appreciating his compliments.

Bentley wouldn't usually appreciate my work like this, but he seems so fascinated with this book and wants to learn more. I'm shocked because he usually only gives a few things he likes about the book and then moves on.

"Honestly just reading other books on criminals and a little advice from a creative source," I say, not giving Slade's name.

"Well, keep up the good work. Just wanted to talk to you about how you're doing, but it looks like I shouldn't be worrying about you. You're doing great."

I stand from my chair and grab my notebook and laptop. "Thank you, sir. I appreciate it, truly. I'm happy I can make you proud."

I leave his office and write for a little more in my office before it's time to head out for the day.

As I'm packing up all my things I can't help but wonder if Slade will be at the apartment or if he is just going to ignore me like he did for the last few days by not coming home.

"Drinks after work today?" Becky asks, sticking her head into my office.

I give her a sad smile. "I'm still not twenty-one yet. I swear once this book is released we will go out for drinks whether it be at your house or you can sneak me drinks at the bar," I promise.

She pouts. "It sucks having a friend slash coworker who can't drink yet. You're basically a baby."

"You just turned twenty-one. You're practically the same age as me." I laugh.

"I know but it's so boring having to wait for you. I can't keep drinking with Adrian, it gets kind of tiresome," she says, talking about her boyfriend.

"Be patient."

She rolls her eyes and says 'bye' before leaving.

I finish packing up my stuff and locking and shutting down my computer before leaving the office.

It's dark by the time I walk out the door and it's moments like this when I'm glad the journey home isn't long.

I still can't help but remember the time where the guy

took me into the dark alley. I thought I was going to get raped, robbed, or killed.

But then someone saved me.

I almost thought he killed that guy just so he could have his way with me before killing me. I can't stop thinking about him. I feel like I keep seeing him around but that's impossible. I won't forget him or how he basically saved my life and I wonder if I'll ever see him again.

Probably not.

I unlock my phone and look through my messages for the day, going on Instagram and seeing what's on my feed.

New York is busy per usual with everyone walking back home from work. I know how to make my way home while keeping my eyes on the floor and avoiding bumping into people while doing so.

As I turn the corner, goosebumps appear on my skin.

I do my best to ignore the feeling of something crawling on my skin while I continue walking home, just trying to get inside the building so that I don't have another situation like I did a few weeks ago.

The feeling doesn't go away after five minutes so I stop and look around.

My eyes catch someone in a black hood. I notice his blue eyes from a few feet away. I'm frozen in my tracks as I stare at him, wondering if he's looking at me.

I furrow my eyebrows and turn around to glance

behind me in case he is staring at someone else but no one stands out. I turn back around but he's gone.

Anxiety creeps up my throat and holds onto it as if I'm starting to suffocate.

I don't think, I just run and the apartment building comes into view.

I run faster as it feels like someone is going to reach out and grab me.

When I get inside the building I take the elevator up to our floor, pressing the seven button a bunch of times so that the doors close.

As I unlock the apartment, I look around the hallway, making sure it's just me. I push the door open and lock it right away once I'm inside.

I rest my back against the door and close my eyes, taking a deep breath, trying to relax.

It's fine.

He's gone.

He can't hurt you.

He already took too much.

9

ISABELLA

"Mommy!" I yell, trying my best to wake her up but she stays still.

I need to get them out.

How will I get them out?

They can't die.

I need them.

I can't be alone.

Who's going to take care of me?

"Mommy! Please wake up! I need you. You can't leave me," I cry, holding mommy's hand while trying to pull her out of the flipped car.

Daddy is on the driver's side, his head against the wheel. I don't even remember how I managed to crawl out of the tiny space.

I have cuts all over my knees and hands and there is no one out on this road that can save us.

Someone save us.

Please.

"You're going to be okay. We're all going to be okay and we're going to go back home and I'm going to get help. I promise. I'll get help." I lean down and kiss her forehead, saying I love her before I stand up. My jeans and shirt are a mess from blood and dirt.

I try not to look back at mommy and daddy as they rest in the car. My eyes go to every detail around me. There is a gas station down the street.

Maybe if I run I can get help?

"Shame," a voice says, making me turn around.

My eyes meet bright blue ones.

He stares down at me, no sympathy in them whatsoever.

"Can you help me? My parents, they need help. I need to get them help before they die. Please help me," I say while crying.

The guy kneels down and tilts his head slightly, almost in a mocking tone. "Now why would I do that?"

His voice sounds haunting, as if he is a bad guy.

Mommy told me never to talk to strangers.

He doesn't seem like a nice stranger. His eyes look like death even though they are the color of the ocean. They just scream bad news.

I need to run.

As if he can read my mind, he grabs my arm and I flinch, letting out a cry. "Let me go!"

He pulls me closer to him, his breath smelling like ciga-rettes. "Be careful Isabella, because I might leave you alone right now. But one of these days, when I find you again, I'm not going to stop at anything to destroy Richard Rossi's life. He'll be up there watching his beautiful little girl die at my hand." he says, gripping my arm harshly, making me let out another cry. "The grand finale will be you, little Rossi."

He tilts his head down giving me a sinister stare before his lips form a creepy smile.

"Please," I whimper, shaking my head and shutting my eyes so he can't see me.

If I can't see him then he can't see me.

"Be ready, Isabella."

I scream.

I jolt away, screaming uncontrollably.

Hands are on me but I can't see them.

All I can see are those sinister blue eyes.

The same blue eyes that destroyed my childhood.

"Isabella," I hear someone say. "Listen to my voice. You're okay," he says, trying to calm me down.

I blink away the blue eyes, desperately trying to erase him from my mind. My eyes focus on the person in front of me.

Slade.

I look around.

We're in my room and he's sitting on the side of my

bed with his hand on my face, stroking my cheek. I feel hot and sweaty from the nightmare.

"Slade," I whisper.

He scoots closer and moves hair away from my face, staring at me intensely. "I'm here, you're okay," Slade assures. I haven't had a nightmare like that in so long. Most of the nightmares I've had lately have just been about what happened in the alleyway. But then the shadow from earlier today must have brought back memories. I lick my lips and Slade watches me as I try to calm down and keep my heart from exploding. "What happened?"

Blue eyes flash in my head making me flinch. "It was a nightmare o-or a m-memory. I don't know." I shake my head lightly.

"A memory?" Slade raises an eyebrow.

"Yea, just something that happened in my past and I guess I still think about it sometimes." My bedroom door is open and I can't help but feel like something is out there.

Slade turns his head, looking at the door and back to me. "What's wrong? You want me to close the door?"

I shake my head. "No, but would it be weird to ask you if you could look around the apartment? And make sure that nothing is in here?"

He nods. "I know there's no one here but I'll check

for you." Slade lets go of me and holds out his hand for me to take.

I grab it and get out of bed while he stands up. I watch him as we walk around the apartment. He looks through every corner and opens every door, except his own, in the apartment. When he's done we go back to my room and he closes the door behind him.

I get into bed and pull the duvet to cover me while he sits on the side of the bed, facing me. "You don't have to worry about anyone coming in here and hurting you." Slade pushes a strand of hair behind my ear. "I will always be the thing you should fear the most in this apartment. No one other than me is allowed to hurt you."

I can't help but smile. "You could never hurt me."

Slade's eyes go down to my lips, licking his own before meeting my eyes. "What did you mean by memory?"

"It was a memory of my parents' death. They died in a car crash," I say but not explaining it in detail. He'll think I'm crazy if I tell him the whole story. "Do you have nightmares?"

Slade nods slowly. "Everyone does. You just have to overcome them, *avtor*." He strokes my hair a few times before he stands up.

My anxiety creeps up my body and before I stop myself I grab his arm making him stop. He glances down at my hand on his arm before looking up at me. "Can you stay? Just until I fall asleep?"

Slade licks his lips before nodding.

I move to the other side of my bed and he gets in, under the duvet.

We're facing each other, not saying anything. I see his eyes tracing over every detail of my face while I do the same to him.

I've never been this close to him. I can feel his body heat radiating onto mine.

And I know if I move closer we'd basically be touching.

I'm not sure why all of a sudden, after not being interested in guys for so long, I'm interested in this one.

"Close your eyes, Isabella."

I smile, hoping he can't tell because it's dark.

But I listen and close my eyes, letting him be the last thing I see.

10

SLADE

A phone buzzing wakes me up from the empty dream I had.

I look at my surroundings and see I'm in a bed, cuddled up next to someone.

My arms are wrapped around Isabella who is sleeping silently.

Her back is to me and I have one arm around her waist and the other under her head, my hand holding hers.

She is sleeping so beautifully.

How can someone sleep while looking like an angel at the same time?

She's lying next to me as if I'm not a monster and I won't tarnish her dreams or soul.

I move my arm from around her waist and my fingers graze her skin making her shiver. I scoot away from her just so she can lay down on her back and I can have a clear view of her face.

Her lips are parted and she is breathing steadily.

I use one of my fingers to trace her features on her face slowly, while also trying not to wake her up.

I'm surprised I even slept.

I was going to leave once she fell asleep but after cuddling up next to her, feeling her warm body against mine, I knocked out.

I don't fucking cuddle.

I don't do women or anyone in fact.

I keep my walls up high so that I don't get fucked up in the end but why is this girl making it so easy for me to let her in?

She is slowly creeping closer to my walls with an explosive to break them all down in one go.

I could have gone another day without sleeping but my body felt relaxed and I couldn't help but fall with her into a deep sleep.

My phone buzzing again makes me groan and look away from her.

I grab my phone from her side table and see that my older brother, Ryker, is calling.

I roll my eyes and answer. "What?"

"Don't give me that tone, *brat*," he spits out. "You've been dodging me and Landon's calls for the past week. We thought you died or went on a killing spree."

"Not yet unfortunately. What do you want?"

"Why do you make it sound like you're busy? Did you just wake up or something?" Ryker asks.

My brother Ryker is the sanest out of all of us.

My dad treated him like gold because he is the oldest.

Everyone loves Ryker because he is the good brother who will do anything to protect his family. I always wondered why our dad didn't just give the Pakhan title to Ryker in his will. But instead of doing things the easy way he wanted me and my two brothers to have a friendly competition.

We each have to complete a task in order for us to get the title. Whoever does it the best wins.

My dad always loved putting the three of us in a competition.

He enjoyed having a fucking show.

"Why haven't you been answering?" Ryker asks.

My eyes go to Isabella, wanting immediately to just hang up on the motherfucker and go back to bed with her.

It's hard not to kiss her while staring at her.

She's just too tempting.

"Is it a girl?" Ryker says, and I can hear him smiling.

"I'm going to hang up on you."

"Wait, wait, wait. I didn't call to tease you." He laughs. "I'm calling you about a kill and also a possible problem."

A possible problem.

The fuck is that supposed to mean.

"Hold on." I rest the phone on the side table and glance at Isabella, admiring her before taking the blanket off me and fixing it on her. She snuggles into the pillow and sighs, still sleeping. I grab my phone and leave her room, closing the door. "What do you want?"

"I have someone I need you to kill for me. He is in New York now. Make it quick. Make it clean. I'll send you the information right now," Ryker says as I step into my room, locking the door behind me. "As for the problem. I just sent you a picture of someone who was walking suspiciously around your apartment building. Your second in command told me about him, but because you haven't been answering your phone, he forwarded me the details and told me to tell you about him." I put Ryker on speaker while watching the video he sent me.

It's a video of a guy in a black hood, standing outside my apartment building.

He seems suspicious as fuck, looking at everyone as if they could be a potential target.

There's a moment where he glances up at the building and scopes out the place.

"Any idea who this guy could be?" I ask.

"No. We don't have a clear view of his face with the hood up so Niko said he's working on trying to trace him."

I lick my bottom lip and nod, thinking.

"Maybe you know this guy or he could be one of your targets' family members and he knows you?"

I doubt it.

I'm very careful with my work and who I kill and how I trace my steps.

To the public, Slade Rykov doesn't live in New York.

He lives in Russia and never shows his face anywhere in New York.

The only time he takes off his mask is in his warehouse building.

I have Niko, my second in command, get all my groceries. I stay in the house if I want to have a drink. I have a little bar cart for myself to make drinks. I don't go out. I don't have friends or invite people over.

The only reason I'm in New York is because of work.

"No, I hide myself so it's impossible."

"Don't be reckless, Slade. You need to be careful. You don't know who this guy is." Ryker lectures.

My dear big brother, always the one to lecture and make sure the family stays safe.

He would be a good Pakhan but one thing he lacks is detachment.

He is responsible and keeps his ducks in order, but his weakness is his family.

And family is the easiest thing to use against a person.

"*Starshiy brat*, trust me I'll be fine. I'm the last person you need to worry about. Make sure to check on Landon. He was the one who was crashing out over a bitch he hasn't talked to in six years." I'm not wrong, Landon has been stalking his ex ever since they broke up. He doesn't get the hint. "You have bigger things to worry about don't you, Ryker? Pretty sure it has to do with a certain Italian. Mmm?"

He says nothing and I take that as my cue to hang up.

Him and the rest of my family have no clue.

They have no clue what I'm capable of doing or how the biggest worry I have is killing everyone in sight.

Just like how Isabella should only be scared of one thing.

And it's the person who is sleeping in the room down the hallway from her.

11

ISABELLA

Work today went by quick.

I made some marketing videos for my book, spoke with the editing team about giving them the first draft soon, and wrote a good ten thousand words.

I would usually write more but because I had other things on my schedule for the day I didn't have much time.

It was my birthday yesterday.

I took the day off and went to Grams' house for lunch and dinner. We spent the entire day together just hanging out and catching up before I got an Uber back home.

She said she's been worried about me even though she talks to me everyday to check on me. She calls me a lot because she's lonely living in that house by herself.

Without my grandpa or my parents there, the house is

super quiet. She spends her days mostly gardening outside or looking after the neighbor's daughter.

We talked about my mom when I was over.

She misses my mom as much as I do since that was her only daughter.

I think about my parents every day, now more than ever after that nightmare.

I walk inside the apartment and all the lights are on.

Slade comes out from the hallway with just a towel around his waist and my eyes widen.

He is using another towel to dry his hair while staring at me. "I thought you'd be home earlier."

I try my best not to stare at his chest or admire his long, muscular arms, water dripping from his wet hair onto his chest.

There is a light patch of hair that leads down to the spot between his legs and his v-line is prominent.

I want to lick the water off of every spot on him.

Oh my god, Isabella, chill out.

My eyes meet his and he smirks while he is still drying his hair. The action makes me want to grab him by the hair and press my lips against his.

"Isabella," he says, making me snap out of the haze. "Where were you?"

I try not to blush. "I just left work not too long ago. I had to stay late to talk to the editing team about when I should be able to hand in the first draft of the book."

Slade saunters towards me and he rests the towel he was using for his hair on the chair beside me. My eyes go down to his v-line before meeting his eyes. "Stop looking at me like that."

"Like what?" I ask, furrowing my eyebrows as if I don't know what he's talking about.

Tempting him.

Trying to see if he'll finally make a move or not.

Or if we'll keep playing this little cat and mouse game.

I haven't seen him in almost five days since my nightmare. Although when I came home from Grams' house on my birthday there was a big bouquet of red roses with a note that said "Happy Birthday, *avtor*" on the island and I knew immediately it was from Slade.

I hate how he keeps leaving for a few days and then comes back like it's nothing.

I have the bouquet of flowers in my room, making it smell like fresh roses.

"You know exactly how." He narrows his eyes on me. "Like you want me to let go of the tight control I have on myself and fuck you already."

My core pulses and my cheeks heat. His pupils double in size when they look down at me. Going down to my lips before meeting my eyes again.

"Why are you trying to fight this?" I ask, genuinely confused.

Obviously he feels it too.

So why is he not letting go?

"Because if I don't, then like I said before, I'll take you, Isabella. And when I do, I don't plan on letting you go. Careful."

"What if I want you to take me?"

Slade chuckles lightly. "Trust me, you won't want me to. It would be smart if you fight this as well." Before I can say something else, my phone starts ringing in my bag. "Better answer that, could be important," Slade says before walking away and leaving, taking the towel with him.

I pull my phone out and see Becky's name. "Hey," I say when I answer the phone.

"You and I are going out tonight. No exceptions or excuses."

I smile while I head towards my room. "Becky, I just turned twenty-one and you already want me to go everywhere with you."

"Of course I do. You're like my only friend. I need to go drinking with someone. Adrian is boring to drink with since he doesn't like going out that much."

"Where are we going?"

Becky screams through the phone excitedly, making me laugh. "Ahhh I'm so excited! Finally I can go out with someone my age!" she says before explaining all the details like what I should wear, what club we're going to, and how we are definitely getting majorly fucked up which I can't stop laughing at. Becky is a cool and fun person to be around. "We will not only celebrate your birthday but also your book that will definitely be hitting the bestseller charts."

"We won't jinx it. I'll text you when I'm ready."

"Perfect, do you want to meet there or get a car together?"

"We can meet there. It will be cheaper than getting Ubers back and forth."

Becky tells me she's excited before we both hang up.

I take a quick shower and then figure out what I'm going to wear.

I decide on a mini skirt with a lace shirt and boots with heels. I'll also bring my jacket since it's New York and I will for sure be cold.

Once I'm done getting ready, I leave my room at the same time Slade exits his room.

He's wearing a pair of black sweatpants, and when he sees me all dressed up, he furrows his eyebrows. "Where are you going?'

"Out."

"Where?" We both walk out of the hallway and into the kitchen where I check if I have all my things in my purse.

"To a club with a friend."

"What friend?" he asks, crossing his arms while keeping his eyes on me.

"Why do you want to know?" I tilt my head, giving him a teasing smile.

If he wants to play the cat and mouse game, I can play.

Slade knows exactly what I'm playing at, so he stalks towards me and puts his hands on either side of me on the island, caging me in.

"Don't fuck with me, Isabella." He leans down.

Our breaths mix and I can feel the heat coming off his body from the shower. I look up at him and I swear I almost forget what I'm about to say.

I shake my head a little bit, trying to get my thoughts together. Being near him is distracting and messing with me.

"Relax. I'm going out with my friend Becky for drinks."

"Where?"

"At some club on 7th Street."

Slade's jaw clenches and my eyes go down to his lips when I see him lick them. My stomach fills with butterflies as he looks almost protective of me leaving the house. "Have you heard of the shady shit they do at that club?"

I furrow my eyebrows. "No. Don't be such a buzzkill. I just turned twenty-one and my friend wants to take me out for drinks. Plus you're always out, god knows where. If I want to leave the apartment every once in a while and have fun I should be able to without your permission. You don't own me."

Slade raises an eyebrow. "I don't?"

"We barely talk. You don't know anything about me," I scoff and roll my eyes at him.

He's being ridiculous.

Slade nods slowly and from the corner of my eye I can see his finger tapping the counter behind me. I bet he is thinking of an excuse to give me not to go.

But he can't do that.

It's not fair.

"Okay," he says.

I look at him in confusion. "Okay?"

He nods and leans away from me. "Okay, but I'm going with you."

"But-"

"I'm going with you. I'm not letting you go to that club without me. Don't fight me on this," he says before leaving so I can't start an argument with him.

He's impossible.

It takes Slade about fifteen minutes to get ready. While he does, I text Becky.

I'm bringing a friend.

Better not be another bitch. It's my night with you.

No it's actually my roommate.

The hot serial killer one?

That's the one.

AHHHHHH COUNT ME IN

You're going to get me in trouble with
Adrian if he comes tonight.

I smile at her text as I hear Slade's footsteps. I look up at him and he is in a completely different outfit.

Slade is wearing a black button up shirt with the sleeves rolled up and black pants with white shoes. My eyes go down to the helmet he's holding and now I'm thinking that the skirt wasn't the best idea. The expensive watch on his wrist looks like it cost more than ten thousand dollars for sure. He doesn't have to style his hair since it's very short and he didn't put any make-up on to hide the scar on his face but I think the scar makes him look more attractive and unique.

He knows he's good looking and that he can get anything he wants by looking the way he does.

I try my best to make it seem like I wasn't checking him out but it's so hard when he looks like that.

"Ready?" he asks, keeping his intense eyes on mine.

12

ISABELLA

The club we're at is playing loud R&B music right now. I can't tell what the song is because everyone is talking loudly and screaming over the music.

Becky brought her boyfriend Adrian with us because I had Slade so it only made sense.

Adrian probably won't be drinking a lot since he is super protective over Becky and wants to make sure she gets out of the club with him instead of throwing up all over the floor.

She is already drunk even though she only had two drinks.

I had one and I'm slowly starting to feel the buzz.

She got a mojito, her favorite drink and a shot of vodka.

I got an espresso martini.

Adrian also got a drink to sip on but I'm not sure what it is.

And Slade got a Moscow mule to sip on.

"Where did you find this club?" I ask, swaying my hips to the music softly.

"One of the guys down in design suggested it to me. He asked if I wanted to go out with him, but I'm basically married," Becky says before glancing over at Adrian.

Adrian and Slade are both at the bar, sipping on their drinks while examining the layout of the club. Adrian is staring mainly at Becky, probably to make sure no one goes near her, while Slade is looking at every single person, on the second floor, first floor, dance floor, bar, everything.

With how much he is keeping his eyes on everything, you would think that someone's out to get him or he's just very paranoid.

"What's going on between you two?" Becky asks, bringing my gaze back to her.

I shrug. "Nothing, we're just roommates."

"Roommates aren't supposed to look at each other like that."

I raise an eyebrow at her. "Like what?"

"Like they want to fuck each other's brain out."

I laugh and shake my head at her.

I've never really dated a guy.

Slade has been the only guy I've ever had a connection with.

Becky doesn't know I'm a virgin because if she did she would just baby me or try to get me to sleep with the first hot person she sees.

But with all of the teasing between Slade and me, the constant back and forth, I'm getting restless.

Slade knows what he does to me too. He just likes messing with me.

Times like this are when I wish I did at least have some sort of contact with boys so that I would stop acting like a prude and just go for what I want, but I get scared and insecure.

I've only kissed one boy and that was during a round of truth or dare in high school.

I barely even remember that night because it wasn't that important to me.

During high school I focused on my studies and myself rather than drama or boys.

"I need another drink. I'm starting to feel sober," Becky says and I agree. All this thinking isn't helping me have fun.

We walk back to the guys, and Becky immediately goes into Adrian's arms while I go up to the bar, standing next to Slade.

The bartender smiles when he sees me as I say, "I'll get

four shots of your best vodka," I say before he nods and gets to work.

"What are you doing?" Slade asks, putting his hand on my arm. Sparks fly where he's touching me.

I look at him and my lips are dangerously close to his face. "What do you mean?"

"I mean, why are you ordering four shots? Don't you think you had enough to drink?" Slade raises an eyebrow at me.

My eyes concentrate on his and I notice how dilated his pupils are. It almost feels like I'm staring into space because of how dark they are.

"I've only had one drink tonight," I say while the bartender comes back with the shots. "Stop being a buzzkill and trying to ruin my night." I grab one of the shots and take it.

Next thing I know Slade comes up behind me and he presses his chest into my back. I arch and his hips press up against my butt, his erection thrusting into me lightly.

His lips touch my ear, sending shivers down my spine. "*Pochemu ty vdrug vedesh' sebya so mnoy kak khuligan?*" he asks with his smooth Russian tongue while caging me in against the bar, his arm trapping me.

I exhale and close my eyes, starting to feel the shot I just took.

Damn, alcohol works fast.

"You didn't answer me. Why are you acting like a brat with me all of a sudden?" he asks.

"Because you aren't playing fair," I answer and turn around to face him, my butt no longer pressed up against his erection.

I know for a fact that Slade is big because of the gorgeous v-line he has that leads to what's between his legs, his rippling body, and his hands.

Guys with big hands always have big dicks.

That's what Becky told me.

"I didn't know we were in a competition," he says, a playful smirk on his face.

I glare at him. "You're so infatuating sometimes. It pisses me off."

"I know, seeing you mad is like foreplay for me. Keep going," Slade teases, leaning closer to me and pressing his erection into me again.

I want to almost pull Slade closer to feel more of him, wrapping his arms around me.

The room starts to feel hot and stuffy with him being so close, his breath hitting my cheek and his nose barely touching mine.

"Oh you want me to keep going?" I raise my eyebrows at him. "You brought me flowers for my birthday, gave me a ride to work, make me dinner and breakfast, help me with my manuscript, flirt with me, touch me, sleep with me when I have nightmares. Should I continue?"

"I'm not allowed to do those things?" he playfully asks.

I feel my face getting red. "You can't do them with the intention of not doing something about it."

The playful demure is gone from Slade and his jaw ticks before he leans in closer to me, pressing his entire body against mine. His hands land on my waist and his lips are right next to my ear.

"Trust me, Isabella, when I have you, you're going to be begging me to let you go. Only reason I haven't staked my claim with you yet is because I want you to enjoy the last bit of freedom you have before I consume your every need."

My head feels heavy when he leans back, his eyes caught on my lips. "I hate you."

Slade smirks again and thrusts his hips into mine. "I want you." Slade grabs one of the shots from behind me and gulps it down without any chaser before backing away from me slowly. "Make sure to enjoy tonight Isabella, because after this, our game is over." Slade walks away and I turn to Becky.

She is making out with Adrian, smiling into his lips while he has her hips in his hands.

If Slade wasn't being such a pussy, that could be us.

I grab the shots I got for them and take both, the burn sliding down my throat. I swear I feel like if I take another one I'm going to gag.

I spin back to the bartender and wave him down. "Give me another two shots."

13

SLADE

I leave her for ten minutes to take a call and she's stumbling on her feet by the time I come back.

I glare at her dark haired friend.

I think her name was Bianca? Becca? Becky?

I don't fucking know and quite frankly I don't give a shit.

We've only been here for an hour and I'm practically losing my mind. The line I took in my room before we left seems like it's doing nothing, neither is the drink I had.

Maybe because you're worrying too much about her, dickface.

I walk up to her and grab her face as she laughs. "What did you drink?" Her eyes try to focus on me, as she squints while smiling at me. "Isabella."

"You're SSSlade, yea?" She giggles, the sound sending

blood down to my dick. "Oh yea, you're a twin. Like three times three," she says while holding up three fingers.

I look behind her at the bartender wiping down the counter. "Hey," I bark, making him stare back at me. "What did you give her?"

He thinks, glancing at Isabella in my hands "An espresso martini and a couple shots."

"How many is a couple?" I ask, glaring at him.

His eyes go to the scar on my face before he focuses back on the conversation. "Like seven?"

My jaw clenches and I grab my wallet, giving him my card. "Take care of their tab, too," I say, pointing to Isabella's friends.

He nods and leaves with my card.

This is reckless.

I shouldn't be out in public without my mask or my helmet, or using my card with my personal name on it. I should be using Niko's card that I transferred funds into but, no. I just need to get the fuck out of here before I grab my gun from my waist band and start shooting up the place.

My eyes catch her friend's, and I walk towards her while holding onto Isabella. "We're going to head out. Are you guys good?"

Her friend smiles and nods before looking at her boyfriend.

"Yea, man, we're good. You guys get home safe," her boyfriend says.

The bartender comes back with my card and I pocket it before holding onto Isabella's waist and pulling her into me. "Can you walk?" I ask, my lips next to her ear.

"I can fly, what are you even saying?" She laughs, gripping to me and stumbling as we walk towards the exit.

She is so fucked up.

I'm tempted to make her snort coke just so she can sober up a little bit. Isabella's talking about anything and everything under the sun as I walk her to my bike. I'm kind of scared to drive with her but luckily the apartment is just ten minutes from here.

We stand in front of my bike as Isabella goes quiet, which concerns me.

She's swaying back and forth while staring at me weirdly. "What's wrong?" I ask, my hands holding her face again as I inspect her eyes. Her pupils are normal so I don't think she got drugged.

She just got really fucked up from the shots she took.

I shouldn't have left her alone, but Ryker texted me saying he had more info on the hooded guy outside my apartment building.

Isabella shakes her head and backs away from me before she leans down and pukes on the side of the road.

I hold her hair away from her face as she throws everything up. "Everything's spinning." She groans before vomiting more. I rub her back and tell her she's fine as she stares at the ground, spitting out the puke.

"Everything all good here?" I hear someone ask from a distance.

A guy with blue eyes watches Isabella spit out the throw up and groan. "She's fine."

"Are you sure man? She doesn't seem-"

"Didn't you hear me? I'm taking care of my girl right now. Fuck off," I grunt before focusing back on her. I don't pay any more attention to the guy as he walks away. "Are you okay, *avtor*?" I ask her, still rubbing her back softly.

Her face and neck are red and she is breathing slowly. "Take me home," she whimpers and looks up at me.

I move her hair out of her face. I grab the helmet and put it on her, fastening the clips. "I'm going to have you sit in front of me so I can hold you and make sure you don't fall okay?" I tell her and she nods. I put on my helmet and sit on the bike turning it on and making the engine roar. I hold out my hand for her. "You're okay?"

She nods. "Yea, just go slow."

I probably won't but she doesn't need to know that.

You can't go slow on a bike.

I help her on the bike and make her sit in front of me, facing me so that I can hold her while I'm riding. When she sits down, the position we're in makes my cock swell with blood.

I swear since the minute I met Isabella, I've had multiple uncontrollable boners like a fucking needy teenager.

The need I have for this girl is unbearable and I have such a tight hold on myself but I'm close to just saying fuck it and going after her.

She pushes her hips into mine and I can't help but groan. I grab her hips, stopping her from grinding into me. "Stop, Isabella, before I fuck you on the bike in front of everyone on the street. I don't care how drunk you are, I'll make you scream my name, *avtor*." I tell her and Isabella shivers.

I hold onto her with one hand and kick my stand up before moving. Isabella wraps her arms around me tightly as I move onto the street. She rests against the gas tank of my bike while wrapping her arms around my waist.

I weave in and out of traffic, trying my best to go fast but also make it back to the apartment in one piece.

It takes me ten minutes to get into the apartment garage.

I stare down at Isabella making sure she's okay as I go into my parking spot. I kick the stand to the ground and turn off the bike. "You okay?" I ask, taking Isabella's helmet.

Her eyes are a little bloodshot and fluttering. "Yea, just kind of tired." I remove my helmet and rest it on the handle bar. "Why do you have to be so attractive?" Isabella tilts her head to the side a little bit.

"What do you mean?" I ask.

"Like you're just perfect, even with the scar. I think the scar makes you more attractive," she says before putting her hand on my face, her finger tracing the line. I flinch when she makes contact with the scar. I'm hoping she didn't notice my reaction.

Her touch feels like fire on my skin, everything in my body in flames.

I need her, I think as I push my hips into hers.

"You like the scar?" I raise an eyebrow at her.

Girls usually do.

When I first got the scar, girls would always look at it before giving me a flirty smile.

None of their compliments meant anything to me.

Compliments in general never meant anything to me until I met Isabella.

"Yea, it makes you unique." Isabella smiles at me.

I help her get off the bike and put her helmet on the handle bar. I hold onto her as we walk back to the apartment. She sways back and forth in the elevator and in the hallway.

When we get inside the apartment I turn on the lights and still hold onto Isabella. "You fucked a lot of things up for me tonight," I tell her, knowing she probably won't remember any of this tomorrow morning with how many fucking shots she took.

"What do you mean?" she asks, looking up at me with those big innocent brown eyes.

I ignore her and just bring her to her room instead. I make her sit down on her bed and grab clothes from her dresser for her to put on. She asks me to help her take her clothes off and I agree, hesitantly.

I first help her take off her skirt and change into sweatpants. Her leather jacket is already off and was thrown onto the floor.

Next is her shirt.

I grab the bottom of it and lift it over her head, leaving her completely bare from the waist up. My eyes go down to her pink nipples and I can see they are erect.

Goosebumps spread on her skin and I can't help but trace the swell of her breast with my finger. She moans and pushes herself into my finger.

I flick her nipple making her shiver. "Slade." Her nipples are pointy and hard when I brush my finger against them. I can't help but smile at her reaction. She's so sensitive, everywhere. I almost want to thrust my dick in her to see how loud she'll scream my name. My hand travels down, tracing her stomach. "Slade, please," she begs and I swear I almost lose it.

"Yesli ty ne budesh' ostorozhen, avtor, ya prizhmu tebya k stene, skhvativ rukoy za gorlo, i zastavlyu konchat' na

moyem chlene vsyu noch'." I say harshly before tugging on her nipple.

She shakes her head. "I don't know what you said but say it again. It sounds hot."

"Stop being a brat," I say before forcing myself away from her.

I grab her shirt and cover her body so I don't take her in my hands and ruin her.

Because I plan on ruining her.

She's fucking begging for it at this point.

14

ISABELLA

My head feels heavy as I open my eyes.

The room is dark but some light is shining through the window. I hold my head, as if that will make the pounding go away, but it doesn't.

I sit up and look around my room, trying to remember what happened last night.

The last thing I remember was dancing with Becky for a little, arguing with Slade, him walking away, and then taking way too many shots.

I shouldn't have gotten so many shots.

Slade was pissing me off and it felt right at the time.

I glance at my side table and see some pills and a glass of water. I take them without a second thought and gulp down the entire glass.

I grab my phone and read the texts I have from Becky.

They are all drunk texts, mostly making sure I got home safe and commenting on how Slade wouldn't keep his eyes off me.

I seriously don't remember anything after taking those shots but I'm sure everything will come back to me slowly.

I just hope I didn't embarrass myself in front of Slade or anyone for that matter.

The smell of food fills my senses.

I slowly get out of bed and carefully leave my room without tripping over all my clothes on the floor.

My room is finally fully unpacked, now I just have random clothes laying around the floor for no reason but I've always been bad with doing laundry.

I open my bedroom door and hear the sound of food cooking in a pan. I walk out and see Slade's back facing me. He's wearing a plain white t-shirt and black sweatpants.

He glances at me before focusing back on the food he's cooking. "Did you take the pills I left?"

"Yea," I answer as I sit at the island and rest my head in my hands. "How embarrassing was I?"

"You couldn't even walk. I had to basically carry you out," he says, and then pauses, which makes me assume he's done but then he says, "and then you threw up on the side of the road next to my bike."

I groan. "No! I'm so sorry, Slade."

"You took seven shots and basically blacked out." He

turns off the stove and starts putting together a burger and fries on a plate. "You're lucky I was there or you would have been showcased on the news for a missing girl alert." Slade places the plate in front of me. "You should be more careful when drinking."

"Why do you have to make everything into a lecture? You've never blacked out before?" I ask, raising an eyebrow.

Slade pauses and his gaze darkens as he thinks about it before turning around. "No."

"Lies," I say before putting a fry in my mouth. "I just turned twenty-one, let me enjoy the mistakes I make."

He cleans up the area where he cooked. "If I let you enjoy them then you wouldn't be here right now, would you?"

"Why are you even here right now? Shouldn't you be somewhere else since you were here yesterday? You're always leaving."

Slade shakes his head slightly. "Shut up and finish eating your burger before I shove it down your throat." My lips part, not believing he just spoke to me like that. He turns his head, and smiles teasingly. "Sorry, should I have added a please in there?"

"Why are you being such a dick all of a sudden?" I glare at him and push my plate away, not even in the mood to eat.

He's making the pounding in my head worse.

"Because you acted stupid yesterday. You think I want to spend my night babysitting someone the same age as me?"

"You didn't have to babysit me. I can take care of myself."

"Sure thing, *avtor*."

"And stop calling me that stupid pet name."

"You're just pissed because I won't kiss you," Slade says as he leans against the counter across from me. "Admit it."

"You're so full of yourself." I shake my head lightly. "I can't believe I thought you were a decent person."

Slade chuckles darkly, almost like there is a meaning behind his laugh. "Trust me, Isabella, I'm the last person you should be calling decent."

I roll my eyes and stand up from the chair. "Whatever. You can have the burger, I'm not hungry anymore." I start walking away.

"Isabella," he says but I keep going until he says, "Isabella," again.

I turn around and raise an eyebrow at him. "What?"

He motions for me to approach. "Come here."

I glance at his hand before looking back up at him.

His face is completely stoic so I can't read him or what he plans to do when I get to him.

"Why?" I ask. "You feel bad all of a sudden?"

"Just for once, listen to me and come here." I roll my

eyes and walk over to him. I lean against the counter in front of him and cross my arms, waiting for what he wants. When we stand there for a good few seconds just staring at each other, I get annoyed and say, "God, Slade, if you aren't going to tell-"

Slade shuts me up by grabbing my waist and pulling me into his body, his lips crashing down on mine. One of his hands is holding my face while the other grabs my waist, pressing my warm body against his.

Butterflies explode in my stomach from how Slade holds onto me as if I'm the only thing he needs.

He kisses me like he owns me and has been waiting to do this his entire life.

It is more animalistic rather than passionate and slow. He is punishing me with his mouth, nipping at my bottom lip, gripping my waist tightly and pulling me into him as if he can't get enough.

I gasp, inhaling sharp intakes of air between each breathless kiss.

Slade turns us so that I'm pinned to the fridge. He grinds his hips into mine and moans as he kisses me, ravishing me.

I wrap my arms around his neck and pull him closer, as if we aren't close enough.

My first kiss didn't feel like this.

I've never had a connection with someone like I have with Slade.

"Fuck, what is it with you, *avtor*?" he says before moving his kisses down my neck, nipping at the skin before sucking it. "I was doing fine before you." I moan in response and close my eyes, enjoying the feel of his lips on me.

"Slade," I whimper when he slides his hand to my throat. He shuts me up by kissing me again, shoving his tongue in my mouth.

His tongue glides against mine smoothly making my knees feel weak and my core tighten, begging for a release.

He tugs my bottom lip, sucking on it before biting it and letting it plop back in place. Slade stares down at me with heat and need in his eyes.

He looks like he is trying to hold himself back from doing more damage to me, not that I would mind.

"That was for being a brat all night yesterday and thinking you could get away with it," he says, tilting his head slightly, his eyes darkening, and his pupils growing. "Oh *avtor*, you have no fucking clue what you've landed yourself into."

15

SLADE

I f my mom saw how much cooking I was doing for this girl, she'd probably start crying, saying how happy she is seeing me care for someone and treat a girl right.

She'd have a stroke from how happy she would get.

It's been two days since I kissed Isabella and I've been home two nights in a row, not including the night she got drunk.

Every day I cook breakfast and dinner.

Every night we sit on the couch together. She's writing while I'm reading a book or watching a show.

And I haven't felt the need to take a line in those few days.

Not even for a kill.

I've had one mission and it was in the daytime while Isabella was at work.

I'm not going to lie, I'm getting restless with not doing anything and taking out my demons.

They demand to be released but I'm keeping them locked up just so I can enjoy my nights with Isabella.

This wasn't supposed to distract me or keep my demons at bay.

Isabella was supposed to be the person to help me get the role of Pakhan, not someone to make food for. I wasn't meant to sleep in her bed cuddling with her so she wouldn't get nightmares, or giving her a rides to work.

None of this was supposed to happen and I feel like the leash is starting to get into her hands.

I need to get back my control.

The door unlocks and in walks Isabella.

She's on the phone, probably with her grandma.

She told me a little bit about her grandma and how she practically raised her since her parents died young.

I had Niko look into it for me around the time of her nightmare when I was watching her sleep, like I do every night, but she doesn't need to know that.

I found out that both her parents died in a car crash in the middle of the woods. Isabella stated in the investigation that her parents saw a man in the middle of the road. They tried to swerve out of the way and ended up hitting a tree and their car flipped.

Isabella went to a nearby gas station to get help.

Then Isabella's statement was about how she saw a

bad man with blue eyes and a hood and how he was going to take her.

Which made me think back to the hooded man who was lingering near my building

Isabella smiles when she sees me, a light blush decorating her cheeks. "Yes, Grams, I swear everything's fine. The book is going well," she says as she walks towards her room.

I focus back on the food.

It's almost done.

Today I made a rice pilaf with my mother's recipe.

Isabella's kind of picky but I know she'll like this.

My phone buzzes on the counter, Niko's name on the screen.

I pick it up and turn the stove on low, knowing I won't pay much attention to the food.

"What?" I answer in Russian.

"I found the name of the suspect outside your apartment, sir," Niko responds in Russian.

Most of my conversations with him are in Russian since he knows Russian better than English.

"Okay, good. Tell me everything," I say.

"His name is Georgio Bandino. He graduated from NYC ten years ago with a doctorate degree in criminal psychology."

I look up and see Isabella come out of the hallway, in more comfortable clothes, shorts and a tank top.

While keeping my eyes on her, I say, "Interesting."

"I thought so too. He worked with the FBI for forensics."

"How old is he?" I ask. Isabella's eyes go to me.

She's not used to me speaking Russian because most of the time I talk to her in English. The only time I speak in Russian is when I'm talking to my family or Niko.

"Thirty-eight. Born and raised here in the US."

"No wonder. All Americans are fucking insane," I say and Isabella's eyes wander down my body.

I smirk at her and motion for her to come to me. She shakes her head and I raise an eyebrow at her, daring her to disobey me.

She decides to listen and slowly walks to me.

"I'm still trying to find a connection between you and him sir. I'm looking through every employee there was at the time he worked at the FBI," Niko says while I grab her waist in my hand and pull her closer to me.

She smiles and laughs silently so Niko won't hear her.

"He doesn't work there anymore?" I ask, my hand traveling up her body, slowly so I can remember how every inch of her feels.

"No. He got fired due to an issue between him and another employee."

My finger traces the valley of her breasts slowly, my eyes meeting hers so I can see what I'm doing to her.

Her eyes are filled with lust and goosebumps spread

over her body as she leans into me. I trace her collarbone while her breathing comes out uneven, probably because she's trying to control herself.

I want to make her cum with fucking Niko on the phone just so I can see how much she can control herself.

"Find out why and how he got fired," I say, trailing my finger back down her body.

Fuck it.

I'm going to make her cum with Niko on the phone.

"Slade," Isabella whispers when my finger stops at the waistband of her shorts.

My eyes go back up to hers and she looks at me with not just nervousness but also temptation, as if I won't fucking do it.

"I tried but that file was locked sir. It seems they have buried that issue deep, not wanting it to come out," Niko says at the same time I shove my hand in her shorts and underwear.

Isabella grabs my wrist when my hand cups her dripping pussy.

She's hot and wet, all for me.

"I don't care. Fucking find a way to get information on that cunt. I want to know who he is."

Isabella shakes her head slowly and begs for me to stop.

Fuck that, not when I'm so close.

I need to feel her.

I need to feel her dripping for me.

And trust me, she's fucking dripping.

I thrust a single finger inside her and she's fucking tight.

Too fucking tight.

A thought crosses my mind.

I didn't think she would be a virgin but at the same time I'm not surprised.

I slowly move my finger out before thrusting it back in.

Isabella's knees shake and I turn us around so that I'm pressing her against the counter.

I hold the phone to my ear with my shoulder and turn off the stove, too preoccupied.

Fuck the food, I'll eat her pussy for breakfast, lunch, and dinner.

"I'll get onto it, sir," Niko says, reminding me I'm still on the phone with the fuckface.

My dick grows with an erection that Isabella caused.

"Oh my god, that feels so good," she whispers while her chin trembles.

I move my finger out and slam in it harder and reach all the way to what I assume is her g-spot. I play with her clit with my thumb, circling it and giving it attention.

"I have to call you back, Niko. I'm busy right now," I say while I watch Isabella fall apart because of my fingers. I hang up and throw the phone on the counter. "You're fucking hot you know that?" I ask, my hand grabbing her chin to force her eyes on me.

She keeps closing them from the overwhelming pleasure but I need her eyes on me.

"Slade-"

I cut her off by taking her lips in mine.

I keep thrusting my finger in and out of her while playing with her clit very slowly, teasingly.

She clenches onto my finger with every thrust, not wanting me to leave her cunt.

I can't help but imagine my dick being in her. I keep grinding against her into the counter.

She is fucking soaking me while she quivers and moans.

I curl my finger into her g-spot and her cries get so uncontrollable that she releases my mouth. She wraps her arms around my neck and holds onto me as I slam into her pussy with no restraint.

"Come on my fingers, *avtor*," I beg, wanting to know what Isabella feels like when she cums.

This feeling is unexplainable.

All I want to do is rip her shorts off and fuck her hard and fast, all night.

I never knew anything with a woman could feel like this.

But it's only with her.

"Slade, it's too much. Ahhh it feels so good." She grips onto my neck.

"Pridi ko mne, avtor." I whisper in her ear and like clockwork, she tightens around my fingers and screams my name. I crash my lips onto her and grind into her as I keep my fingers inside her as she clenches and unclenches while she cums. *"Khoroshiy."*

When Isabella is done, she whispers as I slowly slide my fingers out of her. She stares while I lick her off my fingers.

"Who was on the phone?" she asks after I've licked myself clean.

"My assistant and thank god I hung up because if I didn't, he would have heard you cum and I would have had to find a new one."

16

I'm in a meeting with my team and Bentley.

They are all expecting the book to be finished, which it is. I finished writing the last chapter earlier this week and have spent the last few days just adding my own edits and making sure everything looks polished enough for them.

Usually after the first rounds of edits are done they send it back to me to approve it and then I send it off to proofreading.

The cover draft that I gave them was also approved.

Most of the time with how things work here, we all come up with ideas for the cover but because it is my book I make the decision at the end of the day. They'll add a few tweaks and have some say in what happens in the book though.

When I first started out writing, I'd heard mixed

things about traditional publishing and independent publishing.

I feel with both you can make really good money, the main difference between the two was how much control you have over what you create.

The reason why I went with traditional publishing is because I didn't have an audience and I know with traditional publishing they are good with marketing your book and getting it out there for people to see.

Would I ever go with indie publishing?

Yes and no.

Yes, because I have the potential to earn a lot more money.

No, because the publishing house I work with pays for everything for my books, they market for me, and they give me signings and a bunch of other benefits.

"Bentley told us such great things about this book. We can't wait to go through it," Miranda, who does developmental editing, says as she flips through the manuscript.

I smile at her. "I hope you enjoy it. Honestly I've been hearing really good feedback on the idea, especially from readers who comment on the videos and posts we make."

"Well everyone loves a good psychological romance. They love the thrillers and deranged plots," Matthew, who is a copy editor, says.

Miranda and Matthew have worked with me since I got signed here.

They know how to clean up my writing the best.

"That makes me happy."

"Well, that concludes this meeting," Miranda says, standing up. "We can't wait to read it and let you know our thoughts."

"Same here. I hope you guys enjoy it while editing."

We all grab our stuff and leave the meeting room. Miranda and Matthew leave together since their desks are next to each other while I head to the other side of the building because I still need to grab my bag and laptop from my office.

My phone buzzes as I grab my stuff. After I finish packing everything I take my phone out and see a few messages from Slade.

> When are you going to be home? You should have gotten off an hour ago.

> I feel like I'm going crazy without you here.

I smile at the messages, feeling my heart flutter.

I go inside the elevator and text Slade while the number drops down and then also check my other notifications.

> I'm leaving the office now. The meeting ran over because they were curious about some things with the book.

Everything good?

Yes. I'll be home in 20 minutes.

I pocket my phone when I leave the building. It's dark and there are other people on the street probably leaving from work and going home.

While walking home, butterflies flutter in my stomach as I think about Slade.

I feel like things between us are progressing which I didn't think in a million years would happen.

It's been more than a week since he kissed me and since then he has touched me in ways I've never let anyone touch me before.

We kiss a lot.

Right when I get home from work, he pulls me into his arms and ravishes me against the wall and then the counter. He pulls us down on the couch, against the wall in the hallway, and down into my bed.

He sleeps in my bed most nights and isn't disappearing randomly from the apartment anymore.

He leaves every other day but still texts me that he made food for me. He also helped me finish writing the ending of my book so that I could send it off to the editing team.

He told me that once the book was published he wanted to take me out to a really nice dinner, just us two.

I don't know what's going on between Slade and I.

I know that I care for him and like him more than a friend and I can only hope he feels the same for me.

Sometimes when he touches me he's hesitant until he snaps out of whatever haze he was in and starts to pleasure me.

There are times where I want to help him and I stick my hand in his sweatpants so I can touch him but I get shy. Also, when he stops pleasuring me he just makes me eat right after or distracts me from asking him if he needs help.

I feel his erection when we go to sleep and sometimes he's unknowingly grinding into me while he's sleeping.

I'm close to the apartment building and I round the corner but I stop in my tracks when I see the same hooded guy from a few weeks ago.

The guy I thought I saw.

The one who looks like the guy at my parents' car crash.

He is just staring at me.

The hood hides most of his face, but I can see his blue eyes clearly.

I don't think twice as I turn around and start walking the other way.

I pull out my phone and go to Slade's contact. I check if he's following me. I still see his black hood and blue eyes.

I press Slade's contact and it starts ringing as I put my phone to my ear.

"What's wrong?" he asks, as if he immediately knows.

"Someone's following me," I say, still glancing behind me to see if he's still trailing me and he is.

My steps start to quicken as I try to get lost within the crowd.

"Where are you?"

"I was down the street from the building but I'm walking back towards my office."

"I'm coming. Stay within crowds of people and keep me on the phone," he says as I hear rustling.

I look behind me and the man's closer.

I start running.

"I'm scared. He's starting to walk faster."

"You're gonna be fine. I'm getting on the bike now. You'll hear me. What street are you on?" he says before his bike starts up, roaring from the other end of the phone.

"I'm on 57th."

"Go to the BMW dealership. I know them over there."

I listen and run as fast as I can towards the dealership, wishing for the guy to just give up but as I run he keeps getting closer.

My heart is pounding and I'm fill with so much adrenaline that I don't even feel tired from the running. All I can think about is getting to the dealership so Slade is come and get me.

"I'm coming for you, you fucking bitch! You can't run forever!" the man yells. "Your prince can't save you!"

Once I'm at the dealership, I don't think as I push open the doors and go inside.

"What's going on? Are you inside?" Slade says as I search for the restrooms and then run towards them.

All of the employees probably think I'm insane.

Once I get in the bathroom I lean against the door, catching my breath.

I've never run so fast in my life.

What does he want with me?

Why does he look so familiar?

He looks like the guy from my nightmares, the ones about my parents.

"I'm here, *avtor*. Keep breathing," he says through the phone as tears streak down my face.

My heart is pounding hard and I feel like I can't breathe properly.

"Slade," I cry and close my eyes.

The bathroom door pushes open and I immediately know it's Slade.

A pair of hands are on my face and I open my eyes.

He's still wearing his helmet but his visor is lifted.

"You're okay. I've got you," he says although his voice is muffled.

"Slade, I was so scared. I swear I thought I saw a ghost

from my past following me." I cry in his arms while he comforts me.

"It's okay, *avtor*. I'll find him. I won't let anything happen to you."

He pulls me to his chest and I rest my head against where his heart is, listening to his heartbeats and closing my eyes as if they are a lullaby to calm me down.

17

SLADE

"Why the fuck would I let you go?" I ask, Nicolas, the fucker I'm going to kill tonight.

Nicolas is a twenty-eight year old bodyguard from the Italian Mob.

Ryker sent me his information and requested that I kill him.

Why does my brother want me to kill him?

I have no clue.

All he said is that he needed me to eliminate this guy and that he'd pay me for it.

But I told him not to bother with the money because after the past few weeks I've had, I need a good challenge to keep myself busy.

Nicolas is really good with combat from what Ryker told me.

He knows his weapons and is quick on his feet.

I'm filled with so much pent up anger and fury that all I want to do is smash someone's head into a wall.

And lucky for Nicolas, he caught me on a good fucking day.

I took some pills to calm down my racing heart and the loud voices in my head. Isabella has been consuming all my time and I'm starting to get withdrawals, so I need something to just take the edge off since she wasn't here.

She has no clue that you're a cold blooded killer and you're afraid of her knowing you take drugs?

She can live with the fact I'm a killer.

She'll accept it because she has the same kind of dark and twisted mind as mine.

"Because you won't do shit. You're just some Russian prince that gets bored so he kills people for fun."

I shake my head lightly. "You have no clue why I'm going to kill you. I don't even know why I'm killing you. This is for my brother."

"*Vaffanculo, stronzo,*" he spits in Italian.

My phone buzzes in my pocket. I take it out and Isabella's name lights up the screen.

"My girl's calling so I'm going to need you to shut the fuck up for a few minutes," I say, walking over to him and taping his mouth shut. He struggles against my hold but once I get the tape on I answer her call. "*Avtor.*"

"Hey. I'm probably going to be a little late coming

home. I have another meeting with my team about the book. They said they had some questions for me."

The clock on the wall tells me it's five-thirty.

Fuck I completely forgot that I have to have Niko pick her up.

"Okay. I'm sending Niko to wait for you outside. He'll take you to the apartment."

I can't have another situation like last week happen again.

Niko's been looking into it.

He has been checking all the street cameras, trying to connect the person with the black hood that Isabella saw on the street to the one who was outside my apartment. I'm sure the connection is that they are the same fucking person.

"Okay, where are you? Why can't you come?'

"You miss me already, *avtor*?" I smirk.

"As if." She chuckles.

"I made food for you before I left for work." I walk around my warehouse as Nicolas struggles against the ropes while watching me being a lovesick puppy.

For this girl I am.

What am I doing?

Making meals for her, sleeping in her bed, getting her a fucking five hundred rose bouquet for her birthday, making her cum almost every single day even though what happened in my childhood was supposed to ruin that for me.

She's just a girl.

A girl who's starting to make me feel things I definitely shouldn't be feeling.

"What did you make?" she asks.

"Alfredo pasta."

"That sounds good."

I know she loves pasta.

Her mom and dad would cook homemade pasta for her since they are Italian.

I've learned a lot of new things about Isabella in the past few weeks of constantly obsessing over her and spending time with her.

Her favorite color is red, her favorite movie is Pulp Fiction, her favorite actor slash actress is Angelina Jolie, she had a dog named Charlotte who was a golden retriever but she unfortunately passed away.

She used to live with her grandma before she moved to New York.

She told me a little bit about her parents.

Isabella said that they died in an accident but there is more to the story she isn't telling me, even though I know most of it from the research that Niko did for me.

She would ask things about me and I would tell her some stuff but not in detail.

She has no clue about my real life.

"Why do they want to talk to you? You keep having a lot of meetings at work."

"It's because they are just really interested in the book," she explains. "They want to talk about some of the scenes I wrote, I think."

"Okay, well I probably won't be home until late so don't wait up for me," I say, looking back at Nicolas. He is just staring at me with boredom now. "I'll see you when I come home okay?"

Home.

I've never called that fucking apartment home.

Another thing she has changed for me.

"Okay, bye."

I hang up and pocket my phone.

I rip the tape off of Nicolas's mouth and he says, "Fucking bitch boy. You're nothing."

I throw my fist at his face, knocking it to the side. He spits out blood and smiles.

"Did I hit a nerve?" He raises an eyebrow.

I grab his throat and squeeze, his face turning red. "Why the fuck does my brother want me to kill you? Other than you being a fucking pain?"

"I-I-"

I let go of his throat so he can talk.

"I work for the Italian Mob. I'm Lorenzo's daughter's main guard."

I furrow my eyebrows at him. "Interesting," I say as I

think.

Ryker possibly going undercover for the Italians?

How long has he been planning this?

I'll have to call Landon to see what he knows.

All three of us have secrets but we're close and we tell each other most things.

Only thing we keep hidden from each other is this competition our daddy dearest is making us do so it possibly has to do with that.

When I asked Ryker why he wanted me to kill this guy he wouldn't say.

"They'll know what happened. You can't hide forever, Rykov. The Italians already have a plan to get rid of you pieces of scum. You and your entire family."

"Alright, let's see what you got so I'm prepared." When I go to untie him he head butts me and stands before slamming the chair to the ground.

The chair breaks apart and I fucking curse at Niko for giving me a wooden chair instead of one of the metals ones I always ask for.

My head is pounding as he gets out of the ropes and comes at me.

We throw punches and we kick and push each other around.

I slam him on the floor and strike constant jabs at him as he tries to defend himself and cover his face.

He bucks his hips from under me and throws me off

of him. I get my knife out of my pocket but he knocks it out of my hand and kicks my chest so that I'm down.

He grabs my knife from the floor and stalks towards me.

My head still fucking feels like it's spinning from the head butt.

"You messed with the wrong fucking guy, Rykov," Nicolas says before he gets on top of me and prepares to stab my face but I hold his arms, forcing them away from me. "I'm going to kill your entire family and then find out who your girl is." He slices my cheek making me wince. "And then I'll fuck her on your dead corpse."

Rage fills my body and I throw him off of me. I grab my knife from him and don't think twice before stabbing it in his eye. He screams and cries while I stab him repeatedly, in the chest, face, arms, anywhere I see fucking fit.

His body goes limp after a while but I don't care, I take my anger and emotions out on him until my body is covered in his blood and he's just an open corpse on the floor.

18

I walk inside the conference room after Slade hangs up.

Everyone is waiting on me so my cheeks heat up. "Sorry, I'm a little late." I sit down next to my agent.

Miranda and Matthew, my editors, Coraline, my agent, and Bentley are here in the meeting today.

My editors haven't finished editing the manuscript from what I know. They have made a few edits here and there but aren't done.

Bentley has finished reading the manuscript and he told me he wanted to know a few things about the story before I went home for the day.

Slade said that Niko will be waiting for me downstairs whenever the meeting is over since he doesn't want me to have any more issues getting to and from work.

Thankfully, Slade has been sleeping with me almost every day since I sometimes get nightmares.

I haven't told him the whole story about the car crash or said how that hooded guy with the blue eyes may be connected to that night because I don't want to rehash it.

I want to pretend for a little bit that he isn't out to get me and I still have time left to enjoy my life and live.

"Where did you get the inspiration for your book?" Bentley asks, his facial expression revealing nothing.

He doesn't look mad, just curious.

"Oh, mostly dreams I have or random thoughts." I shrug, glancing around the table at their faces. "Why? Did I do something wrong?" Anxiety crawls up my throat as I start to worry if I accidentally might have stolen another writer's idea or story.

"No, no," Coraline says. "We were just curious because your scenes and some of the chapters remind me of what's been happening in the news lately. I mean they are so graphic and specific so we were only wondering how you came up with it all."

"Mostly dreams. I got help from an outside source as well with some ideas that I was stuck on but I don't watch the news."

"You should. It's a coincidence that you're basically writing what's happening in New York," Miranda explains. "I was thinking about it the other day when editing a scene and I rewatched the news then spoke with

Bentley and Coraline about it and they saw the similarities too.”

I furrow my eyebrows and try to think.

Watching the news always makes me feel a little anxious so I try to not pay attention much to what’s happening on the TV and instead just focus on what’s happening with myself.

“I’ll have to check it out because I don’t know anything about that.”

“That’s what I told them. Isabella’s just a genius.” Bentley smiles at me, looking like a proud father.

I know he is proud.

He always tells me that I’m his favorite in the building. I know he sometimes just says that to make me feel better about myself and my writing.

We talk more about the editing and the cover and how marketing is going. They all tell me I’m doing a good job and to keep it up.

Miranda and Matthew leave and it’s just Bentley and my agent.

“I want to give you a break before you start writing the next book. But I’m curious if you have any ideas for what’s next?”

I have thought about it.

I’ve enjoyed writing this book a lot and I know I’m getting really good feedback so I want to keep writing similar stories to what I’m writing right now.

"Yea, I was actually thinking about extending this world I'm currently writing. Everyone is loving it and romance seems to be popular right now," I explain with a shy smile on my face, wondering what they will think about me continuing this book. "I think I could make this book into a series. Leave the first one on a cliffhanger and add a book or two. Readers love interconnected stand-alones or just series in general."

Bentley smiles at me and glances at Coraline. "And this is why I will continue to praise her." Coraline smiles at me too, looking insanely proud. "Let's fucking do it. Take a breather after editing and let the marketing team worry about getting the book out there and attention. You can relax while we plan some signings for you, and you start working on the next book whenever you feel the inspiration."

Bentley doesn't know this and I won't tell him until I've started writing but I already have the whole story outlined and plotted.

I'm almost ready to start writing it but I do want to take a break and maybe read a little bit since. I don't really like reading while writing because then I'll sometimes get the worlds or plots mixed up.

Plus, I really need to catch up on my TBR.

We finish up the meeting and I tell everyone to get home safe before leaving. When I'm downstairs I see the car that Slade told me Niko was going to wait for me in.

"Miss Rossi," Niko says, opening the door for me as I get in.

I thank him and he rounds the car, getting in the drivers side and then pulling out onto the road.

The drive is pretty quick and quiet.

Niko and I don't talk much.

Rides are silent but he seems nice. Niko is basically Slade's assistant or personal driver.

I'm not really sure but it's cool that he has someone like Niko to help him out.

I tried talking to him the other day but he barely responded and I wonder if it's because he doesn't understand or speak English that well.

He drives to the underground garage of the building while I go to my messages with Slade. I text him letting him know I just got home and ask him when he'll be home.

Things between us are good.

We keep getting closer and my feelings for him grow everyday.

He is so easily able to make me happy and smile.

I can only hope I'm able to do the same for him.

Niko parks the car and then opens my door. "Miss Rossi." He smiles and I take his hand as he helps me out of the car.

"When do you think Slade will be home?" I ask, impatiently.

"I'm not sure, Miss. He had a few things to get to today," Niko says in a heavy Russian accent, struggling to say certain words.

"Okay. Thank you again for the ride. I always appreciate it."

"*Konechno*," he says, smiling at me. "Do you need me to escort you?"

I shake my head. "No, Niko. I'm good, thanks."

We say our goodbyes and I leave to go up to the apartment.

When I walk in, it's empty, not that I'm surprised.

Whenever the apartment is empty, I try not to let it get to me since I'm so used to Slade being home now compared to before.

He is usually cooking while talking on the phone, smiling and winking at me when I walk in.

I go to my room and put my things away before changing into more comfortable clothes—shorts and a T-shirt.

I walk out of my room as my stomach growls, begging for food.

I heat up the alfredo that Slade told me he made.

He already knows me so well even though we've only known each other for around two months.

Time passes by so fast whenever I'm with him and I always want to beg for more.

I have no clue what we are doing and we've never

talked about it. I want to because not talking about it is killing me.

So I won't think about it, I turn the TV on and go to the news channel in order to watch what my team was telling me.

I'm curious how similar my book is to what's happening in the news.

Are they really that similar?

19

SLADE

By the time I get home all I can think about is falling asleep.

I remember before Isabella, I would go days without sleeping but now that I'm so used to sleeping with her every night, I can't go back to that routine where I would constantly be awake and on drugs every single second of the day.

Isabella makes me feel calm enough to rest and close my eyes.

So when I walk through the door, I'm relieved to be back at the apartment.

The door closes behind me and I lock it.

Isabella strolls out of the hallway, excitement on her face until she gets closer and sees the scratch where Nicolas got me.

Motherfucker was probably one of the most annoying

people I've ever had to kill because he is the only one who's ever nicked me or actually made blood spill from me.

"What happened?" Isabella asks as her hands grab my face and she inspects the scratch.

Thank god I took a shower at the warehouse instead of here.

Because if I didn't then she would have seen Nicolas all over me.

And who knows if my Isabella is jealous.

"Relax, I just got scratched walking past a tree branch." I take her hands and bring them to my lips, kissing them. "I'm fine."

She looks at the scratch on my cheek with worry. "It looks deep though. You should stitch it up." She doesn't let me argue with her. Isabella grabs my hand and walks us to her room. I sit on her bed while she leaves and comes back with a first aid kit. "You aren't afraid of needles are you?" I shake my head. "Lay down."

"You really don't have to, *avtor*. I c-"

"Seriously, it's fine. I don't want it to get infected. Then you would have to go to the hospital."

I roll my eyes and lay on her bed.

She sits on the edge of the bed and starts cleaning it up, even though I did that a few hours ago when I got the scratch.

"I've had deeper cuts and they were fine."

Her eyes go to the scar near my eye. "That one?" I nod. "How did you get that scar?" Memories flash in my mind, my father specifically. Nothing good ever comes from looking back on the past. That man destroyed my entire fucking life. I don't want to answer her question but Isabella pushes. "I'll trade you. A question for a question."

"Isabella—"

"You can ask me first. Ask me anything you want."

I think.

There are a bunch of things I want to ask her even though I know almost everything about her.

I want to live in her thoughts so that I know what she thinks about everything and anything.

"Tell me about your parents' car crash." I settle on that one so that I can at least know who the fuck this guy stalking her is.

I can use the information she's providing me for not just my benefit but hers as well.

Her eyes look deep in thought and she tilts her head to the side a little.

"It was dark and we were driving from Grams' house after dinner that night. My mom and dad were laughing about what happened at dinner. I drank my orange juice and I guess it had come out of my nose when I'd been laughing with them." Isabella smiles at the memory, reminiscing. "My mom and dad were holding hands while my dad drove home. He yells about something being in the middle of the road. I remember a horn honking and the next thing I know we crash into a nearby tree." My hand rests on her thigh as she talks. "After some time I got out of the car and was sitting next to my mom whose waist looked dislocated or disfigured, I don't know." She winces and a tear slowly falls from her eye. "I talked to her and begged her to come back but I knew I wasn't going to have a mom anymore, that she was gone. So I got up to get help but when I did I saw this black-hooded man. He was just standing next to me."

Isabella pauses, her hands not stitching me up anymore.

"And then what? What about the man?"

Isabella closes her eyes and breathes out, taking a minute before she starts working on my cut again. "He told me that he was going to come for me. He wasn't going to stop until he ruined my father's life." Isabella shakes her head lightly, probably remembering the horrible moments from that night. "I don't even know him. I don't even know why he would want to ruin my father's life. My dad was a good man. He would never do anything or harm anyone." Isabella finishes up the stitches on my cheek. "I have no clue why this man is coming for me and I don't know how to protect myself against him."

"You don't need to," I say and her eyes meet me. "I won't let anything happen to you." Isabella trails one of her hands down my face and cups my jaw. She smiles softly at me. I reach up and wipe a tear from her face. "I would rather die than let you live a life where you're constantly scared and looking over your shoulder."

I'm connecting the dots between Isabella's dad and this Georgino guy.

Is Isabella's dad the one who Georgino had an issue with?

What was the issue?

"Thank you." She smiles down at me and her finger lightly traces over my scar. "So where did this come from?"

I feel tiny needles prick at my skin, just thinking about that fucking scar. "My dad did it," I force myself to say.

I've never told anyone about that night and I don't fucking plan to.

She's just some fucking girl that I'll eventually fuck and get out of my system.

Whatever it is that she's doing, I'll get over it and she won't affect me anymore and I won't have to care about her so much.

Or at least that's what I try to tell myself but I don't even believe that.

Isabella furrows her eyebrows. "What?"

"My dad wasn't a good person."

"What did he do to you?" she asks, sadness and concern washing over her face.

I grab her hips and turn us over, pinning her to the bed. "Don't worry about it. It's in the past." I am hovering over her, trying my best not to crush her.

"But-"

I cut her off by pressing my mouth to hers. I don't want to think about it.

He died so I shouldn't have to think about all the shit that motherfucker put me through.

I kiss her with all the hunger and need I have for her while my dick starts to rise in my pants. Isabella is not just a want, she's a fucking need.

Ever since I laid eyes on her.

And right now, I just need her to make all of it go away.

All the rage and built up tension.

Isabella melts in my arms and she whimpers as I tug on her lips, wanting more, needing more from her.

My mouth fucking devours her and I grind my hips into her, making her moan. Her arms wrap around my neck and her fingers play with the small hairs at the nape of my neck.

"You're mine. Only I'm allowed to touch you," I say, suddenly feeling possessive of her, not wanting anyone to kiss her or hear her fucking moans, her laughs, her cries, nothing.

She's mine.

I lick her lips before thrusting my tongue fully inside

her mouth and sliding it against her own. I grunt and press myself against her.

My dick feels like it's going to fall off with how sensitive it is from how fucking turned on I am. "Say my name," I say against her mouth while my hand travels down her stomach and into her shorts.

"Slade," she moans.

"Again," I say, my fingers making contact with her pussy.

"Ahhh Slade," she moans.

I shove two fingers inside her and she grabs my wrist as I pull my fingers out and thrust them back in.

"Louder. I want New York City to know whose fingers are inside you and making you cum," I say in her ear, curling my fingers and pounding them in her.

"Slade! Oh my god, Slade! Slade!" she screams and opens her legs wider for me.

I grind against her thigh and mark her neck with hickeys. She feels so soft and warm, all I can think about is fucking ramming her.

By the time I'm done with her, all she'll be able to remember is how my dick made her fucking scream.

"*Snova.*"

"Slade!" she screams as if she can understand me. I pinch her clit and she screams while clenching around my two fingers that are inside her. "Oh god, Slade!" She shakes against me and drenches my fingers with her need.

My lips go back to her mouth as I kiss her and lick her lips.

Fuck she feels so good around my fingers.

I can't help it.

I pull my fingers out and sit up. "On the floor." She's still in a haze as I demand. "Go on the floor and get on your knees."

She does it hesitantly. "I've never-"

"I know. I'll go slow." She does as I say and I rip her shirt off, not wanting that thing on. I want to see her everything. I want her bare for only me to see. I pull my pants down a little and go to stand in front of her. I reach down to pinch her nipple and she whimpers, thrusting her boobs against my leg. I lean down and press a kiss to her mouth. "Keep your hands on my thighs."

She nods and looks up at me with those innocent eyes. She parts her lips, and I don't think twice before sliding my dick in.

I try my best not to thrust all the way into her throat.

"*Yebat*, Isabella." I throw my head back and pull out before thrusting back in. Her grip on my thighs tightens and she groans while taking me repeatedly. "You're doing so good, *avtor*."

I let her keep up at her own pace, trying my best not to start thrusting into her mouth hard and fast. I touch her hair and face, anything to distract myself.

Her tongue traces my dick, exploring it as if she is trying to memorize how my dick feels.

She watches me so innocently as she takes my dick down her throat perfectly.

My brothers have always raved to me about blowjobs but I've never gotten to experience one because when it comes to sex I've always been fucking scared of it.

Becoming intimate with someone after my dad ruined that for me, terrified me.

Saliva trickles from the corners of her lips and I can't help but go with her movements, thrusting in her mouth but not going too far. My dick slides inside her throat for a fraction of a second and I swear I went to heaven.

Her throat feels nice and warm and fucking tight.

"*Ty yedinstvennyy chelovek, kotorogo mne tak sil'no khotelos' trakhnut'*, Isabella," I beg, watching her swallow my dick like a good girl. "I'm going to go hard. Tap my thigh if you can't take it. In advance, I'm sorry for how rough I'm about to go."

Isabella blinks up at me and I take that as my sign to ram inside her.

She takes me deep in her throat and I grip onto her hair tightly.

Isabella doesn't tap my thigh but her eyes water and she looks like she's in pain from how red her face is.

My dick keeps sliding down her throat, again and again and I swear I black out as my release creeps up. My vision turns black and my whole body is close to tipping over the edge.

"Holy fuck, Isabella," I moan, my eyes rolling to the back of my head. My dick swells in her mouth and I fuck her as I would with her pussy. "*Tebe nravitsya moy chlen u tebya vo rtu? Pochemu ty menya ne ostanovish'?*" I say but she doesn't fucking understand me. "Why won't you stop me?"

Isabella doesn't answer me and I don't stop until I see stars in my vision.

20

ISABELLA

I wake up as my alarm clock on my phone beeps loudly, stirring in bed before opening my eyes.

Slade's arms are wrapped around me and I look at my phone and see it's 7:45 a.m.

My eyes widen. "Shit." I move Slade's arm off me and get out of bed.

"What are you doing?" he mumbles, resting his head on my pillow still.

"I'm going to be so late," I say while running around my room to get clothes.

"Just call out sick. You can write at home," he mumbles. "Come back to bed."

"It doesn't work like that," I say even though I can call out sick. "I still have to show up to the office even if I write at home."

"No you don't. Just come back. You won't even make

it to work on time."

"I can try." I start to throw my clothes off. "I can't believe I slept through my alarm."

His arms wrap around my bare waist and I jolt from the contact. Slade's lips attach to the side of my neck, probably creating a new hickey.

I still have the hickeys from two nights ago all over my chest and neck and I've had to use a shit ton of makeup to cover them.

"Slade-"

"Just today. You deserve a day off from writing. And if you really want to write you can, just stay in with me," he mumbles in my ear before pressing soft kisses on my neck. As if he knows I won't deny him, he walks us towards the bed and pins me down. "Tomorrow you can go back to being miserable." He trails kisses down my neck.

Since two nights ago where he fucked me with his fingers and fucked my mouth with his dick, it's almost become a routine for us.

He can't keep his hands off of me.

And instead of going to work at night he's been here with me.

I don't know what he does during the day but when I get back home, he's here and starts making out with me against the wall and then we have dinner together.

I love it.

I can't deny it.

I love spending time with Slade and I want to spend all of my days with him.

The way he takes care of me, cooks for me, makes sure I'm comfortable when I'm writing, he just does everything right and it's hard to not want him.

I wish I could be here with him at the apartment instead of working all day.

"Stay with me, please," he begs, still kissing me.

How can I refuse him when he begs and kisses me like that?

"Where's my phone?" He reaches over to the little table and hands it to me. I text Coraline that I won't be coming in today because I don't "feel well".

When I'm done, Slade grabs my phone and puts it back on the table and then adjusts us so that he's lying on his back and I'm on top of him.

"I thought we were going back to sleep?" I ask while he still is pressing soft kisses on my neck.

"We are, but I need to do something first," he says before sticking his hands down my pants and underwear.

"You're so bad." I chuckle.

"How bad, baby?" He smiles against my throat.

"You keep leaving marks."

"I need people to know you're mine," he says while biting my neck.

I whimper and rub myself against his fingers that are just resting against my pussy, teasing me.

"You're making me call out."

"You're being overworked and under-fucked, I'm trying to help you."

I blush and hide my face in his neck.

"Let me help you," he says as a single finger slips in. I moan and move my hips against it. "I can help you, Isabella. I can make you cum, again and again and again, until all you can think about is my dick inside you."

"Oh," I moan as he strokes my folds and inside my pussy. He's teasing me and I'm so desperate for him. I just want him to shove his fingers inside me and make me see stars. His fingers hover over my opening, pressing and flicking but not pushing a finger in. "Oh my god, please Slade." I press my hips against him. I move my head from his neck and hover my lips over his. "Please Slade, make me cum. Please," I beg, whimpering while I try to chase his touch.

"You want me to make you cum, *avtor*?" he breathes against my lips, pressing a kiss to them quickly before nibbling them.

"Yes, please, Slade. I'll do anything." Next thing I know, Slade is shifting down the bed and he grabs my thighs and moves me up his chest. "What are you-"

"Sit on my face, Isabella," he says, his breathing sending heat to my pussy and making the core clench.

I've never done this before.

What if I smell or I don't taste good?

"But-"

"Syad' mne na litso, chtoby ya mog zastavit' tebya konchit' tak sil'no, chto ty budesh' umolyat' o bol'shem, avtor," he says in Russian, I don't have a clue what he's saying but I lower myself to his face and his tongue pokes out and licks my opening all the way to the hood of my pussy. I grab onto his hair and moan loudly. "So the only way for you to listen to me is when I speak Russian? *Da?*" His hand wraps around my thigh and pushes me further down onto his face.

He stares at me with hooded eyes as he licks and sucks me dry but I keep drenching his face with my need. He thrusts his tongue in and out of me, tongue fucking me.

He goes harder, not stopping no matter how much I plead for him to.

"Oh my god, Slade!" I yell as my orgasm rocks through me and I'm clenching on his tongue.

I'm shaking from my release as he licks and sucks everything.

Black dots appear and I shut my eyes as I grind against Slade's face.

"I could watch that forever," he mumbles and glances up at me. "I could eat this pussy for the rest of my life and die a happy man." Slade legit moans when he licks me and I look behind me and see his dick, rock hard, making a tent in his pants.

"Slade-" I breathe out.

"I love how horny and needy you are for me. You respond to me so well. I know exactly how to make this cunt cum with my tongue, fingers, and soon my dick too."

I get off of him and the bottom half of his face is drenched with my cum. Before I can respond he grabs me by the throat and pulls me towards him.

"You're going to take my dick and when I'm cumming inside you're gonna take it so fucking well, isn't that right, *avtor*?" he asks me with dark eyes, appearing deranged and desperate.

His eyes are still so familiar to me. I can't pinpoint where I've seen them before, but I know there is darkness in there.

And the story behind the scar and what he won't tell me only adds more to the mystery of Slade.

It doesn't matter if I change my mind about him and don't want him anymore.

Slade Rykov will never let me get away from him. I'm his.

21

ISABELLA

Ever since I had that meeting with my team about the book being similar to what's happening in the news, I've been doing my own research.

I'm on my computer right now and Slade is next to me, reading.

Since he's been helping me with my writing, he's been next to me. He started reading my books recently. He bought them himself and has a few of them on his bookshelf. He's read most of my books and sometimes he'll ask me questions about them and whatnot.

The videos I watch about the missing people and the murders make me feel like bugs are crawling on my skin.

The way the bodies are disfigured and the torture methods the reports describe are so similar to my book, it is genuinely concerning.

Comparing my book to the news makes me think that

I could have committed the crimes even though I know I didn't.

Now I understand why Miranda and Matthew were staring at me weirdly.

There was a recent murder two weeks ago.

He was stabbed over thirty times in the stomach and his organs were basically splattered all over the floor.

His name was Nicolas Venedi and they say that he was a guard for Sydney Bianchi. She is the daughter of Lorenzo Bianchi.

He owns multiple businesses around the world and is a tycoon. He is known for possible mafia relations but everyone is too scared to go after him because of how powerful he is.

I research more about the other victims that were killed recently.

There is one where a club owner named Mitch died after being cut everywhere on his body, similar to what Slade told me about for my book.

His club was next to the place where I was cornered by the guy in the alleyway before I was saved by that masked man.

A man who's eyes I can't get out of my head.

"What are you looking at?" Slade asks and I hide the tab, going back to the document where I'm outlining my book.

I look at him and put on a smile. "Just thinking of what to add for my next book."

"Do you need help? What were you thinking?" he asks, placing a bookmark in between the pages and resting it on the coffee table.

"Well, I think in this book I'm going to have both of the main characters take down the whole human trafficking organization. In the last book, he saved his girl and now the girl wants to help him destroy the organization."

"Sounds like it will be good."

I smile and nod. "Yea, I'm just trying to figure out what will be in each of the chapters."

"More torture?" he jokes with a playful hint in his eyes.

His dark eyes with the scar near one of them.

It's hard to try and pin where I've seen his eyes before but I can't think straight when it comes to Slade.

For the past week I've been looking at him differently, especially after every news video or report I read, since he was the one who gave me the ideas for chapters and scenes in the book.

I'm suspicious but for some reason I still enjoy every second with him.

The dinners, the rides to and from work, the moments where all we do is kiss and touch each other.

I don't want to think of Slade in that way but how else

would he know about these murders and torture methods?

You'd have to be deranged to come up with this kind of stuff.

But when I stare into his eyes I can't help but think he can't be capable of doing all that.

I shrug. "We'll see."

Slade rests his hand on my knee and my core tingles.

Every single time he touches me, even if it's innocent, my body automatically reacts and wants him instantly.

There are times in bed when I've wanted him to just break his control and thrust into me and sometimes I beg for it but he just ignores me and makes me come with his tongue or fingers instead.

I think he might be scared. I don't know why he would be, but I have a feeling he is. Why wouldn't he have sex with a girl who is literally begging for it?

I don't think Slade is a virgin like me. He doesn't seem like one especially since he knows how to play with my body so well.

But why else would he be scared?

"I have a question," I say, putting my computer to the side and turning to face him on the couch. "Where did you get all of those ideas for the torture and murder scenes?"

His eyebrows twitch but he looks calm and his hand on my thigh doesn't tense.

Instead he runs his hand up and down my thigh, stroking the inner part, dangerously close to the spot between my legs.

He presses his tongue to the inside of his cheek. "I've seen what's been happening on the news so I thought back to that and twisted it into my own way."

"What do you think about it?" I ask curiously.

Slade shrugs. "I don't know. Shit like that happens every day."

"But it's scary that things like that are going on here. Like aren't you scared of him breaking in and murdering you next?"

Slade shakes his head lightly. "I don't think he would murder us."

I furrow my brows at him. "Why do you think that?"

"Because from what I've been seeing, he's only murdering bad people. Like pedos, traffickers, or people who have also killed, so I think you'd be fine."

I tilt my head to the side a little. "You think?"

"Yes, *avtor*. You're safe." He grabs me by my thighs and makes me sit on top of him. His erection presses up against the spot between my legs and I almost roll my eyes from how good he feels against me. "Why are you asking me these questions?" he asks, running his hand through my hair and trailing his eyes all over my face.

I shrug, giving him a small smile to cover up the real

reason. "I don't know. I'm just curious about your thoughts on certain things. You have an interesting mind."

Slade raises an eyebrow at me. "An interesting mind, huh?"

I nod and wrap my arms around his neck. "Yea, I mean you have intriguing points of views on certain things. Sometimes I wish I could go inside your mind and know what you're thinking about."

"What do you think I'm thinking about?" He lifts his chin with a smirk on his face.

I blush. "I don't know. Sometimes I think you're thinking about how dirty you are."

He looks at me with amusement. "Dirty?"

I laugh. "Yea, like how you have to take two showers every single day, sometimes three."

"I like being clean. Is that so wrong?" he defends himself.

"You probably think about what to cook for dinner."

"I want to make sure you're being fed right, *avtor*. Nothing wrong with that," he answers, twirling a strand of my hair with his finger. He adjusts his hips under me and I immediately blush when his erection presses hard against me. I can feel every ridge of him through his sweatpants. "What else?"

I look down at his lips and when I look up to meet his eyes, they are on my lips.

His jaw ticks and he leans closer to me but I don't let him touch my lips.

"I feel like you sometimes think about what you want to do to me."

"Yea? Like what?" he asks, his eyes filling with lust and that same darkness I keep seeing.

I gulp and say, "Like fucking me."

"I do."

"Then why haven't you?"

"Because I don't want to hurt you. All I do is hurt people. I can't be gentle. You're the only person I want to be gentle with and sometimes I can't even do that with you." He runs his hands along my bare thighs almost teasingly.

"What if I don't want you to be gentle?"

His erection grows beneath me when I say that. "You have no clue what you're doing. You have no idea what kind of person you're tempting, Isabella."

"I feel like I know you pretty well," I say while playing with the small strands of hair at the back of his neck.

He's been growing out his hair.

It's still pretty short and you can't really style it but he doesn't have a buzz cut anymore.

"You really don't." He leans in, his lips hovering over my own. "And if you're not careful, I'll take advantage of what you're offering."

Maybe it's because I feel daring, maybe it's because

I'm fed up with him pushing himself away from me, or maybe because I'm just stupid, but I grind my hips against his.

"I do." I press my lips to the side of his and start trailing them down his neck slowly. "I want you, Slade."

"*Blyad'. Ty ponyatiya ne imeyesh', chto sobirayesh'sya trakhnut' ubiytsu,* Isabella," he says. Even though I can't understand anything he says, I feel needy for more. Whenever he is talking in Russian on the phone, I can't help but watch and listen. Him speaking Russian makes me want to do anything he says without question. "*Ty khochesh' trakhnut' ubiytsu,* Isabella?"

"Yes, please," I beg, not even knowing what I'm agreeing to.

"Just remember you asked for it," he says before grabbing my throat and crashing his lips down on mine.

22

ISABELLA

His lips ravish mine hungrily in a desperate kiss. It's like he's trying to prove me wrong with this kiss, how he can't be gentle and that he's a rough lover.

But maybe I need someone who doesn't treat me like a doll, and Slade doesn't.

He gives the perfect amount of slut and princess treatment.

"You're a fucking temptation, *avtor*. I was trying to stay away from you, but no, you have to go in and ruin it all," he mumbles against my lips before biting and tugging on them.

I moan and grind myself against him which earns me a grunt from him.

He grabs my thighs and wraps my legs around his waist as he stands from the couch.

I don't pay attention to where he's taking me while he kisses me and lets his hands explore my body.

He sets me down on what feels like my bed and lets go of my lips. "I'll try to be gentle but I can't promise I will be," he says before taking off his shirt.

I admire his tattoos and the way his muscles tense and flex.

He leans down and I wrap my arms around his neck and he kisses me again. He's tugging on my lips and tasting every inch of them, not letting his tongue miss a spot.

The only time our lips disconnect is when he's taking off my shirt. The rest of my clothes are somewhere on the floor of my room and his fingers trail down to my bare pussy.

He groans against my lips. "You're always so wet and ready for me, *avtor*."

I moan as he slides two fingers inside me, stretching me wide. "Slade."

His other hand runs up and down my body, feeling every inch and making me hot and achy with need. "Your cunt wants me so bad, Isabella. She is swallowing my fingers perfectly and she's so so wet and fucking ready for me," he says as he thrusts his two fingers in and out.

He's filling me while playing with my clit, getting me wetter.

He fucks me with his fingers in a savage and rough rhythm and when he curls them I feel my release building.

"Slade, I'm going to-"

"Cum baby. I love when you cum. You tighten around my fingers so strong, I can't wait to fuck you, *avtor*. You can take it, my good girl, right?"

"Yes, Slade. Keep going." I clench around his fingers, seconds away from my release.

Slade fucks me faster until I'm screaming and wrapping my legs around him.

His erection digs into my stomach as I grind into his fingers. Our breaths mix with one another's as our lips lightly press against each other.

He lets go of me and pulls his fingers out before moving his head down to my pussy and before I can ask him what he's doing, he licks from my opening all the way to the hood of my pussy. I moan so loud, all of New York can probably hear me.

"Slade! Oh my god!" My core tightens on nothing and I thrust up into his face.

He pushes his tongue inside me before groaning. "*Yebat, Isabella. Tvoya kiska na vkus kak moya.*"

"I want you to teach me Russian," I say.

He moves up my body after he's done licking me and smirks down at me. "Why, so you can eavesdrop on my conversations?"

"No, so I know what you're saying while we do things like this."

"Trust me they are all good things." He digs in his pockets and thinks for a second before saying, "I don't have any condoms."

"What do you mean? I thought you would have some." I furrow my eyebrows.

Since I'm on birth control, I'm okay with him going bare, as long as he's clean and he pulls out.

"I've only been with one person before you, Isabella, and that was when I was eighteen years old," he says, looking at me intensely.

My heart tightens.

I would expect him to allow women to worship his body but I guess I was wrong.

I nod and gulp. "I trust you."

He nods too and pulls his sweatpants down, revealing his long and hard dick where the tip is leaking pre-cum.

His tip looks so large and purple, almost angry appearing from how turned on he is.

"I'll pull out," he gets on the bed and positions himself between my legs. "*Nezhnyy*," he whispers to himself.

"Kiss me."

He looks away from where our bodies are about to join and looks up at me with lust and darkness in his eyes.

He leans down and presses his lips against mine hard. One of his hands goes to hold my hip and his other holds himself up so he doesn't crush me.

"*Medlennyy*," he whispers as he eases himself in. I squeeze my eyes and wrinkle my nose as he sheaths himself fully inside me. He strokes my hip as he goes deeper and I feel like it'll never end until his hips finally meet mine. "*Blin, izvini.*" He pulls out to the point where I can't feel him and then he roughly thrusts inside me.

Pain explodes in the lower half of my body as he drives into me over and over again.

Slade doesn't feel like Slade anymore. It's like he blacked out and a monster has taken over.

"*Ty takoy tesnyy, avtor, blya. Ty tak chertovski khorosho menya beresh', chto ya ne khochu ukhodit',*" he whispers in my ear before taking my lips in his and thrusting a little faster.

My nails dig into his arms as I hold onto him while he rocks into me, going a little harder and faster each time.

My mouth parts against his as I moan from the pain and pleasure. "Slade," I whimper. His hold on my hips tightens and he rams inside my pussy fast and hard as if I triggered something. "Oh my god, Slade! Slade!" I scream, scratching at him.

He grunts with every harsh thrust. He removes his lips from mine and sucks on my neck, leaving marks everywhere.

"This body is mine." He trails his hand down my stomach. He presses a harsh kiss on my lips. "These fucking lips are mine." Slade puts his hand between us and presses his thumb against my clit. My pussy stretches around him. "This cunt belongs to me." He grabs onto my throat and fucks me like an animal, like a monster. "Tell me you're mine, Isabella."

My eyes open and they connect with his.

His eyes are filled with darkness and carnal desire.

My walls clench around him as I say, "I'm yours."

"Again." He thrusts harshly. I'm sure he's leaving bruises.

"I'm yours, Slade."

His grip on my neck is rough and almost threatening but I'm not scared.

If anything I'm fascinated.

He doesn't treat me like glass, he fucks me like a madman and like he isn't scared of breaking me.

Slade goes faster, not stopping or giving me a break even after I've cum around him. He tenses inside me before he pushes himself away. Spurts of his cum land on my stomach as he strokes his dick in front of me.

"Isabella," he says my name like a prayer while cumming and I can't pull my eyes away from him, fascinated with how godly he looks. He tries to control his breathing while I lay my head back and close my eyes. I could take a ten hour nap. Slade adjusts on top of me and

I open my eyes and stare at him with confusion. "You didn't think we were done, did you?"

23

ISABELLA

Slade is out getting groceries while I'm reading.

It's the weekend and usually on the weekends I write but since I finished writing the book, I'm reading one of Becky's books that she released a few months ago.

I've been meaning to finish one of her new books but every time there is a scene where the main characters have a steamy moment I can't stop thinking about Slade.

We had sex for the first time a week ago and since then, that's all we've been doing it seems.

Right when I walk through the door of our apartment, he grabs me by the waist and starts making me cum by his fingers before bending me over and thrusting inside me.

We've had sex in the shower before he cleans every inch of my body, on the island in the kitchen, the couch when he distracts me from outlining or reading, in my bed all the time, even when I'm sleeping he thrusts into me by surprise.

We've had sex everywhere but his bedroom.

I still haven't stepped foot in there but every day I'm itching to just take a peek.

I told Grams about him.

She said that I sound happy and that she would love to meet him one of these days over dinner. I tried telling her that it's not really serious between us yet, to which she told me to give her his number so she can talk some sense into him.

I did talk to Slade about what we were doing a few days ago.

"Slade," I say and he turns his attention away from his book and towards me. "What are we doing?"

We're in the living room, laying next to each other on the couch just relaxing.

"What do you mean?" He furrows his eyebrows at me and puts his book down, bookmarking it.

"I mean what are we doing? The sex, the touching, the dinner, the motorcycle rides? I just want to know where we stand with each other."

"You stand with me. You're mine."

"Okay but what does that mean? What do you mean when you say that?"

He turns so he can fully face me. "I mean, no one else

can touch you and be with you besides me. Same goes for me."

I smile at him and bring my hand to his face so that I can touch him. I always feel close whenever I feel his skin on mine.

"So we're together?" I raise an eyebrow.

"Ty moy," he whispers, looking down at my lips and then meeting my eyes.

"What does that mean?"

"You're mine."

"Ty moy," I repeat and he nods with a sweet smile that makes his dimples appear.

He leans in and captures my lips in his, and we forget about both of our books.

The next day when I came home from work, Slade had cooked us a steak dinner and put a candle in the middle of the island to make it romantic and he'd gotten me a 200 rose bouquet with a note saying *"Ty moy."*

The night was romantic and he knows me so well, probably better than Becky even though I've known her longer.

I trust Slade.

I trust him enough to protect me, not hurt me intentionally, and just be patient with me like I am trying to be with him.

We're still trying to figure each other out.

I've never been in a relationship and from what I've

gathered, neither has he so we both are going into what-ever we are doing blindly.

We're both trying to be patient with one another.

My phone rings beside me on my side table. I pick it up and see there is no caller ID.

"Hello?" I answer.

Usually I don't answer calls from unknown numbers but I'm waiting on a call from a lawyer.

It's for research purposes.

I'm not suing anyone but I need help on outlining my book since I will be including a lawsuit and I want to write that whole part of the book as accurately as possible.

The lawyer I'm trying to get a hold of is a young female criminal defense lawyer who is based in New York.

Her name is Maddie Walker and I heard she is one of the best.

"Hello?" I say again, not hearing anything.

I'm about to hang up when they finally answer.

"Little Rossi," he says, in a low and almost deadly tone.

"Who's this?" I ask as my heart starts racing.

"You know exactly who I am."

A flash of blue eyes and a black hood appear in my mind.

"I told you I was coming for you didn't I?"

"How did you get my number? Who are you?" I ask while anxiety creeps up my neck.

"Your little boyfriend knows who I am. I'm surprised you don't."

I feel the butterflies in my stomach when he mentions, I assume, Slade being my boyfriend. I mean we are together but we haven't said the 'boyfriend' or 'girlfriend' word. Even though Slade says I'm his and that's basically the same thing.

"You killed my family. That's all I need to know."

"Tsk tsk tsk. You don't even know half of the story, little Rossi. But that will be told another time. I need your boyfriend off my back."

A tear slides down my face. "What do you want from me?"

"First, get rid of that fucking lunatic boyfriend of yours. Then maybe we can strike a deal. I'd rather be alive than waste my breath killing you."

"Why would you want to kill me?"

"Because your dad fucked everything up for me! It's payback time, little Rossi," he yells and I try to muffle my cry. Visions of the car crash hit me all at once. My father's head against the steering wheel, the upper half of my mother's body, lying halfway out of the car, practically disfigured, and then, his bright blue eyes staring straight at me with the intent to hurt and destroy. "But one thing at a time. We first need to fix this issue with that fucking Russian boyfriend of yours."

My heart races thinking about Slade.

"What do you want?"

"The news has been crazy lately. Haven't you heard? All of these people dying and no suspect yet? He for sure knows how to hide his tracks but I'm thinking a certain author knows all about these crimes since she did write them all in her book, right?"

"How do you-"

He cuts me off. "Your boyfriend isn't the only one who was stalking you, little Rossi."

Slade.

The murders on TV.

The book with all the crimes that were all just a coincidence.

Nothing's making sense.

It's all too much.

"What are you even saying?" I cry, my mind going in circles.

"I'm saying your boyfriend's a fucking murderer. Either send him to jail or I'll fucking slit his throat in front of you," he says before hanging up the phone.

My phone drops from my trembling hand and all I can do is cry.

I scream and cry and have a panic attack, stressing about what this all means.

My heart is racing. Everything is suddenly too bright, too close. I need more room.

Everything is wrong.

Slade can't be a murder.

He can't.

He's not that type of person.

He's the type of person that cares for me and is gentle with me.

He buys me flowers and cooks me food and takes me to work.

He does so much for me.

"The victim has skid marks all over his body."

"His tongue was dismembered and shoved down his throat."

"The victim's penis was shoved in his gluteal region."

"Body parts were found scattered around the victim."

"Yea, I would include some torture scenes but I have no idea how to write a good one or any ideas for torture."

Slade shrugs and tilts his head lightly. "Cutting off his dick and shoving it up the ass is a creative one."

The tears all of a sudden stop and I look at my door, waiting, trying to convince myself why going into Slade's room would be a good idea.

How going into his room would make all of this thinking go away.

It can't be true.

Slade wouldn't do that.

He wouldn't keep this from me.

I don't think as I get out of bed with robotic movements and go straight for his room.

My whole body shakes and my vision is impaired as I try to focus and stay calm.

I stare at the door knob, my hand hesitating before I just say fuck it and twist the knob, pushing the door open.

It's dark in his room.

Everything is black.

His bed is in the center of the room with black silk sheets and a black comforter.

He has a desk and a bookshelf on one side. I walk towards it, seeing if I can find anything.

His desk has his laptop, pens, paper, and other supplies, all neatly put together like he's some sort of psychopath.

My eyes go to his bookshelf and all of my books are there. I furrow my eyebrows and grab one of the books.

Why would he have my books here even though he has them on the bookshelf in the living room?

I flip through the pages and find all kinds of notes.

Notes on every single page, trying to connect the stories I write to me.

As I'm flipping through, I find a photograph.

I pluck it out and it's a picture of me on the street.

I'm walking home from work while reading.

The book drops from my hand and a tear falls from my eye.

What the fuck?

What the fuck?

What the actual fuck?

I back away and stare at the other side of his room.

One of the doors leads to the bathroom and the other, I'm assuming, is his closet.

I open the door to his clothes and find an average closet. He has all of his clothes neatly organized by colors, mainly black, white, and gray, some blue shirts.

He has a dresser in the middle of his closet.

The drawers are filled with regular stuff like underwear, socks, belts, and very expensive watches.

When I get to the last drawer it's locked with a passcode.

I try random numbers but none of them work. I put in the numbers of my birthday and my heart drops when it pops open.

I open the drawer and I see everything he's hiding from me.

He's a liar.

All he did was lie.

And he did it so well.

24

SLADE

Niko has been blowing up my phone since I started torturing my target.

He usually never calls me so much because he knows not to bother me unless it's an important issue or about Isabella.

My target's body is lying on the floor with his eyeballs neatly placed next to his body along with some other parts of his body.

I'll let my fucking team deal with it.

I need to see what Niko fucking wants.

I'll fucking shower when I get to the apartment. Hopefully Isabella isn't there.

"You better be blowing up my phone for a good fucking reason," I say as I walk towards my bike and put my helmet on.

"Sir, we have a problem," Niko says in Russian, the phone call connecting to my helmet.

I stick my phone on the holder and start the engine. It vibrates underneath my body.

"What is it?" I ask, my jaw clenching.

"Your safe at the apartment was broken into. I got a security alert. Didn't you get it?"

No.

Probably because it was lost among Niko's thirty missed calls.

God fucking damnit.

I pull out of the warehouse grounds and race back home, going over 100 mph and cutting through cars.

"Fuck. Did you check the cameras?" I ask.

He hesitates and breathes harshly. "Isabella is the only one in the apartment, sir."

"God fucking-" I zoom down the street. "I'll be there in fifteen minutes. Make sure she doesn't leave that fucking apartment."

I drive fast and reckless, trying to beat the traffic home.

When I finally get to the building, I turn the bike off and swing off of it in a hurry. I rush to get to the apartment.

The door is unlocked and I don't hear her so I jog past her room where the door is open but she isn't there. My bedroom door is also wide fucking open, which it never is, and my heart drops to the pit of my stomach.

I slowly walk inside, trying my best to stay calm and not freak out.

I almost wish I fucking took coke before I killed and tortured that son of a bitch or at least before I got here.

I look at my closet, where the safe is.

My closet door is open, the light shining through.

My steps are small and quiet as I step towards the closet, making sure not to make any sound in case she gets startled and tries to run.

Isabella is sitting on the floor, crying as she stares at all of the guns, knives, and bullets in the drawer.

Fuck. Fuck. Fuck.

I take one step closer to her but the floor fucking creaks and she turns around.

She stares up at me with frightened eyes.

There are two ways this could go.

She can either be fucking furious and act crazy or she can cry and just understand.

I guess we're about to find out.

She stands and tries to run out of the closet but I grab her by her waist and pull her into my arms.

She starts screaming and struggles against my hold. "Let me go! Let me go! Let me go, Slade! Please, let me go."

"I'm not going to hurt you, relax," I whisper in her ear but that doesn't do shit. She tries to fight me and elbow me in the stomach but her little attempts are amusing at best. Her hip grinds against me and fuck, her acting crazy, while also being scared, sends a jolt of excitement all the way down to my dick. My cock twitches and I rub it against her. "Keep fighting me like this and I'll get the wrong idea, *avtor*."

"You're fucking horrible! You killed them! I can't believe I—"

"Isabella." I whisper in her ear and walk us towards the bed while she still struggles against me. "Tsk. Tsk. Tsk. You need to calm down. I can explain."

"Explain what? You're a murderer!"

I push her on the bed and pin her down, resting my hips against her and holding her wrists.

My erection presses against the spot between her thighs, but she doesn't pay attention to that.

Isabella tries to get her hands out of my hold.

She's determined, I'll give her that.

"I already told you a while ago, Isabella, that I'm not the kind of person you think I am."

"You kill people!" she cries, still trying to fight me even though it's really doing nothing.

I tilt my head to the side a little bit and furrow my eyebrows. "I kill people sometimes. You're over exaggerating. Really."

Her eyes widen. "You're fucking crazy! You have photos of me too!"

"Okay, look I have a lot of explaining to do. I know that, but you need to calm down Isabella. I'm not going to hurt you. I would never hurt you."

She shakes her head. "You lied to me. You lied about who you are."

"No, I never lied to you, Isabella. I just didn't tell you shit because I knew this was how you were going to react."

"No! This is something you tell someone when you first start talking to them. So all of this 'contracting stuff' that you were out doing was all a lie! It was all a facade."

"I never told you what kind of contracting I do. So again I didn't lie, stop saying I did. You're starting to piss me off," I say, my hands tightening around her wrists, warning her.

She seriously has no clue what I can do to her.

"Fuck you-"

I cut her off by pressing my mouth on hers.

This is the only way to shut her up.

My lips ravish her in a rough and demanding kiss. She pauses and almost kisses back before she starts to pull her lips away from me.

Her face scrunches up and she struggles against me but I keep kissing her, not letting her get away.

"*Uspokoysya i prosto day mne tebya potselovat'* Isabella," I say against her lips but she doesn't fucking listen to me.

When I imagined how this conversation with Isabella would go, it was completely different from this.

But she'll learn to be okay with it. She'll learn to understand me. She'll learn.

I wince when Isabella bites my bottom lip.

I can taste iron.

I grunt and move away. "I didn't know biting was a kink of yours?" I raise an eyebrow at her, and instead of laughing like I'd hoped she would, she brings her knee up and tries to thrust it into my groin. Instead she just punches my stomach, not really doing anything. "Come on, baby. If you're going to hit me, at least make me bleed again."

"Screw you, Slade."

I sigh and shake my head.

Looks like I have to do this the hard way.

I get off of her and she runs to my bedroom door. I open my side table drawer and grab the small injector.

By the time I leave my room she is putting her shoes on by the front door.

She is rushing and still a sobbing mess.

Right when Isabella puts her hand on the door knob, I wrap my arm around her waist, pull her into me and stick the needle in her neck.

"Slade." Her speech slurs and she goes limp in my arms.

I put the syringe on the island and pick her up, carrying her down the hallway to my bedroom.

Damn this girl can put up a good fucking fight.

Just thinking about it makes me want to take her to a random location, maybe the warehouse, and let her run away from me until I catch her and fuck her.

We'll try it out once she starts to calm down.

For now, I've got bigger things to worry about.

Like keeping my little *avtor's* mouth shut.

I lay her down in my bed and put the covers on her to keep her warm.

My lips touch her forehead. "You'll see, Isabella," I whisper and sit down next to her on the bed, rubbing small circles on her back.

I grab my phone from my pocket and open Landon's contact.

I press it to my ear as it rings. My eyes go to Isabella, admiring her sleeping form as he finally answers the call on the last ring.

"*Mladshiy brat*! Long time no call!" Landon yells. "I'm sure you fucked up on something so tell me what it is."

"It's a fucking girl."

"Ahh who's the unlucky girl?"

25

ISABELLA

My head feels like an elephant stomped on it. It's pounding so hard and dizziness consumes me as I toss and turn in the bed. It's almost like I'm hungover but stronger.

Was everything that happened a dream?

My eyes are so puffy like I've been crying non-stop.

I open them and see Slade staring straight at me.

We're in his room and the memories from earlier hit me all at once.

My stalker calling me and saying that Slade is a murderer.

Me going into Slade's room and searching through his things and finding the weapons.

Him coming home and admitting everything.

"Don't scream, unless you want me to give you a

reason to." He narrows his eyes at me, waiting for my next move. My muscles tense as my heart rate picks up. He scoots closer to me and runs a hand down my back, making me flinch. "I won't hurt you. I don't know how many times I have to tell you, Isabella."

Slade's hair is wet and I assume he took a shower after he knocked me out.

"You killed people," I say while tears start to form in my eyes.

"They deserved to be killed, trust me," Slade says, with no emotion in his voice.

He has his walls up and is showing me no sign of the Slade who took care of me, who made sure I was safe and happy.

This Slade has the dark voided eyes that I've seen many times before.

And who knows what he is capable of.

I shake my head. "You can't decide that."

"Isabella, I told you that my life isn't what you thought it would be."

"You never gave up information about yourself so what was I supposed to think?" I sit up in his bed and scoot back until I'm pressed against the headboard. "All of those people you killed, Slade." I shake my head lightly and rest my face in my hands. "I wrote about their deaths."

He moves closer and when his hand grabs my jaw, I flinch and stare up at him.

His touch still feels the same but looking at him I know everything is different.

This isn't the man I was starting to fall for.

This is just a lookalike.

"I was just trying to help you, Isabella, I would never intentionally hurt you and you know that."

I shake my head, again. "No, Slade. You have to turn yourself in."

"That won't do anything. I'll be out within a day."

I furrow my brows. "Who are you? Is Slade even your real name?"

Slade's lips lift in a small smirk. "Yes, *avtor*. There are a lot of things you should know about me and we'll get to that but so much is about to change for you right now."

"Are you going to kill me?" I ask, my lips quivering.

"No." He runs his hand down my hair and then strokes my cheek. "Why would I do that? I don't want to kill you, Isabella, I want to keep you. You're mine. How many times do I have to say this?"

"I barely even know you." I move his hand away from my face. "You have lied about so much. I don't know the real you. You kill people-"

"I kill bad people. You're overreacting."

My eyes widen. "Overreacting?"

"Isabella, in my world, this is a day to day thing." He shrugs like it's nothing.

"I can't, Slade. I can't do this." I push him out of my way and get off of his bed. Before I can walk out his door he grabs me by my waist. "Slade-"

He cuts me off by pressing his demanding mouth against mine.

I rest my hands on his chest ready to push him off but he keeps going, roughly moving his lips against mine over and over.

I can taste the metal from the cut on his lip from where I bit him yesterday.

He fucking deserved it, the piece of shit.

Touching me with soft caresses with the same hands that murder and torture people.

One of them is against my throat, not squeezing, just holding his hand there, as he walks us back towards the bed. His lips are intoxicating, distracting me from the fact that he is not a good person, not even a decent one.

"Let go of me. Please," I beg, still not kissing him back while he tries his best to pull a kiss from my lips.

Slade trails his kisses down my jaw and to the side of my neck. "I will never let you go," he says, darkly, almost like he is daring me to try and run.

I will.

But I have to be smart about it.

"Who are you?" I ask him.

He bites my neck making me moan as I try to move away from him. "Your worst nightmare." He lets go of me and stands. "Run."

"What?" I furrow my eyebrows while staring up at him.

"I want you to run, Isabella." He tilts his head, as if he's bored. "I'm giving you a ten second head start to put your shoes on and run. Don't make me say it again."

I don't think, I run.

I slide on my white vans that are near the doorway and grab my phone before opening the front door and running out. I probably have five seconds until he starts chasing after me. He has his shoes on and is way faster than me. My heart races as I take the stairs down to the parking garage.

I can leave through the gate there.

When I get inside the parking garage I unlock my phone, ready to dial 911, but I get knocked over and feel him on top of me, his erection digging into my butt.

"Slade-"

"Shhhh." He leans down and presses his soft lips to the back of my neck. "You don't want people to hear you." It's morning and I'm sure people will be waking up soon to go to work. His strong hand grips my hair and pulls. "I'm going to fuck this cunt while you scream and beg for me to make you cum, *avtor*."

He wastes no time shoving my shorts down and positioning me so that my ass is in the air. One of his hands pins my wrists above my head while my face is pressed against the concrete.

"Slade! Please! No!"

"Keep begging, *avtor*. It only makes me want to fuck you more."

Slade's belt buckle echoes and when I look back at him, he pulls his cock out.

My eyes go to his face which is covered by a ski mask. Deja vu hits me again and the night I got cornered in the alleyway comes to my mind.

"You-"

He cuts me off with a rough thrust inside me.

I scream and my walls tighten around him.

I wish I could hate how he makes me feel but I push myself back into him, my body craving more.

"My *malen'kiy avtor*, you love what I do to you. You love how I take you like a monster in the dark and fuck you like an animal," he says while forcing himself into me over and over again.

My whole body shakes with adrenaline and his rough hands touch me everywhere and anywhere.

"Slade," I moan, my saliva falling to the concrete as he fucks me rough and hard.

His thrusts are punishing and I know that this isn't about me this time.

This is about Slade making a statement that I'm his, no matter if I want to be or not. He is after his own pleasure and probably couldn't care less whether I cum or not because he isn't doing this for me like he has the other times.

It's all about Slade and what he wants.

Everything comes back to me.

He knew my job and where I work without me ever telling him, the amazing deal on the apartment, his eyes that have haunted me ever since that day in the alley, everything.

"Ty tak khorosho prinimayesh' moy chlen, Isabella. Ty moya, tvoye telo znayet eto, i tvoye serdtse znayet eto. Skoro ya ubedlyu tvoy tvorcheskiy um," he spits in Russian even though he knows I don't understand a thing he's saying.

My pussy throbs from his unknown words and my vision narrows. I feel like I'm going to pass out from how hard he's going.

His strong hands grip my ass, pulling me into him each time while he grunts and moans. My need for him drips down my legs with every thrust.

My body's a fucking traitor.

"Slade, oh my god!" I say as my whole body tightens up and my pussy walls clench around him tightly.

"Fuck, that's it, *avtor*. You're so tight and so perfectly mine, baby. Cum with me," he says, slamming into me once more before pressing his hips against mine as his warm semen fills me to the brim.

I can't move as Slade pulls out but when his semen runs down my thigh, I realize that he wasn't wearing a condom and he came inside me.

26

I can't believe I even let him fuck me, especially in the parking garage where anyone could walk in and see us.

He keeps looking over at me, probably scared that I'll run or scream but I have no thoughts in my brain.

All that's going through my mind right now is the image of our cum running down my leg.

I am on birth control but I'm still paranoid about getting pregnant because I'm too young to take care of a child and can barely afford to live on my own in New York.

Not to mention the dad would be a murderer.

The elevator bells dings and Slade walks out, pulling me with him with his hand on my arm. We turn the corner and he curses and then backs us into a wall.

"What's wrong?" I furrow my eyebrows at him.

"There's a cop," he says, licking his lips as he thinks. My eyes go down to his lips, secretly wanting to taste them again. "Did you call someone?" He looks down at me with a hint of a glare.

I shake my head. "No. The guy who's been following me. He called me and told me about you and said that if I don't call the cops or send you to jail, he's going to handle it his way."

Slade's jaw ticks and he slams a fist above my head, making me flinch.

A single tear falls from my eye as fear floods me.

Slade seems pissed. His jaw is clenched and his pupils have grown in size, looking like that dark void again.

He raises his head to look at me. "Here's what you're gonna do. Deny everything. You don't know what I do. All the advice and details I gave you, you got that from the news. You don't know what I do outside of the apartment. You're gonna forget what happened last night. I don't know what they will ask you regarding me but pretend you don't know anything. Got it?"

"Slade-"

"Isabella, tell me you understand?" Slade cups my face, so my gaze goes to him up. He wipes a tear from my cheek and his eyes soften. "I can't lose you so tell me you understand."

I nod. "Okay."

"I promise, when I have the time, I will explain everything to you. But right now I need you to stay calm and listen to me, understand?"

"Yes, okay," I say, stupidly.

Slade nods and grabs my hand, pulling me out into the hallway.

Two officers stand right in front of our door like they are just waiting for us. As we walk closer to them they turn their heads to look at us.

"Hello, officers, what can I do for you?" Slade says, tightening his grip on my hand.

The officers stare at me. "Miss Isabella Rossi?"

"Yes," I say, trying to stay calm.

"We need to have you brought in for questioning," one of the officers says while my heart rate speeds up.

My eyes go to Slade, silently questioning him but he just stares at the officers with a blank face, not revealing anything.

—

I'm sitting in the interrogation room, waiting for the detective to come in and question me.

They allowed me to get changed really quick before leaving with them. I was able to wipe the semen off my leg and freshen up, thank god.

Slade wanted them to give him a reason why they were

taking me but they said it will all be explained at the station.

He was about to have a fit over it but I told him that it was okay and to calm down.

Slade came in with me to change while the officers waited outside. He was pissed and also anxious but tried to remain calm.

Slade said he will figure it all out before letting me leave with both officers.

They put me in handcuffs but said it was procedure.

There is a knock on the door before it opens and in walks two detectives, wearing suits. "Hello, Miss Rossi, right?"

I nod. "Yes, sir." I smile.

"My name is Detective Wren and this is my partner Detective Johnson. The reason why we brought you in today is because we need to ask you some questions about some killings that have been happening in the city."

My heartbeat speeds up.

Stay calm.

Slade said he will get me out of this. He'll handle it.

The serial killer will handle it.

The serial killer who fucked me like an animal not too long ago and came inside me without any hesitation.

"Okay."

"So you have recently been writing and marketing your new book called, *Long Lost Love* and from what we gathered, this book is about a serial killer whose girlfriend got kidnapped and now he is going around killing and torturing people." Detective Wren says and I nod, trying to stay calm. "So what's alarming is that there are multiple similarities. The details of the killings and torture methods that have been happening around New York match up to your book. We were curious and it looks like an anonymous caller was also concerned as well."

"That makes sense." I nod. "I know it might seem suspicious but I was getting ideas from the news, that's all."

They both nod, writing down what I'm saying along with other things probably. "What gave you the idea for this book?" Detective Johnson asks.

"Usually for book ideas I get them from movies or dreams."

"Okay, now we just want to ask you where you were on these days if that's okay. Just so we have all of our tracks-"

There is a knock on the door before it opens and an officer pops his head in. "Sorry, to interrupt but there is someone here for Isabella Rossi," he says before a young, beautiful girl with a pencil skirt showing off her gorgeous tan legs and a white button up top walks in.

She looks familiar, but from where?

"My client won't be taking any further questions at the moment," she says, making me raise my eyebrows.

Since when do I have a lawyer?

"Ms. Walker, we didn't expect to see you here," Detective Wren says, his face losing its color.

"Well, I didn't expect you to start questioning my client but at the same time this has happened before so I'm not surprised." The girl glances at me and smiles softly. "Isabella, you can come with me."

I get up but before I leave with her, Detective Wren stops me. "If you know anything that might help with this case, please don't hesitate to reach out." He smiles at me.

I nod and leave with the woman.

"I'm so sorry about this. I know you're extremely confused but trust me it will all make sense once Slade-"

"I want to speak to my fucking wife!" a familiar voice yells, cutting the girl off.

What the hell?

Wife?

We turn a corner and Slade is yelling at a poor old man at the front desk.

"Oh my god," I say while imagining Slade pulling out a gun and shooting him. I run over to him and grab his arm. "Slade." He glares at the poor old man. "Let's go. I'm done."

Slade looks over at the girl walking over to us. "What happened?" he asks her.

"They aren't pressing charges. I spoke with a sergeant. They were just curious and wanted to question her about her book. They have no real cause so she's in the clear." She smiles at him softly.

"Thank you, Maddie, seriously."

She nods.

Maddie Walker.

She is the lawyer I was trying to contact for my book.

She looks at me. "Isabella, your name sounded familiar and now I know why." She hands me her card. "On there is my personal phone number. Call me with any questions you have or if you need anything."

I take it and smile at her. "Thank you."

She nods before staring at Slade. "Remember, I never helped you today."

Slade rolls his eyes. "Whatever, he won't know."

I furrow my eyebrows at Slade but he ignores me and keeps staring at her.

How does he even know her?

Who is she?

Did they date?

That's not possible because Slade never dated anyone before me.

"He better not, Slade. I don't want to get involved with him and his messes."

Slade gives her a sarcastic look. "Sure thing, Maddie. Family dinners suck without you," he says before grabbing me by my waist and pulling me towards the front door.

There is a big black SUV parked outside and I realize he's taking me to it. "No, Slade," I say, stopping.

"Stop being a brat and keep walking," he says, grunting.

"No, you-"

He brings me towards him and my hand lands on his chest. "Don't be fucking stupid, Isabella."

I glare at him and he just tugs me towards the car. He opens the door and I get inside, sitting all the way at the other end of the car.

Slade slides in and slams the door closed, his whole body tense and his jaw ticking. "To the airport, Niko."

I widen my eyes at him. "What?! Slade, no! Go back to the apartment," I demand but he doesn't listen. I glance at Niko through the rearview mirror. There is another guy in the passenger seat but I know he won't be any help. "Niko, go back to the apartment!"

He gives me a sympathetic glance but continues driving.

I stare at Slade and he's on his phone, ignoring my demands.

Slade types a few times on his phone before he puts it to his ear.

He speaks in Russian so I can't understand shit.

I need to think.

I need to get out of here.

My eyes search the car, trying to find something that can help me get out.

There's a gun in Slade's pocket.

Slade is still focused on the conversation with whoever is on the phone with him.

I don't think twice as I reach over and grab Slade's gun and point it at his head.

The car jerks to a stop and the guard in the passenger seat aims a gun at me, the safety clicking off.

Oh fuck.

27

SLADE

I hear a safety clicking off, pretty sure that it's Alexei's as he points it at Isabella.

I keep fucking clenching my jaw and my entire body is tense.

I need to calm down and relax because if not I'm going to shoot someone without thinking.

Someone might fucking die today who I'd regret killing.

"I'm going to have to go, Lan. I need to take care of something," I say in Russian before hanging up and looking at Alexei. "Put your gun down."

"But sir-"

"Do I need to say it again? Put your gun down before I grab it and shoot you in the skull." I glare and he lowers his gun slowly while he keeps his eyes on Isabella. "Niko, continue driving to the airport. Both of you, pretend you're deaf and don't pay attention to anything back here. If you hear a shot, don't fucking shoot her. Do you understand me?"

"Yes, sir," Niko and Alexei say.

Alexei is still kind of new to working for me and our family.

I scouted him while he was in the special forces and I saw his potential.

After training with my guards, I wanted to give him a shot at working closely with me.

I turn to Isabella who still has the gun pointed at me.

I'm not worried.

The gun probably still has the safety turned on because Isabella doesn't know how to handle a gun.

She'll learn.

After I make her cum all over said gun.

"*Avtor*, put the gun down," I say calmly.

"No, let me go, Slade. I can't go anywhere with you."

"You'll like Russia, trust me. Just put the gun down. I don't want you to hurt yourself," I say but Isabella doesn't listen.

Motherfucker.

I had to choose this one.

I had to choose the one who disobeys and doesn't fucking listen to me.

Since Isabella doesn't show any signs of standing down, I take the gun from her hand, toss it into Alexei's lap, and grab her waist to pull her closer to me.

"No!" she yells while trying to scoot away from me. "No, Slade! You have to let me go! I can't go to Russia!"

"Isabella, it's the safest place for you right now. By my side, especially since that fucking creep is still out there and until I kill him, you aren't safe." I rub her shoulders to calm her down. "And don't ever, ever fucking point a gun at me. Do you understand?"

"You can't kill him, Slade. You have no right," Isabella yells, ignoring everything I just said about the gun.

She legit does not give a fuck.

I shake my head lightly. "What did I tell you in the apartment? You have no clue what kind of person I am. Don't provoke me, Isabella." My lips graze her ear. "You remember the last time you provoked me don't you?"

I still can't stop thinking about her, on the floor in the parking garage with her ass in the air, her shorts pulled down her legs.

Just thinking about it makes my dick hard.

I grab her and pull her onto my lap so that she knows what she's doing to me. "You feel that?" I adjust her position, teasingly thrusting up into her. "I was just inside you less than two hours ago. My cum is still probably sitting in your pussy." I whisper in her ear.

She turns her head glaring at me still. "Yea, about that. We need to have a talk."

I raise my eyebrow at her little attitude. "Okay, give it to me."

Isabella nervously glances at my men in the front seat before looking back at me. "You came inside me," she whispers in my ear

"And? You are on birth control so why are you worried?"

"Because I can't have a possible baby with a murderer."

A smirk lifts my lips and I chuckle softly. "Oh you're going to be having a lot of my babies, *avtor*."

She smacks my chest. "Take me home."

"No. You're coming with me to Russia. Deal with it," I say, wanting to just be done with this conversation but I know she is going to keep arguing with me, even while we are in Russia.

"Slade. You can't force me to go to Russia with you."

I raise my eyebrow at her. "Really?" Her eyebrows are furrowed in a furious way and her face is turning red. She is mad and annoyed but I couldn't care less. I tighten my lips and nod slowly. "Okay, Isabella." I dig through my pocket, trying to reach for the box that I bought two weeks ago.

"What are you doing?"

I pull out the velvet box, opening it and taking the ring out. I grab her left hand and slide the silver engagement ring onto her ring finger.

"No, Slade. You're crazy!" she says, taking her hand out of mine.

"If you take it off, I'm going to fucking brand you instead. So keep this on," I demand.

"No, Slade." Tears start to form in her eyes. "This is all insane. You have to think about this," she pleads, looking at me with those begging eyes that make me almost want to say 'fuck it' and let her go, but screw that.

She's mine.

"I have," I say in a defiant tone. "You'll be my wife and stand by my side until death do us part."

"Why are you doing all this?"

"Because if I let you have a choice you would run, Isabella. Right?" I raise an eyebrow at her. She doesn't say anything or show any facial expressions, keeping her facial expression blank. "There are many reasons why I'm doing this. The main one being that no one will touch you once you have the Rykov name. That name protects you, not just from you getting questioned by the police, but from your fucking stalker. You'll have guards twenty-four seven and be protected. I'll make sure nothing happens to you."

"But why?!" She furrows her eyebrows, looking genuinely confused and scared.

She'll get over it.

I slide my hand around her throat, not squeezing, but holding her. My eyes connect with hers. "Because the moment I saw you, Isabella Rossi, I knew you were going to be mine. Only fucking mine."

28

He locked me in the bedroom of the plane.

Right when the car stopped in front of the entrance of the plane, I opened the door and started running.

Slade caught me immediately, so I didn't even have any sort of chance at escaping. He held me as he got on board and took me straight to the bedroom and locked me in here.

I'd been banging on the door for a good twenty minutes as the plane took off before I gave up and just laid down on the bed.

I have so many questions and complaints for Slade but I'm sure he doesn't care.

I should have ratted his ass out to the detectives but as Slade said, he would have been out of jail the next day.

So that tells me that he is a powerful person with a lot of money.

I knew he had money because of the apartment, his clothes, his watches, Niko, and other signs.

I just didn't know how rich he was. But now that we are sitting in, I'm assuming his plane, and he is ordering everyone around, he is loaded.

I hear the door unlocking, making me sit up in bed. Slade walks through the door with a glass of water. "Are you calm?"

He sets the water down on the small table inside the room. "I don't like you." I glare at him.

"Lying isn't good, Isabella," he says while leaning against the table and crossing his arms, making his biceps bulge.

"All you've done is lie to me, Slade!" I yell.

"We have a lot to talk about. I know that. I just needed to get you out of New York."

"Why won't you let me go? I won't say anything if you just let me go, Slade."

He shakes his head. "I can't do that Isabella."

"Why not?" I ask, looking up at him with pleading eyes.

He walks towards the bed.

Once he's right in front of me he tilts my chin up, stroking his thumb along my jaw. "Because you're mine."

"Stop saying that." I move my face away from him,

but his hand grabs my throat and pulls me up until his face is right in front of mine.

"I'm not going to stop, just because you can't accept it, Isabella. You're mine. I've claimed this body over twenty times in less than a month already. So if I want to have you, I'll fucking take you," Slade says before his lips fall on mine.

He presses me against him with his hand on my throat, squeezing it every so often so that I know he's controlling me and this thing between us.

The spot between my legs pulses without my control.

God I fucking hate him.

"You won't be able to keep me forever, Slade."

"Watch me," he says before pushing me onto the bed. Slade gets in between my legs and I can't even protest because his lips are on mine again as he holds himself above me.

He presses his hips into mine and I can't help but grind into him.

He groans in my mouth and grinds back against me.

Electric shocks zap where our lips meet and I feel him stealing all of my oxygen, just taking and taking until I'm left with nothing.

Slade is commanding and everything in my body says I should stay away from him, but then when he puts his hands on me, I can't help but melt into his hold.

His hand slides inside my pants, his fingers running up

and down my underwear. He trails his kisses down my neck and moves my shirt up so that his lips can pepper kisses along my skin.

His teeth graze my nipple and I gasp, squeezing my eyes while he massages my boob with his lips, licking my nipple with his tongue before biting on it again.

Every time he sends a small bite or suck to my breast, there is a zap of pleasure in my pussy making me grind against his hand which he uses to rub me through my underwear.

He's teasing me.

He pulls my underwear back and then lets it hit me. "Oh, Slade!" He leans up and covers my mouth with his.

"I don't want them to hear you. I don't want anyone on this plane to know how you sound."

As he kisses me, he starts to slide my pants down my hips, disconnecting our lips just so he can pull them all the way off and throw them on the floor.

He spreads my legs with his hands, holding them down to the bed as he looks at my glistening pussy. I feel so wet and ready. All I want him to do is shove his fingers inside me so I don't have to think.

It's wrong but my body craves him.

He gives me one glance before he leans down and spits on my pussy.

I moan and throw my head back against the pillow. "Oh my god, Slade!"

Slade stares up at me with hooded eyes as he licks me and thrusts his tongue inside me. *"Eto moya kiska, da?"* he says while he licks from my back hole all the way to the hood of my clit. I try to close my legs but Slade doesn't let me. *"Otvet'te mne."* Slade's finger slides inside me slowly.

"Oh! Slade! Yes! Yes!" I arch my back off the bed and my hands land on his hair, pulling him closer as I practically ride his face.

He thrusts his finger in and out of me while rubbing my clit along his tongue. I moan while he grunts in response, sending a vibration between my legs.

Slade sucks and licks every spot, his finger thrusting in and out of me at a fast pace.

I clench on his fingers tightly and I pull him closer, trying to get more as my release is coming.

"Slade. Please!" I beg, needing to cum already.

He lifts his head to look at me. "Tell me you're mine."

I stare at him, figuring out if I want to give this asshole the satisfaction of making me cum.

After all he's done to me in the past two days, and somehow I just keep letting him do whatever he wants. I should be scared, not wanting him to touch me for however long he can.

"Tell me you're mine or I'll take my fingers out and edge you every single day until you admit it," he warns.

I'm about to tell him to fuck off but he comes up from between my legs and his face is in front of mine. His fingers are sliding, thrusting inside me slowly, enough to bring me to the edge but not enough to cum.

"*Skazhi, chto ty moy,*" he begs, his lips hovering over mine.

I glare at him. "Fuck you."

Slade smirks and nods before pressing his thumb on my clit, my walls tighten around his fingers before he pulls them out.

I scream and tears run down my face from the sudden loss. "Bad girls don't get to cum." He comes up on top of me and hovers his face over mine. "You and I are gonna have a lot of fun in Russia."

29

SLADE

She's still fighting me.

She was fine during the plane ride, probably because she knew she wouldn't be able to do anything and it was pointless to fight. But right when we got off the plane, she tried running until I grabbed her and threw her over my shoulder.

I took her to the car that was waiting for us and locked the doors as soon as we got in.

Niko has my gun so that Isabella won't try anything stupid like aiming a gun at me again.

Currently we are still in the car, almost to my family home where I grew up.

I haven't been home in years.

Last time I was here was when my dad died which was when I was a little over eighteen.

Last time I saw my mom and Angel was when I left

and I haven't been back here and they haven't gone to the U.S.

My brothers, I've seen in New York a couple of times.

Ryker usually stays in Russia, conducting business, but from time to time he'll come and check on me while claiming he is in the U.S. working.

Landon moved out right when his long lost love broke his heart. He ran after her to New York, stalking her but not doing anything. He conducts business there to stay close to her, even though he said it's because he is trying to expand the family business.

Even though we both live in New York we don't talk to each other much since I like being by myself most of the time and Landon is really only ever concerned about himself and his long lost love.

Ryker is the brother that cares and checks on all of us because of his big brother tendencies.

My family knows I'm coming back home today because I told Niko to let them know. Landon said he'll be stopping by as well since we should all have a family reunion. Plus, he's a nosey fuck and wants to know who I'm bringing home.

So this should be fun.

"Where are we going?" Isabella, asks with some attitude.

"My childhood home," I answer while looking at my phone, going through countless emails. "I told your boss that you're taking a trip and won't be back for a while. You'll be writing while you're here so he doesn't worry."

"You talked to my boss?" She widens her eyes. "Slade, you can't do that! That's my job!" she says, getting pissed off.

I put my phone in my pocket. "Yes, I talked to your boss because I can't have him or anyone else questioning what's going on with you while I have you here. For all they know, you are on a writing retreat, clearing your head."

"How am I supposed to work on a book when you are forcing me-"

"Last time I checked, I'm not stopping you from writing. You are. You're the one who is arguing with me instead of focusing on your writing. The estate is quiet and my mom makes really good food. You'll like it there and have some peace and quiet and a bunch of time to write while also getting our wedding ready."

"Wedding?! I can't get married. I'm only twenty-one!"

"Who said you can't?" I raise an eyebrow at her.

"I did. I'm not ready for that Slade. I can't marry you. You're a murderer and god knows what else. You have been keeping so many things from me, I don't even know who you are."

"You will learn. I'll explain everything."

"You keep saying that." She crosses her arms over her

chest like a toddler and turns to face the window. "I'll never marry you."

"Never say never, wife."

I admire her pissed off face.

I don't know why but her being fired up and ready to attack someone, does things to me.

I love seeing this side of her.

Her ears get red when she's mad and her eye twitches too.

She has that fucking sparky attitude that makes me want to fuck it out of her and show her who's really in charge between the two of us.

I watch Isabella until Niko pulls into the estate gates.

The grass is green and flowers are blooming in the front yard.

There are multiple cars lined up on the driveway and Niko parks next to my mother's Cullinan. "Whose cars are these?" she asks while staring at every supercar.

"Me and my brothers," I answer and her jaw drops. "When we get in there, I can't have you disrespecting me. I know you are mad at me right now, it will pass, but until it does you will not disrespect me in front of my men or my brothers' men. You'll be respectful to my mother." She glares at me. "You keep your attitude and that bratty side for inside the bedroom, where it's just us two. But out here, keep your mouth shut and don't pull that disrespectful American bullshit. If you do, you'll be punished."

"Punished how?" She raises an eyebrow, daring me, tempting me.

I smirk and slide my hand onto her thigh. "You'll find out the kind of person I've been trying to hide from you." I grip her thigh tightly and gasp softly. "Behave."

I kiss her cheek before reaching over and opening her door. Niko is outside and lends her a hand as she gets out.

I follow her out and close the door behind me while staring up at my childhood home.

The place hasn't changed.

Except my cars, which look like they have been washed since I first left here.

I wish I could have taken my cars with me but in New York, traffic is terrible, which is why I take my bike everywhere.

Isabella scours the estate and looks at all the cars, amazed and probably confused.

I grab her hand in mine, and she turns her head. "Come," I say as I walk us towards the front door.

Before I can grab the handle, the door opens wide revealing my mother.

Angela Rykov looks like she hasn't aged a day.

I'm pretty sure she has some Botox but my mom has always been a beautiful woman and looked very young.

She always took care of herself.

"Oh my goodness, my baby." She smiles before

coming over to me and throwing her arms around me. I let go of Isabella's hand and hug my mom back. She smells like home and suddenly I realize how much I've missed my mother. "It's so good to have you home, baby," she says in Russian.

Isabella is going to have to pick up on the Russian to understand everyone at the house.

They can speak English but not as good as me and my brothers since we spend a lot of time in the U.S.

My eyes go to Isabella and it looks like her facial expression has softened and she isn't glaring at me anymore which is a good sign.

"Mom, I want you to meet someone," I say, letting go of her. She glances from me to Isabella and smiles at her. "Her name is Isabella."

"You're absolutely stunning," my mom says, with her strong Russian accent. "How did Slade find such a beautiful girl like you?"

"He got lucky I guess," she jokes.

My mom hugs her. "Sorry, I love hugs." She squeezes her tightly. "I can't wait to show you all of Slade's baby photos. He was such a troublemaker, my son."

She grabs Isabella's hand, stealing her away from me, and they both walk inside. I watch as my mom talks to her while holding her hand.

My mom loves physical touch.

It's her main love language along with cooking for people she loves. Which is probably where I got my love of cooking for Isabella from.

"I'm having Alexei bring in the bags now. Did you want your bags and hers in the same room?" Niko comes up from behind me.

I nod. "Yes. Put them in my room."

"Of course. Also, I'm having someone keep an eye out for Georgino Bandino," Niko says.

"You found out more information about him?" I say, not looking at Niko, instead keeping my eyes on my girl and my mother.

"I'm connecting the dots between him and Isabella's dad. I'll have a full report for you tonight."

"Good. Make sure the house is guarded. I want guards covering the whole perimeter."

"Yes, sir," Niko says before leaving.

I walk inside the house, feeling all sorts of emotions.

Flashes of my dad and my memories as a child haunt me.

I freeze when my eyes go to the foyer.

"I always knew it'd be you, Slade. I always knew you'd be the one to do it, you little devil," my dad spits in Russian.

My mom is crying on the floor next to him and my hands now have blood on them.

My brothers and sister can never know.

"If it isn't the little devil," a familiar voice says. Ryker walks out of the hallway where the main office is. "*Mladshiy brat*, you and I have a lot to chat about."

30

ISABELLA

Slade's room looks just like his room in the apartment but it's a little bit bigger.

He has a large bookshelf, a closet, his own bathroom, a small shelf for all of his expensive cologne, and a full length mirror on the wall across from his bed.

After talking with his mom for a good hour yesterday and her making me some food, Slade said it was time I get rest because of the long day I had.

He showed me his room and told me to go to sleep and that I'd see him tomorrow. I was about to ask him where he was going and if he was coming to bed but I stopped myself.

I shouldn't care.

He kidnapped me.

I turn to the side he would have slept on, but it doesn't look messed up or like Slade came to bed.

I don't know why that bums me out.

Even though you shouldn't be because he literally kidnapped you and is a serial killer.

After talking to Angela and learning what she had to say about Slade, I'm starting to see him differently. She makes it seem like he is innocent and an angel and her baby.

She talks about him as if he is just a regular person who doesn't kill or torture people.

I get out of Slade's bed and go to the drawers. Slade said that all of my clothes are already put away and if I need anything else, to look in the bathroom.

While I was in jail getting questioned for his messes, he was probably packing up all my shit for this trip.

As I start to think about everything he's done in the last three days, anger consumes me again.

My skin feels hot and all I want to do is cry and trash his room.

Anger at him and anger at the fact that he isn't who I thought he was.

He seems like such a different person outside the apartment.

Like the guy I met who would help me with my books and sleep with me to chase the nightmares away is gone.

I change into a pair of leggings and an off the shoulder sweater. After brushing my teeth and hair I leave the room and find my way downstairs.

When I saw Slade's cars in the driveway, I was thinking about all of the possible reasons why he might be so loaded.

The cars, the guards, the house, the apartment, the expensive cologne and watches, everything.

How does he have so much money?

He said he would explain everything to me but he has barely talked to me.

All we've been doing is arguing because I can't let go of the fact that he lied and kept things from me.

After making the wrong turns and getting lost in the wing, I finally find the stairs.

I walk down the long stairway, still shocked about how large and grand this house is.

Multiple art pieces are hung on the walls, probably expensive ones.

When I get inside the kitchen I see a young girl and boy making out against the counter. The girl has long black hair that the boy is wrapping around his hand as he pushes her into the counter.

I feel like I should say something but I don't want to intrude on their moment.

I'm about to turn around and leave when the boy's eyes open and he lets go of the girl. The girl tilts her head before turning around to stare at me.

She glares at me. "*YA mogu vam pomoch'*?"

"I don't speak Russian." I give her a small smile, hoping that it will stop her from glaring daggers at me.

"I asked, can I help you? Who even are you?" she asks, looking at me up and down like I'm some sort of trash.

I lick my lips and try to not let her get to me.

She looks like a teenager.

And teenagers are fucking mean and ruthless.

"She's my guest, Angel. Be nice," I hear a familiar voice say before a hand slides onto my waist and pulls me into a hard chest.

The girl's face lights up. "Slade?! When did you get here?" She beams and runs towards Slade, going to hug him, making him let go of me.

I'm gonna assume she is a sister or some sort of family because of how he is hugging her.

He smiles down at her with a softness like he did with his mother. "I got in last night. I didn't tell you because I wanted to surprise you."

"You should have told me." She punches his shoulder lightly. "I'm glad you're back."

He nods and glances at the boy in the kitchen. "Who's this little shit?"

"My boyfriend. His name is Dimitri and we met at school," Angel says while staring at Dimitri who is still standing in the kitchen, with hearts in her eyes. Slade is glaring at him while Dimitri is giving him a blank stare, like he couldn't care. "Don't glare at him. He's nice and treats me well."

Slade looks down at her. "He better or else I'll cut his dick off and shove it down his throat."

Dimitri shows no signs of distress or worry.

And Angel just laughs as if he's joking but after what I've seen from him, I don't think he is.

Every time he gets mad I'm scared he'll just pull out his gun and start shooting people.

"Oh stop it. You're the one who came here with a girl that we know nothing about." Angel glares at me, her nice and playful expression gone. "*Chto eta suka zdes' delayet?*" she says in Russian but I know for a fact it was nothing nice.

Slade's expression darkens and he lowers his eyes to Angel, giving her a deadly look. "*YA ne pozvolyu tebe tak razgovarivat' s moyey budushchey zhenoy. Yeshcho raz proyavish' k ney neuvazheniye, i ya pozovu sobak, chtoby oni rasterzali tebe litso. Nakonets-to ty smozhesh' poprosit' moyu mamu o plasticheskoy operatsii.*" he says in a low and threatening voice.

Angel's mouth parts, as if she can't believe he just said that to her. "That's not nice, Slade."

"Then keep your mouth shut, Angel," Slade says before grabbing me by the waist and pulling me to his side. "I'm not joking around about this."

Angel rolls her eyes. "Whatever. I'm taking Dimitri to my room. Your little *podruga* ruined our makeout sesh."

It's nine in the morning.

Why is a teenager having a make out session with her boyfriend in the kitchen?

Shouldn't she be in school or something?

Angel gives me a sassy smile before going over to her boyfriend, grabbing his hand and walking them out of the kitchen.

I turn to look at Slade. "Who was she?"

"My sister Angel. Don't take anything she says or does to heart. She's always been a bitch." He slides his arm around my waist and pulls me closer to him. "How'd you sleep, *avtor*?" he asks, his other hand reaching up to put a strand of hair behind my ear.

"Fine. Where were you?"

"I had to talk to my brother. We had to catch up."

"All night?" I raise an eyebrow at him.

"Why? Did you miss me?" He smirks down at me.

I roll my eyes. "No. I was just trying to see if I was able to escape or not."

"Escape and you won't get your wedding gift," he whispers, glancing down to my lips.

I glare at him. "I'm not marrying you, Slade."

He sighs as if what I'm saying is an inconvenience for him. "How many times do I have to tell you?" Slade steps into my space and his lips hover over my ear as he whispers, "You're going to marry me. You're going to have my kids. You're stuck with me, Isabella. The sooner you accept that, the better."

"I don't want to. I'm not ready. You still haven't told me anything about yourself. Like how you have all this money, why you kill all these people, hell we haven't even had a first date."

"You want a date, *avtor*?" He smirks.

I narrow my eyes on him. "I'm not happy with you."

"Well sucks to suck. Our wedding is this Friday. You're going to be trying on dresses I found for you tomorrow."

My eyes widen and my jaw drops. "What? You're insane. No," I say, getting out of his hold and running away. But before I can get far, Slade grabs me and swings me over his shoulder. I scream, upside down, his ass right in front of my face. "Slade, put me down! Put me down, right now!"

Slade sends a slap to my ass, making me yelp. "Stop being a brat. My brother and mom are sleeping and you're going to wake them up."

"You can't just slap me on the ass."

"I can do whatever the fuck I want to you." He grunts as he takes us up the stairs.

I hold his waist, starting to feel a little lightheaded.

He walks into his room, closes the door behind him and finally rests me on the bed.

I feel like I'm going to faint when my head hits the pillow. "You're impossible."

"You're being dramatic."

"When are you going to let me go, Slade?" I ask him, with the same pleading tone again. "I promise I won't tell anyone."

He gives me those same dark eyes, glaring at me. "Stop," he says quietly but there is a lot of authority in that one word. "When will you stop and just accept the fact that I'm not letting you go?"

I sit up in the bed and furrow my eyebrows. "When will you stop keeping things from me and just tell me who you really are?"

His jaw ticks and he licks his lips. "If I told you who I am and the stuff I've done, you wouldn't want me. You'd be scared of me and that's the last thing I want, Isabella. I don't want to hurt you or scare you. But I just don't know how to get to you." He rests his hands on his hips while staring at me.

I didn't get the time to check him out in the kitchen.

But now I notice how good he looks, especially standing and staring at me like that.

He's wearing black jeans and a plain black t-shirt with an expensive belt and watch.

His dark tattoos showcase his long, muscular arms.

"Maybe start telling me things, Slade. Instead of letting me be scared of you after finding out you're a killer.

You don't tell me anything. How am I supposed to trust you if I don't know why you did the things you've done?"

I'm still scared of Slade but I know he won't hurt me.

He cares about me, I know that.

But I just need some sort of glimpse into his mind to know who he is.

It's obvious I'm not leaving anytime soon, no matter what I do. If I leave, he'll send his guards after me or he'll come for me himself.

His eyes stay on mine as if he is thinking .

Trying to think of what to do and how to help me.

"And if I do, will you run? Will you be scared?"

I lick my lips instead of answering.

Because I don't know.

I don't want to hurt Slade.

I wish things could go back to how they were before, hanging out at the apartment, reading and writing together while making food.

We could cook dinners together and just hangout.

But he ruined it by forcing me to come to Russia and marry him.

Slade nods and then slowly walks out of the bedroom.

31

ISABELLA

I thought I'd be at least twenty-eight years old when I would have my dress fitting for my wedding.

But I'm freshly twenty-one, recently not a virgin and already getting married.

To my roommate who is a murderer and some sort of lord or dark prince or something.

"Oh, Isabella! This one is absolutely gorgeous." Slade's mom, Angela beams while browsing through each of the dresses.

Angel is here as well, sitting in one of the chairs while scrolling through her phone.

Angel looks just like her mother, with bright blue eyes and dark brown hair. Slade has some similarities to his mom but he probably looks more like his father.

I've never seen his dad and I want to learn more about

Slade and his father's history but this morning I didn't see Slade.

I knew he came into the bedroom because there was steam on the shower glass.

I had breakfast with Angela and Angel before we went to check out the dresses in one of the many rooms in this huge estate.

I'm shocked that Angel is with us because I would expect her to be at school since she looks like she is still in high school because of how young she looks.

Slade said he wants me to try on dresses here since he doesn't want to risk me leaving the house.

There are a ton of different dresses and I love every single one, especially how elegant they all are. But picking the dresses and knowing I'm being forced into this, it isn't really the same.

"What are you thinking, dear?" Angela asks, smiling at me.

I force a smile on my face. "There are so many to choose from."

"I know, it's a lot to take in. I was in your position when I was your age." She gives me a sympathetic look. "I met Abraham, Angel and the boys' dad when I was 20 years old. He was the love of my life, or so I thought."

"What happened?"

Angela glances behind her, at Angel, who is distracted

by her phone. "I found out that he worked for the Bratva."

My heart pounds hard and fast in my chest as I try not to freak out or call Slade to start yelling at him.

"I've heard rumors and stories of the Bratva but I didn't think it was real. I thought it was all just talk and when I first saw him kill someone, I was terrified." She grabs my hands.

"Did you try to run?" I ask, hoping she says 'yes' because it would make me feel a little better about running, not seeming crazy for doing so.

She nods. "Of course. Any sane person would. But I couldn't escape. I was forced to marry him and after marrying him I saw his true colors. Things only got worse after we had Ryker, Slade's older brother."

I've seen Ryker around.

He looked like he's in his late twenties or early thirties when I first saw him. Short beard and a nice haircut. He looks mature and definitely older than Slade.

I know for a fact he works out because you can literally see his biceps through the suit he wears.

Everyone in Slade's family has perfect genetics.

"How did he get worse?" I ask Angela.

"He just wasn't acting the same. I knew Abraham had this darkness in him that I was careful of but I never knew he would take his aggression and that darkness out on me."

I start to worry but I try to hide it.

What if Slade is the same way?

From what Slade has hinted at, his dad wasn't a good person.

He hated his dad and now that Angela is saying that he was terrible, it makes me wonder how Slade will be when he gets older.

I'm pretty sure Angela can see the concern on my face because she touches my arm and says, "Oh dear, I didn't mean to scare you with Slade. You have nothing to be worried about when it comes to my son."

"I like Slade a lot, don't get me wrong. And I know you're his mother, I shouldn't even being talking to you about your son-"

Angela shakes her head. "Darling, it's okay. I understand. But with Slade, you really don't need to worry. I've raised all of my boys with love and care and to show them how to treat people. Abraham did have Slade and Ryker under his wing more than me. I did as much as I could to save both of them from turning out like their father. I think that's why Landon is a little more level headed since he spent most of his time with me."

Slade has a good heart.

I've seen it.

I've felt it.

But I also know that when Slade wants something he'll do anything he can to get it.

"How was Slade around his father?"

Angela's eyes flash with something, a hurtful memory possibly. She sighs and says, "Slade had it worse than the other boys. It's because he was the youngest so Abraham thought he could manipulate Slade the most."

"And did he?"

"He tried, but Slade is a strong person. He has a strong heart and knows right from wrong. Don't get me wrong, he has demons. Everyone does, but his are louder than most." She looks back at the dresses. "Out of all of my sons, Slade has always and will always be the strongest one. He is a good person with a good heart as I keep saying. I know you're scared like I was when I was your age but trust me, Slade is the best person you can be with in the kind of world we live in."

"But what if I don't want to be in this kind of world?" I ask her, desperate to figure how to get out.

I like Slade, more than I should admit but I love myself more and know what kind of life I want to live.

Angela smiles at me sweetly. "He chose you for a reason, dear. Best thing I can say is try to be patient with Slade. He's been through a lot and he deserves to be happy. I know you'll do the right thing by him but also by yourself." She rubs my arm and looks back at the dresses. "Now enough of this sad stuff, let's pick out the perfect dress for you.

32

SLADE

I keep my eyes on Isabella as she walks into the bathroom.

Her long wavy hair is in a bun and she's wearing sweatpants and a tank top. She has no makeup on and looks like she is about to get ready for bed.

We've barely talked after last night's little argument.

She had her dress fitting earlier with my mom and Angel watching her while I spent all day in the office with Ryker and Niko discussing Georgino Bandino.

There is no sign of him anywhere.

Niko is watching the street cameras in New York and he hasn't found one sighting of him.

I don't know what Georgino is capable of and because he is after Isabella, I want to be careful with how I go about this.

"Isabella?" I say making her turn her head to finally

give me her eyes. I'm sitting in the large tub right now, relaxing but I'd rather have her next to me. "Come."

Her eyebrows furrow and I already know she is about to give me attitude. "Why?" she says with sass.

"Because I want to hold you?" I raise an eyebrow at her, waiting for Isabella to just give up on the back and forth bullshit and relax with me. "I'll tell you whatever you want to know if you just lie in the tub with me. I won't try anything."

I'll try not to try anything.

Isabella thinks for a second before she gives up the fight in her head and starts stripping. I keep my eyes on her, admiring her beautiful body that is perfect just for me.

Her nipples pucker as the cool air hits them while she walks towards the tub. I hold my hand out for her and she gets inside the warm tub.

She sits down between my legs and leans against my chest while I wrap my arms around her waist and hold her.

I rest my head on her shoulder and kiss her on the side of her neck. My hands can't help but run all over her body —her breasts, stomach, hips, and fucking thighs.

"See, not bad."

"I can feel your dick poking my butt," she says and I see a hint of a smile wanting to spread on her lips.

I smile and press my lips against her shoulder.

After our talk yesterday, I was pissed.

And scared.

I just wanted to know if Isabella would ever not be scared of this lifestyle I live or me.

It's not like I'll hurt her.

I would never hurt Isabella.

She is the one person I want to keep safe and I'd do anything it takes to ensure she is.

She said she needs to know more and for me to have patience.

The first thing is possible, I can tell her everything. But patience?

We may as well just kill each other at that point.

"You know when I was a kid, I wasn't treated like one," I say softly while one of my hands goes on her thigh, stroking her soft skin. "My dad always treated me like an adult. He did that with my brothers but he pushed me around more because I was the youngest and he saw himself in me."

"What was your dad like?"

My body tenses and I shift, uncomfortably. "He wasn't a good man. That's why I am the way I am. He taught me to be like this. In my world, there are no good people. My world is black and white. I never said I was a good person and my dad ensured that was the case."

"What things did he make you do?"

The pulse in my neck quickens and I feel the need to throw up, vomit creeps up my throat as I think about it.

That fucking bastard ruined my life.

He fucked me up.

"I'm doing all of this for you, malen'kiy d'yavol."

"You're my very own weapon."

"Me and you are going to rule the world, Slade. Just watch and see."

My lips shake as I open them to say, "He did a lot to me. He made me do a lot of things I didn't want to do."

"Like what?" Isabella asks, appearing concerned and almost sad for me.

"Just fuck her already Slade. You need to lose your virginity eventually. I can't have my son be a goddamn prude."

"But I don't want to. I'm not interested in that shit," I *tell him before glancing back at the whore he got for me.*

Having sex or doing anything intimate with someone feels wrong and makes my skin crawl.

I feel uncomfortable whenever someone is touching me or vice versa.

I wait for my father's response but he ignores my stare and says, "Do whatever it takes to fuck him. I'll wire you more money." My dad puts a hand on my shoulder. "Try to enjoy her malen'kiy d'yavol. I paid a lot of money for her."

I remember that night so clearly.

She took me in the room, put some shit in my water and made me drink it to get me to relax and then she got to work.

I don't like thinking about that night because if I do, I feel uncomfortable in my own skin and like I'm still a victim.

I don't want to be treated like a victim.

Especially a victim of my father.

"Things you'd have nightmares about."

Isabella puts her hand on my jaw and my eyes focus on her. "Hey, tell me. These are the things I said that I want to know about you. I want to know what makes you, you."

I nod.

This better be the fucking way to get to her.

I swear to god, the need to have her, to keep her is so strong I'll do anything.

"He made me kill, he made someone fuck me when I didn't want to, he got me and my brothers involved in a competition to rule the empire he built. He called me little devil but he was the one who turned me into one."

She looks at the scar near my eye. "You said he did that. How?"

I shake my head—all of it is too much. "I-I can't." I stumble on my words. "*Yebat',*" I curse, thinking about him.

Isabella slides her hands over my hands that are holding her and I realize that I'm shaking. "He's not here anymore."

"He will always be there, Isabella." I point a finger to

my head. "He's always in there, taunting me, fucking with me. Even though he's dead, he's still haunting me."

I can't tell Isabella I did it.

She can't know I killed him.

If she did, I can't imagine how she would see me.

She strokes my jaw and gives me a sad look, like she pities me. If it was anyone else, I would have told them to fuck off and that I don't need their sympathy but I want hers.

I want everything from her.

Before she can say anything else, I press my lips on hers and grab her waist, adjusting her so that she is facing me with my dick between her legs.

My dick is pulsing beneath her and all I want to do is thrust up into here and show her how much I physically need her.

Isabella kisses me back and her arms go around my neck, pulling me closer to her. My hands roam her smooth wet thighs as she starts to grind against my dick.

"Ride me," I whisper against her lips.

My hands go to her hips and I gently push her down. Her walls wrap around my tip tightly. I grunt into her mouth, wanting to sheath myself fully inside her.

"Slade-"

"Fuck me, *avtor*. Use me."

Isabella's breathing hitches and she slowly slides down onto my dick, moaning and struggling to stay still.

When her hips meet mine, I can't help but moan loudly in her mouth. My dick feels like it's right at home in her pussy. She pants against my mouth and grinds on top of me, getting used to my size when all I want to do is pull out and ram inside her.

"Oh my god," she moans. I move my lips down her neck, sucking on her skin. "Don't give me marks."

I don't mean to glare at her but I think I do. "Why not?"

"The dress reveals my chest."

"Perfect, that means my marks will show everyone that you belong to me," I say, gripping her hips and pulling her up before slamming her down.

Her eyes roll and her mouth parts as she melts on my dick.

Once I start I can't stop.

Isabella tries to take control but I hold her hips down while thrusting up inside her.

My control slips away with every thrust inside Isabella. Her nails dig into my shoulder and I'm pretty sure everyone in the house can hear her moans even if they are on the other end of the house.

"Oh my god, Slade! Slade! Slade!" she screams while my balls tighten.

"Yes, Isabella. Keep saying my name." My release is coming closer, like I'm going to tip over the edge. My mouth latches onto one of her boobs and I bite her nipple, making her yelp. "You're fucking addicting, baby," I say before going over to the other nipple and biting it. "I will never get enough of you," I moan.

Her pussy clamps down on me and she opens her mouth, screaming while she cums around me.

I put my mouth on her and swallow her moans while we move together. Her pussy tightens and basically grips my fucking dick to the point where I can't thrust in and out of her.

She's soft, warm, and addicting.

Her hips rock against mine. My dick presses against her g-spot, reaching deep inside her.

My hands trail all over her body, giving her breasts the attention they deserve.

I pinch and rub her nipples, making Isabella throw her head back and moan, thrusting herself against me.

It's so tight and wet and warm.

Her walls soak me, and pleasure fills my entire body before my cum spills in her.

Our kissing is sloppy and fast but passionate.

We kiss for what feels like forever all while my dick starts to grow, ready for another round.

"*YA nikogda tebya ne otpushchu,*" I whisper.

33

SLADE

"**K**eep your eyes on every airport in or near St. Petersburg, even the surrounding countries," I say to Niko.

He reported that he saw Georgino at an airport in New Jersey and I have a feeling he is headed for Russia.

How did he find out we were in Russia? No clue.

I made sure Isabella's phone didn't have a tracker or anything while she was sleeping and he doesn't know shit about me, or at least I don't think he does.

"Of course, sir," Niko nods before leaving me and Ryker alone in the office.

"You sure are doing a lot for this girl."

"She's nice to have around." I shrug.

Ryker is sitting in the chair behind the desk, watching me while I'm standing next to the window, trying not to break shit apart in this room.

I woke up this morning with my arms wrapped around Isabella.

It was the first time I was able to have a good night's sleep since we got here. After we were done in the tub, I carried her to the bed and fucked her with her head shoved into the pillows.

After talking to her last night about my father, I needed a way to get everything I was feeling out.

I haven't gone on a mission or killed anyone since we left for New York so I'm on edge.

And not snorting any cocaine doesn't help either.

I had to stop with the lines because I know that if Isabella didn't like the fact that I kill people, she would hate to know that I do or have done drugs.

"Are you having withdraws or something?" Ryker asks, raising an eyebrow at me.

Yeah I'm having fucking withdraws.

Withdraws from a girl with vanilla, rose scented perfume and a long wavy hair that I love tangling my fingers through.

I narrow my eyes on him. "No I'm not having fucking withdraws. I'm fine."

"Then stop stressing out. For a girl you just like having around, you sure are doing a lot. It seems like you feel more for her. I mean come on, you're marrying her on Friday after knowing her for what? Three or four months?"

I shake my head at him. "You won't get it, Ryker."

Ryker has lived through his twenties basically. He should be the one who has to settle down, but of course my dad knew I had trouble with women and that's why he decided my required task would be to marry someone and have a kid.

Last time I saw Ryker with a girl was a few years ago when he came back home high as fuck from a party. A girl tucked under his arm as he swayed and she laughed.

He usually keeps his relationships private because overall he is a pretty private person. He talks to Landon more than me.

I just stick to myself and mind my business.

"You're only twenty-one and you want to marry this girl? I just don't get it," he says.

"I can't explain what I feel for her. And I'm not going to try with you, so drop it."

Ryker stands up, fixing his shirt. "The girl doesn't want to be here. You should let her go and live her life. Don't stick her into your messes, Slade. Look at what happened to Landon."

I roll my eyes. "Landon's fine. Trust me, whatever he's got going on with his girl, it'll die down."

"Okay but you're not like Landon. He's more level headed while you don't even think 100% straight half the time." Ryker walks around the desk and up to me. He puts his hand on my shoulder and I keep my eyes on him.

"I worry about you. I don't want you to marry this poor girl and end up killing her just because she's pissing you off or wants a normal life. She isn't made for a world like ours."

I glare at him. "Well then she'll get used to it."

Ryker sighs, disappointed, shaking his head lightly. "Whatever Slade. You do you."

A line wouldn't hurt at the moment.

"Well, we shouldn't be late for family dinner," Ryker says.

I rush out of the office, not waiting for him.

Ryker doesn't know me.

He doesn't know what I've been through or my current struggles.

So fuck him and his advice.

The only person who overpowers my dad's voice in my head is Isabella and I'm not letting her go.

I walk down the hallway and go into the dining room, since dinner is starting.

My mom told us that we'd be having dinner together tonight as a family. She wants Ryker and I to take a break from work and join them for dinner because we haven't had a proper family dinner in a while.

My mom is sitting at one end of the table while Angel and her boyfriend, Dimitri, are on one side of her. Isabella is across from them with an open chair next to her, probably for me.

"Oh, *malysh*. You're here. Where is your brother?"

"He's coming now, mom." I kiss her head and then take my seat next to Isabella. I slide my hand onto her thigh. "How was your day?"

She shrugs. "It was fine. I mostly spent it in the room reading."

I know she's still trying to get used to all of this and it will take some time but I'm positive she'll be okay.

This morning, I left her in bed after kissing her forehead. The only other time I saw her today was around lunch when I went to check in on her and see how she was doing.

My mom is spending a lot of time with her, ensuring she is comfortable. She's the best, always making sure her guests are treated well and cared for.

"Are you sure you're doing okay?" I throw my arm over her shoulder and rub her softly.

"I'm doing the best I can, Slade." She gives me a forced smile.

I nod, knowing that's all I'm going to get out of her.

Ryker strides in and sits at the other end of the table. "Let's eat, *da*? I'm fucking starving." Workers come in with food and they put it on our plates. While they serve us, my brother decides to use his big fucking mouth and say, "So, Isabella, what are your thoughts on the wedding?"

Isabella and Ryker didn't really speak when she first

came here because I was too busy having Ryker help me with the mess with Georgino.

"Um, there isn't much to talk about. The dress is beautiful."

"Oh wait until you see it, Slade. You're going to fall in love," my mom says with a bright smile, always trying to make the tension disappear.

I feel like I'm already falling and I don't want to.

It's scary to fall.

I've never been afraid of heights but this is a different kind of a fall.

One where you have no clue what the outcome will be or if someone is going to be there to catch you and help you up.

I smile at Isabella. "I'll marry her even if she wears a trash bag."

My eyes go to Ryker and I see him silently judging as my mom talks to Isabella. Angel is just in her own world, ignoring everyone but her boyfriend.

"How did you two meet?" Ryker asks, challenging me.

"She was about to get killed and I saved her," I say in a stoic tone, not giving much information away.

"A hero, my brother."

I glare at him. "Do you have something to say?"

"*Mal'chiki,*" my mom sings. "Not in front of Isabella. We want her to feel welcomed here. Ryker, mind your own business and stop worrying about your brother."

Ryker chuckles. "I'm just curious is all." Ryker looks at Isabella and all I want to do is stab him in the fucking eye. "My apologies, Isabella. This is the first time any of us has seen Slade with a girl so we're all a little shocked."

Isabella gives him a fake smile and shakes her head lightly. "It's fine. Don't worry about it."

I run my hand up and down Isabella's thigh and she gives me a soft smile before I continue glaring back at Ryker.

I'm warning Ryker to stay out of it.

When it comes to Isabella I don't want anyone getting involved.

And if Ryker keeps fucking with me, not even us being blood will save him from what I have planned.

If someone told me that I'd be standing in a wedding dress, about to walk down the aisle, at twenty-one, I'd have called them crazy.

I literally lost my virginity, like, less than two months ago and now I'm about to get married.

The days that have been leading up to this have been very nerve-racking.

I've been feeling like the end is coming but it's just my wedding.

I'm getting married to a murderer and trapping myself in an organization I can never leave.

Slade is involved in something way bigger than I've ever experienced in my life. I don't belong in his world. I can't just be okay with people killing other people.

I know Slade has been through a lot and I wish I could

help him through his issues but he doesn't want help, he wants me.

He slept in a separate room last night because he thinks that the wedding traditions are fun, and even though it's not the wedding I'd hoped and dreamed for, he still wants to make it somewhat special for me.

I think it's sweet but I'm still wary of him.

I don't know how to act with him.

He is so consuming it's hard not to want him or do whatever he says.

I need to be careful or else I'll be in trouble.

He's going to rip my heart out and make it his.

The bridal processional song starts playing. I look to my side and see no one, because I have no one.

My parents are dead, my grandfather is also dead, Becky and Grams are in the U.S., and I have no other family.

It's just me.

I have spoken with Grams and Becky a little bit since I first got here, just so they know I'm okay.

Slade told everyone I was away on a writing retreat and when I called my Grams she tried to get as much information out of me as possible.

When she asked about Slade and when she can meet him, I made up some lie, but in reality I have no clue.

I don't know what my future will hold.

I used to think it would be calm and sane with no drama or issues but since Slade, life has been hectic.

I start walking down the aisle while I take in my surroundings.

We are in a castle-like venue and Slade let me choose the decorations I thought would look best at the very last minute.

I mentioned to him what food I like and what I want at the reception.

I kept trying to tell him to forget about it and that I don't want to do this and that I'm not ready but he didn't care.

There are a bunch of guests here which is surprising since it was such a last minute wedding.

Almost everyone here is part of Slade's family.

His mom, sister, and Ryker are sitting in the front.

There is a gentleman next to Slade's mom. He looks to be around Slade's age, maybe a little bit older.

Is that the other brother?

My eyes finally catch Slade's.

He has a clean haircut going on and he also shaved his scruff.

He appears very put together and not like your day to day scary murderer but it's those dark eyes that always get me.

When you stare into his eyes, you know trouble is coming.

He holds out his hand to me which I take. I stand in front of him and give him a nervous smile while he stares at me intensely, admiring my natural makeup, my curled hair, and my dress.

"Ty samaya krasivaya zhenshchina v mire," he whispers and I blush.

I don't understand him but I know it's all good things.

His mom is slowly trying to teach me Russian.

She said since I'm joining the family it's a must that I understand their language and I don't disagree.

I want to eavesdrop and understand what everyone is saying. I feel left out whenever they talk to each other.

The priest starts speaking in Russian and I don't understand a thing he is saying so I don't pay attention. I just observe all the people in the room that Slade surrounds himself with and all of the decorations and flowers.

"You look perfect, Isabella," Slade whispers.

I turn my head to him and smile. "You look like you don't kill people in your spare time."

He smirks. "I haven't killed anyone since we left New York, *avtor.*"

"Why?"

"Because you don't like it. I'm trying to make this all as easy as possible for you. And even if I do kill someone I won't be telling you."

"Why did you have to do all this? You still never told me."

Slade grabs my hand and he strokes my skin with his thumb. "Because I need to keep you safe. This is the only way to do so."

I stay quiet, knowing that if I ask him to let me go, he'll get mad.

"Have you guessed what your wedding gift is?"

"No. I have no clue what it could possibly be."

"You'll like it." He nods as if he's sure.

"Give me a hint." I smile.

"It's something that every bookworm would want," Slade says before paying attention to the priest.

"What he's saying?" I raise an eyebrow at him. I'm the only person here who can't speak Russian and he knows that.

"He's talking about what should be expected of you as a wife and me as a husband."

"We never talked about what we're even doing after the wedding."

"You'll see, *avtor*. Be patient."

"*Beresh' li ty, Slade Rykov, Isabella Rossi v zakonnyye zheny?*" the priest asks, staring at Slade.

Slade nods. *"Da."*

When the priest moves his eyes to me, my anxiety starts up again and I feel like I'm going to faint or fall into Slade's arms.

"A ty, Isabella Rossi, beresh' li Slade Rykov v zakonnyye muzh'ya?" he asks me.

I freeze, not knowing what to say.

I know what he is asking me and what I'm supposed to say but am I even ready to answer that and basically sign my life away?

"Say, yes," Slade says.

I lock eyes with him and he looks at me, desperate for me to say yes.

Like he'll do anything in the world to make me.

I lick my lips and take a deep breath before glancing back at the priest.

I nod and push out a shaky, "Y-Yes."

The priest's gaze pauses on me as he raises an eyebrow.

He's probably wondering if I'm doing this against my will.

Which I both am and am not.

He looks away from me and back at Slade. *"Slade, mozhesh' potselovat' nevestu."*

Slade doesn't waste any time before taking one step towards me and pressing his hard and demanding lips on mine. He moves his lips, deepening the kiss in front of a good fifty people but Slade doesn't care.

He ravishes me, claiming me as his.

Forever.

Till death do us part.

35

SLADE

Isabella nervously plays with the ends of her hair while looking out the window of the car.

She cracked her knuckles a few moments ago but after she got all of the cracks out, then she decided to move onto her hair.

She's nervous.

The reception dinner ended not too long ago.

During the meal, Isabella stayed by my side the entire time while she got to meet some of my family and friends.

A few of them scared her because they talked about missions and killing but I shut them down and moved on to the next person.

I don't want Isabella hearing any of that because if she does then she'll get frightened and start over thinking like crazy.

When Landon saw her, he started teasing me because

his "baby brother" finally got hitched first out of all my siblings.

Everyone thought Landon was going to be the one getting married before all of us.

But after his first love broke his heart, a relationship is not in the cards for him. He doesn't care about anyone but himself and he makes sure everyone knows that.

I grab Isabella's hand and hold it in my lap. "Relax," I whisper, making her look up at me. "You're fine. It's all over."

She nods slowly and bites her bottom lip lightly.

If I didn't know her, I would have assumed that she killed someone with how nervous she is acting.

Why is she stressing so much?

That's a stupid question because I have been stressing out since the moment she moved into my apartment.

"Where are we going?" Isabella asks.

"Your surprise."

"I still can't guess what it might be. I've been thinking about it through the reception."

I bring her hand up to my lips. "I promise you'll love it. It'll make your time here easier."

And just like that, she is bummed out again and staring out the window, probably thinking about her life back in New York.

I know she misses her old life and I wish I could give that to her.

Maybe I'll get her Grandma or Becky to visit.

Niko drives into a quiet neighborhood and goes all the way to the top of the hill where the house I bought a very long time ago still stands.

None of my family know I have this house. I wanted to keep it as discreet as possible so it could be a safe space for me, and I want it to be the place I'll grow old and raise my future children in.

I had it renovated while I was living in New York so that by the time I was ready to come back to Russia, it'd be here waiting for me.

It's about ten minutes away from my childhood home so I'll be able to visit and see my mom and sister as much as I want but I have the privacy I always wanted especially from my family.

"What is this place?" she asks as the gates open.

Niko drives in and she can't look away from outside the window.

"My house. I've had this place since I moved out."

After Niko stops the car, he gets out to open the door for Isabella.

I slide out of the car and immediately go to her to hold her waist.

"Is this my gift?" she asks.

"No. Your gift is inside."

I pull her by our locked hands to the front door.

Isabella is still in her wedding dress so she is holding

her dress up with her other hand. Her heels are forgotten in the car because she was complaining that her feet hurt when she got in.

I unlock the door and open it, letting her walk in first.

She admires the large foyer with the high ceiling and the painting that almost covers the entire wall. "How do you even afford all of this?" she asks while walking further inside the house into the living room.

"I bought this with my dad's money when he died. He gave each of me and my brothers a trust fund. We get some money when we turn eighteen, when he dies, when we turn twenty-one, and then when we complete the tasks he assigned for us."

She raises an eyebrow before asking, "What is the assigned task?"

"No one can know other than my brothers and the executor of my father's will."

"Have you completed your task?"

I tilt my head to the side. "Almost. I'm not quite done yet."

"Can I have a hint?" She gives me a teasing smile, trailing her hand over the enormous couch in the living room.

I give her a small smile and walk closer to her. "It's about my future. It's about something my dad never thought I could do."

She looks suspicious but doesn't ask any questions, thank god.

Because I think if she begged enough I would tell her and she'd probably be pissed at me. She'd think that I'm using her when in reality I've never felt this way about a girl.

Sure this was all about the competition and the little task my dad set up for me at the start but I knew when I saw Isabella, that she was it for me. She was the only girl that I could be with and have this kind of connection with.

Everyone else disgusts me.

I grab Isabella by the waist, having had enough of this back and forth with her.

It's time to consummate our marriage.

She yelps when I hold her bridal-style in my arms.

She laughs, throwing her head back, and I make my way to the stairs. "Where are you bringing me?"

"To your gift. You're almost as impatient as me."

I skip steps up the stairs, rushing to get to the room so I can chase her and fuck her.

I want to follow her around the house, trying to find her, stalking her, scaring her.

I want her to expect me but to be surprised when I force her on the floor and shove my dick inside her.

When I get to the door where her gift is, I put her down and she giggles. "You're impossible."

"You're my wife now. It's time I treat you like you are."

Her smile fades like she has once again remembered what this is between us.

But to me this is more than just me forcing her to marry me.

She's mine now and no one can take her away from me. No one can take me away from her.

She gives me a small smile as I open the door. She walks in and her eyes widen as they trace each corner of the room.

"Slade," she says in awe. There is every book you can think of in this library that I built. Originally it was for me but after meeting Isabella I knew she would love this room. So I'm giving it to her. "What is this?"

"It's yours." I close the door behind me.

This library has a spiral staircase leading to the second floor

There is a desk and the books are all organized by the name of the author. The room has natural lighting from the glow of the moon with the giant window in the middle of the library.

"There's no way. You're giving me this?" She turns her head to look at me.

"Yes. You love books and I love seeing you happy. It has every book you can think of." I walk towards one of the shelves where the R's are. "And I have an entire shelf just for your books. Your very own shrine."

She smiles, but there's a hint of sadness. "Slade, this is amazing. I can't believe you did this. Thank you."

I nod. "Anything for my wife." I stalk towards her, grab her hand, spin her around, making her back touch my chest. "Anything you want, Isabella. It's yours. All you have to do is ask."

She rests her head on me. "You're playing at this wrong."

"How?" I whisper in her ear and trail my hands up and down her body.

"Because you can't keep giving me stuff and expect me to be okay with all of it, Slade. That's now how a relationship works."

I roll my eyes. "Alright, you want me to treat you the same way you treat me, Isabella? We can play that game. I don't want you to open your mouth unless it's to moan my name, choke on my dick, or ask me to make you cum," I say before dragging the zipper of her dress down.

The fabric puddles around her and she moans as the cold air hits her sensitive skin. Goosebumps cover every inch of her body and she brings her arms up to hide herself from me. I pull her to me and slide my hand down to her pussy.

"Tsk, tsk, tsk, can never be too wet can you Isabella?" I whisper in her ear.

I rub her clit in circles before shoving my finger inside her with force.

"Slade!" she moans, holding my wrist as I work my finger in and out of her.

"You're fucking soaked, *avtor*. You're a fucking slut for me, aren't you?"

"Oh my god." She turns around and wraps her arms around my neck, pulling me down so I can kiss her.

I can't resist having her lips on mine so I lean down and my mouth covers hers. My tongue immediately slips inside her mouth and the kiss turns from clean and slow to sloppy and desperate. Our teeth clash. Breaths hitch. Every second tastes like hunger we've both been starving from.

She moans and everything in my body goes crazy.

All I want to do is make love to her.

I want to show her the stars and make her cum so many times—to the point where she'll beg me to stop.

I'm still fingering her but in two seconds I'm about to replace my finger with something much bigger. My dick is aching and her pussy is soft and warm and wet.

All I can think about is fucking her and making her pussy throb.

I pick her up and wrap her legs around my waist, carrying her towards the nearest wall.

She tightens her legs around my waist and plays with my hair while we kiss.

Ever since I've grown my hair out, Isabella loves threading her fingers through it. And because she keeps touching it and can't stop giving me those eyes, those pleading eyes that beg me to make her feel good and make her forget that we aren't fucked up, I decided to keep it at this length.

"Fuck me, already. Please, Slade," she begs right as I slam her against a bookshelf.

"Do you deserve it? You've been a brat lately. I've done so much and you fucking give me attitude or shut down on me," I say before trailing my kisses to her chest. Wedding's over, that means I can leave as many marks as I fucking want. I use my free hand to rip my belt off and shove my pants down. I line my cock up with her pussy and look up at her face. "You want me to fuck you, *avtor*? Beg for it."

I press my tip against her opening and she whimpers, her legs shaking around me. "Slade."

"Fucking beg, Isabella. Please just do it," I say, shallowly thrusting into her, teasing her but not giving us what we both want. "Beg me to fuck you."

Her eyes roll back and she rests her head against the shelf. "Fuck me, Slade. Please, I need you so bad."

I don't waste another second.

I bury myself in her with one deep thrust, then set a brutal rhythm that makes her gasp.

She takes every inch of me like she was made for it—

and I fuck her like it's the last time I'll ever get to. I use one of my fingers on her clit, flicking it as she moans and screams my name.

Her muscles pulse and her mouth opens wide.

I explore her breasts with my hands and mouth, massaging and licking them before sucking her nipples in my mouth. I bite softly on her sensitive skin.

"Slade! Oh my god!"

"Yea, keep going baby. I'm your fucking god!" I smile against her skin.

I brace myself with one hand on the wall while holding her with my other, slamming into her with need.

With brutal thrusts, I ram inside her to the hilt, hitting her g-spot every time. Isabella screams so loud I'm pretty sure she's going to end up losing her voice.

Every inch of her body is tight and filled with pleasure.

"Slade, that feels so good!"

She drags her nails up and down my back, marking me like I'm doing with her. I wince as I approach the edge.

I swear with Isabella I feel like a teenager with how fast I cum.

"Look at me when you cum. I want you to see who's making you feel like this." I release my hand from the wall and grab her neck, forcing her gaze to meet mine.

Her eyes are glazed with lust and she looks like she's going to pass out.

I rock into her while still playing with her clit. She

clenches around me and then releases, and does it over and over again.

She digs her nails into me, coming while tightening on my dick. I can't help but follow right after her, tipping over the edge.

I shudder and my entire body relaxes as I cum inside her.

Pleasure sweeps through my body and we breath hard into each other's space but not saying anything.

We don't need to.

We both know where we're headed.

And it's a dangerous road.

36

ISABELLA

I can feel someone's eyes on me before I even fully wake up.

Soft sheets are wrapped around me and as I open my eyes, bright light shines through the window and blinds me.

I turn my head and see Slade staring at me with a blank face. His finger strokes my arm softly, as if he's mesmerized by me.

"What time is it?" I ask.

"Who cares?" he says before wrapping his arm around my waist and pulling me closer. "I'm not done with you yet."

I put my hands on his chest. "Slade, no. You went at it with me like three times last night. I'm sore." I groan as he moves me on top of him and makes me sit on his dick, his erection poking me through my underwear.

"I can make it better, *avtor*," he whispers as he leans forward and latches his lips onto my breast.

My boobs feel sore and bruised from his attack on them last night.

He is insatiable it seems.

I know without looking at my chest that I have marks everywhere because of him.

When he bites the skin on the side of my boob I whimper from the pain and then moan when he licks and sucks the spot.

"God, I love the noises you make," he mumbles against my skin. "You're so responsive to me. I can do the littlest thing to you and you come undone."

"Slade," I groan and push away from him and cover myself with the sheets.

He glares at me before whipping the sheets away from my chest. His eyes lock on my boobs and the glare disappears.

He's such a boy.

His fingers touch the marks on my body. He looks so fascinated with every hickey and bite mark.

"Did you ever truly like me Slade?" I ask, unable to stop myself.

It's a question I've been wanting to ask for a while now because it's all I can think about.

Was I just a pawn he wanted to use for his own pleasure?

Did he marry me to save me?

None of what he's doing makes any sense so it only leads me to wonder.

Slade's hand trails up my arm and he grabs a hold of my neck and pulls me closer to him. "If only you knew the things I would do for you. The lengths I would go for you. I don't just like you, Isabella."

Before I can question him he claims my lips.

I always love how Slade kisses me.

It's like he demands my attention when he puts his lips on mine and only wants me to focus on him, only ever him.

Slade isn't the type of person to want to share attention.

And he shows that through his kisses.

He moves my underwear to the side and feels how wet I am. "Mmmm, you're always wet for me, *avtor*." He groans.

"Slade. I feel so sore," I whimper before I get off of him and run away to the bathroom.

When I first saw this bedroom, I was so in awe over it.

This room matches Slade so well with all of the black accents and décor.

His bathroom is huge. There is a bath and separate shower that is probably bigger than my closet at the apartment. There are two sinks and a toilet at the far end. His floors are black marble which makes it look so luxurious.

Even though there is so much room in here, I can't run very far.

I go into the shower, hearing Slade coming behind me.

Before I can close the shower door he stops me and steps in, towering over me.

"Wait-" He cuts me off by kissing me and pushing me against the wall, knocking the air out of my lungs.

He turns the shower on and I yelp from how cold it is. He protects me from the water while still kissing me, running his hands over my breasts and down to my hips.

"Keep running, Isabella, it only makes me want you more."

I try to fight by pushing him away and punching his chest, but he keeps touching me, making my body melt and want to give in.

His fingers spread my pussy and he plays with my clit before his fingers slip inside me, deep and unrelenting, curling exactly where I need them.

I moan and go on my tippy toes as he hits my g-spot. "Slade, please."

"Please, what? You want me to make you cum, my *malen'kiy avtor?*"

I shake my head, not wanting to say it.

His hand grabs my throat and he moves a finger to press down on my clit, punishingly. "Say you want me to make you cum. I want to hear you."

"No, I can't," I say, whimpering and grinding against his fingers. "Please, Slade."

His lips hover over my ear as he says, "I'll fucking tie you to the bed and edge you until you fucking beg, Isabella. Don't test me."

He pinches my clit and I scream.

"Okay, please! I want to cum, Slade!"

"Eto moya khoroshaya devochka," he says before ripping his fingers out of me. "Get on your knees."

My mouth parts.

He just made me beg him to make me cum and now he wants me to suck him off?

Does he have mood swings or something?

"What-"

"I don't think I made myself clear. Kneel," Slade demands. I keep my eyes on him as I get on my knees. "Because you made me wait, I'm making you wait." He holds his dick and gives it one long stroke before pressing the tip to my mouth. "Open."

I part my lips slowly, as he slides into my mouth and his dick hits the back of my throat, making me gag.

I look up at him and his brows are furrowed as he stares down at me with lust. His hand grabs my hair as he pushes my head back and forth on his dick. "Fuck, Isabella, your fucking mouth."

My core is pulsing with need and all I can think about

is him slamming deep inside me and fucking me the way he always does.

Rough. Unrelenting.

Like he owns every inch of me. I ignore how bad my body wants him and lock eyes with Slade as he keeps thrusting into me.

I can't breathe or even think when he speeds up his pace, his hand gripping my hair tighter.

I wouldn't be surprised if he pulled out some strands.

Tears swell in my eyes and I stare up at him, pleading for him to give me mercy and just start fucking me.

His cock is hard, swelling with need after each thrust. He hits the back of my throat, repeatedly, not giving me a break.

My thighs quiver.

I want him inside me.

He pulls out as if he can hear me. "Fuck, I need you."

He pulls me up by my hair and picks me up to wrap my legs around his narrow waist.

Slade slams into me in one go and my walls clench around him tightly and the pain from being sore feels good with the pleasure of him inside me.

"Oh my god!" I moan in pain.

I gasp as he fully sheaths himself inside me.

"I'm going to fuck you and you're going to cry for me, *avtor*."

No matter how many times Slade is inside me, I'll never get used to him.

Pleasure and pain spark and tangle in my body and my orgasm builds with every thrust.

He's so perfectly big and thick and reaches every part of me that no one else can.

Literally and figuratively.

I get addicted with every touch from him no matter how many times he puts his hand or lips on me.

He grabs the back of my neck and punishes me with a harsh kiss. His lips press against mine and he explores my mouth with his tongue. My eyes roll to the back of my head and my core tingles as I get closer to the edge.

We're both wet and dripping from the shower.

He is sliding his hands all over my body as water drips down from the both of us. Steam is in the air from how hot the water is pouring on us.

Slade hits my sensitive spot, again and again, not giving me a break.

I'm so close and am so sore from how many times this man has made me cum in the last 12 hours. His dick tenses as I clench around him.

I know his release is coming soon.

I know when he is about to cum because he always tenses a few seconds before. Then I feel his veins pumping with blood before he spills inside me.

Slade groans as he empties his seed inside me and he presses his face against my shoulder while moving slowly.

I can feel his fast and erratic heart beat slow down as he stops his thrusts and just rests inside me.

No matter how hard I try to make myself see the bad in Slade and hate him, my body and heart never can.

It's like they both already have fallen for the devil while my mind is the only thing holding out.

Slade is an addiction I can't step away from.

He's a craving and a need even though he's the last thing I should want.

Slade pulls out of me with a groan and his seed drips from my pussy. Our mixed together cum runs down my leg.

"You can't keep coming inside me, Slade," I say, making Slade glare at me with those dark eyes. "I can't have kids right now. Not when we should fix what's happening between us."

Slade licks his lips and nods slowly before towering over me. "You're going to be carrying all of my kids, Isabella. Whether you like me or not, I know what this wants." He points to my chest. "I'm not going to listen to what's up here." He motions to my head. "Because everything that is telling me is a bunch of bullshit. I know what you really want. You're just scared," Slade says before walking out of the bathroom.

37

ISABELLA

For the past four days, Slade and I have been staying at his house.

His siblings don't drop by and neither does his mom.

We cook together and read together.

We lay down in bed and sometimes do nothing but talk.

There is tension between Slade and I and I can feel it and I'm sure he can too.

I don't tell him how much I miss Grams or that I want to leave and he doesn't tell me how he'll do anything to keep me here.

There is a boundary that we've set for each other but it does feel like something is missing.

He keeps cumming inside me. No matter how much I tell him not to, he still does it and doesn't care.

He's crazy.

It's like he's trying to trap me and make sure I stay stuck with him.

We've maybe had one argument since I got here and that was about how I wanted to go out and explore.

He got mad at me because I was putting myself in danger by wanting to leave. The black hooded man is still out there. I asked Slade about him and all he said was that his name is Georgino. The name doesn't sound familiar and I don't know why this man would want to hurt me.

I don't know what his mission is or what he wants to accomplish.

All I know is that he wants me because of my father.

But after my argument with Slade yesterday, he said I could go to a local bookstore today with Angel and a guard.

When he mentioned Angel I was shocked because I thought she didn't like me.

He told me she likes reading so she would want to come and it would give us a chance to talk and possibly become closer.

I walk down the hall from the foyer to Slade's office.

I've been in here once when Slade was giving me a real tour and showing me everything in the house.

The library is by far my favorite room. There is a large window above the shelves that gives you a beautiful view of the backyard and everything beyond it.

Slade built a beautiful house and you can tell it's his vibe.

I knock on the closed office door and hear him say, "*Voydite.*"

Which means come in in Russian.

He's been speaking to me in Russian a little bit more.

Small demands or sayings.

I walk in and he is behind his desk looking through files.

He lifts his head up and his eyes catch mine.

He always stares at me so intensely that I feel nervous when standing in front of him.

Slade puts his files into a folder and he sets it to the side before beckoning me with his fingers. "*Prikhodit'.*"

I do as he says and walk towards him. When I get close enough he wraps his arms around my waist and places me on his lap.

"You're still going to the book store today?" he asks. "Fuck, you smell good. I'm tempted to make you stay." He presses a soft, teasing kiss to my neck. "Vanilla and fucking roses."

"Yea. Angel is already here, waiting for me in the car," I say, resting my hands on his arm wrapped around me.

"Okay." He leans away from my neck and stares up at me. "Call me if you need anything. I'll be here with Landon and Ryker."

He presses his lips to mine softly before thrusting his tongue in and devouring me.

I slide my arm around his neck and lean into the kiss, not getting enough of him.

I don't think I ever will.

"And tomorrow, me and you are going on a date," he mumbles against my lips.

I lean away, smiling. "Really?"

Slade nods. "Yes. You will love it, trust me." He pats my thigh. "Now go before I make you stay." I kiss him, helping myself, showing him how happy a simple date makes me.

I've never been on a date before and the fact that Slade, a brooding serial killer wants to take me out, gets me excited.

I stroll out the front door and a black Cullinan is parked out in the driveway. The guard stands outside the door and when I walk up to him he greets me before opening the door.

Angel is on her phone when I get inside the car.

"Hi," I say softly, trying my best to be nice even though she is the complete opposite.

She turns her head and smiles. "Hey. I didn't know you were a bookworm." She pockets her phone and gives me her attention.

Angel seems like such a completely different person from the one I met when I first got here.

"Yea. I'm an author so books are my specialty."

"Slade never told me any of this. Honestly it's hard to find girls to hang out with who like books, especially since I rarely talk to anyone at school. I'm careful with the type of people who I hang out with," she says and I feel like I'm getting whiplash with how she's acting with me.

We talk a little more throughout the drive to the bookstore.

I'm trying not to be in awe because of the car we're in.

I'm not used to the nice houses and nice cars, or the grand wedding I had. I was never poor or anything and I'm grateful for the things I have but then I look at Slade's lifestyle and realize how far money can take you and that there are different levels to wealth.

The bookstore we go to has some Russian name so I don't know what kind of books it will have.

Angel says that this is her favorite one to shop at whenever she needs new books. They have a good English section but she reads almost all of her books in Russian. If they don't have the book in Russian that's when she'll get the English copy since there are good English books she said.

This bookstore isn't huge. It's a nice, small, cozy shop. They have a café in this shop which I love since it would be a perfect place to read books while having a cup of coffee or a pastry.

"What kinds of books do you read?" I ask Angel, trying to make conversation as we look at books.

I learned that the guard who is watching over us today is named Boris and he has been a trusted guard of Angel for a while now.

He is just following us around while also keeping his eyes peeled at everything around us.

"I mostly like romance books. Mystery and thriller are good too but I'm a true romance reader at heart."

"I have a friend who writes dark romance books. I wonder if you've read any from her."

"What's her pen name?"

"Rebecca Grim."

Angel's eyes light up and she smiles before nodding. "Yes, I have a few of her books. She writes really good plots. I sometimes get bored of romance stories and I wish there was a little action in them and her books give me just that."

"She's great. I love her books. I rarely read romance but hers I've always been a fan of."

"What kind of books do you like reading?"

"Probably the same as you. I mostly write psychological thrillers but I do love a good romance from time to time. I think a lot of people do because they wish to have the kind of love that exists in books."

"Oh my god! Yessss! I totally agree with you. I love my

boyfriend and he does a lot for me but god, the things I would do for a fictional boyfriend."

I almost laugh because of how ironic that is.

Slade reminds me a little of a fictional book boyfriend.

I mean I technically wrote about him as if he was a fictional character in my book. A lot of girls want a guy like Slade to spend their whole life with.

Slade has a dark and mysterious aura to him. He has tattoos, muscles on every part of his perfect body, his hair is not too short or too long. He's rich and has a possessive personality that girls would die for. And let's not forget about the scar that makes him look deadly.

Not to mention he kills people which tends to happen a lot in dark romance books.

"I find it ironic how you live this life and still want a badass fictional boyfriend," I say.

"I'm pretty sure for every reader, no matter who you are or what kind of life you live, books will always be better than real life. You don't have to think in books because it's fiction and in a fictional world, there are no consequences," Angel explains. "I love my boyfriend but he isn't who I want to marry. He's my first boyfriend and he treats me well but I don't see him being my future husband."

I nod, understanding her a little bit.

I like knowing how readers think so I can see if they

think like me or not. Everyone has a different point of view on things.

Angel and I spend a good fifteen minutes walking around the bookstore and talking.

She's actually a pretty nice person when she doesn't hate you or act like a bitch.

She tells me bits and pieces about her childhood and how her and Slade got into a lot of trouble as kids.

They were closest in age so of course they are close with each other.

"I'm going to go buy these and then I can meet you at the car?" she asks.

I nod and she leaves.

I'm not buying any books because I would feel guilty using Slade's card, even though he gave it to me.

He said because we are now married, I basically own everything he owns and what's his is mine.

As I scan the books on the shelf my phone buzzes.

It's an unknown caller making the blood in my body freeze. I slowly swipe my screen to answer and put the phone against my ear. "Hello?"

"Little Rossi," Georgino says on the other end. My heart starts racing and I look around to find Boris. He is in front of the bookstore doors, scanning everywhere. "Do anything stupid and Angel Rykov dies."

A tear falls from my eyes. "What do you want?"

"I wanted your boyfriend in jail and you dead but because you didn't listen to my directions and covered for him at the police station, you got away. That's bad, little Rossi."

"I don't want any trouble. Please," I beg but he doesn't care.

"Then you should have done what I said."

"Why are you trying to kill me?"

"I already told you this. Your dad took something of mine. So I had to return the favor and take everything from him. And I'm not stopping until I have his only daughter. If you give yourself up now, I'll spare the Rykovs."

I shake my head and tighten my lips.

I need to be brave. I can't have him see me acting weak.

"Please."

"I will get to you Isabella. I will just have to kill people along the way," he says before hanging up and a few seconds later a shot rings in the air and the glass window shatters.

People scream and take cover.

My eyes go around the bookstore trying to find Angel.

The guard is protecting her and getting her out of the building to the car.

I need to leave.

I run towards the front door and another shot rings out as a bullet grazes my arm. I wince and cover the wound with my hand.

My arm stings from the bullet and blood won't stop dripping down my arm.

There are people yelling in Russian around me and screaming but all I try to focus on is getting the hell out of here without dying.

There is only one reason why this bookstore was shot up and that's because of me.

"Ms. Rossi." I flinch as an arm covers my back and I realize it's Boris. He brings me to the car while still shielding me.

When I get into the car I feel a huge relief.

Angel looks like this is an everyday thing for her.

She doesn't seem that affected.

Angel is staring out the window as police cars drive by.

Boris gets in the car and speeds off, already hitting 130 kph.

"How are you so calm right now?" I ask, still keeping pressure on my arm so that I don't faint.

I'm surprised the bullet didn't pierce through my arm but it graze my pretty good to the point where my arms on't stop bleeding.

"I'm used to the threats." Angel shrugs. "One time we had a home invasion because of a spy and I remember my dad taking all of us to a safe house," she says casually. I forget that this is literally her life. She is used to this and knows that she's safe and protected. "But also remember, it isn't me they are after." She gives me a knowing look.

The drive to the house is quick since Boris is speeding. He is also speaking Russian over the phone, probably to Slade or Niko.

When we arrive, Slade is on the porch waiting for us.

Once Boris parks the car, Slade comes over to us and opens the door, his hands on my face immediately. "You're okay. I've got you." His eyes go to my hand that's holding my arm. "She's been hit." He gives Boris a furious look. *"Ty grebanyy idiot."* He curses before picking me up bridal style and rushing toward the house. I cover my face in his chest and try to calm my racing heart. "Are you okay?"

I shake my head. "He called me, Slade. He wants to kill me."

He takes the steps up to our room. "I won't let that happen, don't worry."

"He said he'll go after your family if I don't surrender myself."

"Shut the fuck up, Isabella. You're not surrendering yourself." Slade grunts and when we get to his room he kicks open the door and gently places me down on the bed. "I told you a thousand times already. I'm not letting you go." He holds my jaw and makes me look up at him. "I'm not letting that Georgino fucker get you and I'm never letting you go. Do you understand me?" I lick my lips and nod slowly while trying to contain my emotions. Slade goes to the bathroom and comes back with a first aid kit. "Take off your shirt."

I lift my shirt, leaving me only in my bra.

He asses my entire body, making sure there are no other injuries He sits on the bed next to me while I silently watch him as he takes care of the wound.

I wince when he presses an alcohol wipe to my arm. He stares at me with worry before continuing.

"Is this what your life is like?" I ask.

"What do you mean?"

"I mean this whole mafia thing. Angel seemed so calm in the car."

Slade shrugs. "I've had worse things happen to me. It takes a lot for something to faze me."

"Like what?"

Slade looks up at me, his hands pausing. "Like losing you." He sighs and puts the alcohol wipe and band aid down. "I feel like if I lose you, I'd go insane."

"Even if it means you'd lose yourself in the process?"

He scoots closer to me and puts his hand on my cheek. "I'm prepared to lose everything for you, Isabella. You say I'm controlling you but you have no clue what kind of control you have over me." He strokes my cheek and his eyes go down to my lips before meeting my eyes. "You have to trust that everything I do for you is for a reason. I don't do it just because I want to have some weird control over you, it's because I want to make sure you stay alive. Because I can't lose you."

I lick my bottom lip and I see Slade's eyes go down before meeting my eyes again. I don't say anything so he lets go of my cheek and works on my wound, silently.

38

SLADE

"So we know he's in St. Petersburg. How do we get this guy off our backs?" Ryker asks, sitting in the chair across from my desk.

"I don't know why you guys haven't put the girl as bait and just lured him out. Obviously he wants one thing and that's her so why are we dancing around the solution?" Landon is sitting next to Ryker, a little pumped up with aggression and adrenaline.

He's on a wild streak right now.

I shoot daggers in Landon's direction. "You know I won't do that so don't bring that shit up again. You wouldn't put the love of your life in danger would you?" I raise an eyebrow at him.

A smirk appears on Landon's face. "So you love the girl now?"

"Don't start, Landon. You're the one who fucked

things up with your own relationship. Don't bring Isabella into this mess or else I swear to god, our relationship won't save you from me."

He just gives me a teasing smile. "I'd like to see you try *brat.*"

He really shouldn't test me since I broke my loyalty to my dad before I left Russia and that was to protect myself and my mother.

I'll fucking destroy the entire world for Isabella if she wanted me too, no questions asked.

I sigh and rub my forehead. "This isn't why I brought you both here. I need you guys to just fucking find this Georgino guy for me. I'll take care of the rest."

"Why should we help you? It's not like you've spoken to us in the past three years ever since dad died," Landon argues.

It was for a reason, motherfucker.

"Landon, stop," Ryker says calmly. "We're going to help Slade, alright? It's not like this is hard." Ryker looks at me. "But Landon's right about the bait. We should use Isabella and lure him out just so we can make this quick and easy. Once we get Georgino, it's in your hands and we're done."

Fuck.

My jaw ticks in annoyance and frustration.

They both don't get it since they have never been put in this position.

Landon probably thought about it before him and his ex broke up but he's confident in himself and knows he can protect her.

The only way I feel like I can protect Isabella is to hide her away from the world and make it where it's only us two.

It's been two days since the bookstore incident. She's been staying in our room or the library, reading or watching TV.

Most of the time I'm with her instead of with my brothers but I need to get this shit resolved so that she can get out of her funk.

I also spoke with Becky to convince her to come over here.

Once Becky's done with her manuscript she'll pack a bag and I'll book a flight for her. She did argue with me and asked me what's going on with Isabella and I told her that all will be explained once she gets to Russia.

I have too much shit to worry about right now to worry about not just Isabella but Becky too.

"Okay. But if we do this I want to take precautions. I want as many of your men and my men there. I don't care if it's a waste of their time being there for only one guy, I want as many men as I can get to surround us when we use her as bait. I'll train her and make sure she's ready too."

"Finally we can agree on something." Ryker rolls his

eyes. "Are we done?" Landon asks, looking bored and like he wants to leave already.

He can fuck off.

"Yea. I've got things to do anyways." I stand up from my chair and leave the office with my brothers.

They see themselves out the front door and I go upstairs to where Isabella is hopefully getting ready.

Because she's been in a funk, we haven't gone on the date I planned for us. So I brought it up to her last night and she said she would be okay with going on a date today.

I slip inside our room at the same time she walks out of the bathroom.

I stop in my tracks and check her out.

She is wearing lacy stockings underneath a black dress.

I whistle and shake my head slowly at her. "You look..." I walk towards her.

Isabella blushes and her hair falls over her eyes.

She enhanced her curls which makes her look absolutely stunning but different in a good way.

"Hopefully that means good," she teases.

I rest my hands on her hips and pull her closer to me. *"To, chto ya khotel by sdelat' s toboy v etikh chulkakh."*

Her face turns red like a tomato as she blushes uncontrollably. "I'm going to assume that what you're saying is good."

"Trust me it is." I nod. "I could get down on my knees and eat you out right now."

She laughs and shakes her head.

I grab her hand and admire my ring on her finger.

I'm surprised she hasn't taken it off but Isabella is a good girl and she follows directions well even if she doesn't want to.

"Where are we going?"

I'm already dressed. I got ready before the meeting with my brothers because once they left I wanted to go and spend the rest of my night with Isabella.

"One of my favorite restaurants that has the best view overlooking the city." I check the time on my phone. We were cutting the reservation close. "Are you ready to go?"

She nods and grabs her gray coat from the bed.

Before we leave, because I can't help myself, I grab her by the waist and kiss her.

I lick off her lipstick, grip her waist, and grind against her. When I try to deepen the kiss and demand her mouth to open, she pushes away from me.

"Stop, you're going to ruin my makeup." She giggles.

"I'm going to ruin it by the end of the night, so it doesn't really matter."

I hold her hand as we walk outside to my car.

It's a blacked out Mercedes GT63.

One of my absolute favorite cars to drive along with my BMW M4.

I open the door for her and she smiles while getting in.

I slip into the driver's seat and start the engine, making it roar to life.

"You have so many nice cars," she says while looking at the interior. "I never thought you'd be this rich."

"I don't like to show it off. That's why I usually use my bike."

"Where is your bike? Back in the States?"

I pull out of the estate grounds, a blacked out Escalade is following behind me with Niko inside.

It's just a precaution.

I'm paranoid to a fault and just want to have a good first date with Isabella and I'll do anything to make sure that happens.

"Yea, but I'm getting it transported over here as we speak. Shouldn't be long until it arrives."

"Why did you move away from Russia anyways?" Isabella asks and I know it's an innocent question but the reason haunts me almost every single day.

My mom and I haven't talked about that night and we never will.

I don't want to remind her of those memories that likely still terrorize her to this day.

"Because I did something bad," I let out, trying to focus on driving instead of this conversation. What will she think of someone that killed their own father? "But I don't regret it. I never will."

"What did you do?"

I rest my hand on Isabella's thigh, needing some comfort.

"If I told you, you would be scared of me. I don't want you scared of me, Isabella. I'm trying my best to be good for you even though I'm not. I've done bad things. Really shitty things."

"Even if I am scared of you, you said you wouldn't let me go. Just tell me. I understand that you do things for a reason and I don't agree with you on some of the things but like I said, I understand." She nods, keeping her eyes on me.

My jaw clenches and anxiety rushes through my body. "You just won't give up will you?"

"You're the same way. You can't just keep making me tell you things and not tell me anything." She raises her eyebrows at me.

"You don't want to get through dinner first?"

"It's a first date. First dates are meant for getting to know each other."

"Yea, but not to get into the deep stuff."

"You made me tell you about my parents' death and the nightmares."

I grip her thigh and she smiles as a blush covers her cheeks. "Okay." I nod. "Not right now though. Let's enjoy the date without any family drama or deep shit. I want to have a real first date with you."

Isabella nods. "Okay." She holds her pinky out in front of me. "Pinky promise?"

I smirk at her and lightly chuckle. I hook my pinky with hers and her smile widens.

She locks the promise by putting her thumb against mine.

"I promise, *avtor*. I'll tell you everything soon."

Things have been calm ever since the bookstore incident.

I don't really go out that much even though Angel tries to get me to go to the bookstore with her. I'm just not comfortable with leaving the house knowing that if I do I'll be targeted.

I don't understand why Georgino wants me.

He said it's because my dad took something from him but what did my dad take? My dad wasn't a bad man.

He loved his family deeply and did everything in the world for us. He could never be a bad person in my eyes.

Slade said that I shouldn't worry and that I'll be okay.

Today he wants to teach me how to use a gun and also fight to defend myself.

He mentioned it last night when we were in bed. Slade

doesn't want another bookstore incident happening and me not knowing what to do.

All I want to do is go back to my regular calm life, writing books in New York, talking to Grams, and hanging out with Becky.

I don't want to bring it up to Slade because I know if I do, it'll start an argument and we haven't been arguing lately.

Eventually when this Georgino thing blows over, me and him need to have a long conversation.

Our date last night was nice.

He took me to a favorite restaurant of his before we went on a drive.

We then went on a walk in one of his favorite parks that has a lake.

Then he carried me inside the house and fucked me until I was screaming his name and begging him to stop.

I'm sore between my legs but he's still making me go to the gym and work out with him.

I'm meeting Slade at his home gym right now.

He showed it to me when I first got here almost two weeks ago. It's crazy to think that I've been in Russia for almost a month.

When I walk inside, I see Slade checking the magazine in his gun before aiming it to check who knows what.

He's dressed in just plain black shorts and that's it.

Showing off his rippled chest, long arms, and thick

muscular legs. Just looking at him makes me want to blush because of how sinful he looks.

Slade is a criminal wrapped in sin and beauty.

It's hard not to be attracted to him or his aura.

The home gym is very nice and has a luxury feel to it.

It's also really big.

It holds treadmills, stair climbing machines, arm and leg workout machines, a weight bench with weights, and a huge fighting ring.

I walk inside the gym and go towards Slade. He glances up from the gun and it's his turn to check me out now.

All I'm wearing are black leggings with a black compression t-shirt. Nothing special but the way Slade looks at me makes me feel like I forgot to put clothes on.

He always stares at me with such fascination in his eyes.

Like he never wants to stop looking at me.

Sometimes I think Slade wants to put me in a glass box in his room and keep me inside it to stare at me whenever he wants.

Little does he know, that's not how a relationship works.

"You ready?" Slade asks and I nod. "First, I want to teach you how to shoot a gun. Have you ever shot one?"

"No. I've shot a BB gun but that's it."

"It's pretty easy once you get the hang of it." He

shrugs and he puts the gun in his waistband before grabbing another one from the little table next to him. "We're going to go outside to shoot. Niko has a set up for us out there."

We leave the gym and go to Slade's backyard.

He has a pretty big backyard with a nice big pool and seating area.

Behind all of that is a big open area of grass with trees in the far back.

He owns such a huge property I can't help but wonder how much it cost him to renovate and buy all of this.

He has more money than God so I would assume that buying a house is like pocket change for him.

We get to the set up that Niko made for us.

There are three dummies with targets on different areas of their body all lined up at different distances and then a table right next to us with ear protection and bullets.

"Alright. I'm going to show you how to load and unload a gun. I think that will be harder than actually shooting."

He holds up the gun and shows me all its parts like the magazine, the safety mechanism, and the barrel.

It's hard to keep up with what he's saying about how to load and unload the gun.

He talks about how to hold it and when to shoot, and all of the safety things that everyone should know.

"Sounds pretty straightforward."

"I'm giving you the easiest gun to use. It's just a basic Glock 19." He hands me the gun and it's pretty heavy in my hands. "You just slide the barrel back before taking the first shot. To release the magazine you press this little button here," he says, showing me the button as I hold it in my hands.

I've held my dad's gun plenty of times and he had wanted to teach me how to use one but I'd always been too scared.

"What kind of gun is yours?"

"It's a Sig Sauer. One of my favorite guns." He pulls it out of his waistband and hands it to me after making sure the safety is on. He grabs the Glock from me and allows me to check out his gun. His is way heavier than mine mostly because of the light at the top. "I also have bigger guns but I usually use those for when I go on missions and need something big and quick but I always keep this one in my pocket everywhere I go."

This is the gun I grabbed from his pocket and aimed at him in the car. I definitely wouldn't have known how to reload it or handle it.

"I'm going to shoot and then I'll guide you." He grabs the gun from my hand and hands me the Glock. "Back up and put the ear protection on."

I do as he says and right when the ear protection is on he starts shooting.

He shoots and reloads the gun quickly and smoothly and for some reason seeing him firing his gun while being almost half naked is such a turn on and makes my insides turn.

He concentrates on the targets he's hitting and every single one is a bullseye.

When he's done he turns around and looks at me, smiling at my reaction. "What do you think?"

I shrug and try to hide my reaction but it's hard especially as he's staring at me like that. "That was cool."

"It's your turn now." He walks over to me and clicks the safety on his gun before putting it on the table. "Alright, so you remember how to load and unload it?"

"Yea."

Slade nods and he motions for me to go up to the target. Slade's chest touches my back, his hands on my hips and his hot breath on the back of my neck.

"I can't shoot when you're touching me." I already know he's smiling.

"It'll be a good challenge."

I do my best to ignore him and aim my gun at the target.

"Be ready for the force. It's going to recoil and kind of push you back a little bit."

I take my first shot and he was right about the recoil. I feel the power in my arms and shoulders as it shoots.

I didn't hit a target so I keep going, trying to keep my sight aligned with what I'm trying to shoot.

When the magazine is empty I replace it with another before I start shooting again. Slade still keeps his hands on me, his head right next to mine.

I probably can't hit any of the targets because of him.

When the magazine is empty I turn and glare at him. "You distracted me."

"*Avtor*, that wasn't distraction. That was just bad aim. I can show you distraction if you want me to?" He raises his eyebrows at me and I just shake my head. "Replace the magazine." I do as he says and turn around to face the targets. "Now, focus on the target and try not to let your arms move when the bullet releases." He puts his hands on mine and helps me with my aim. "*Strelyat'*."

I shoot the gun and I don't recoil as much with his hands steadying my arms.

After a few rounds he lets go and watches me silently.

I still recoil but not as much as before because I'm used to the force.

I turn around and look at Slade with a shy smile.

He gives me a proud look. "Good. You just need to be faster when reloading the gun but you're getting the hang of it." He walks up to me and takes the gun from my hand. "Now, I can show you what a real distraction is."

"What about the fighting?" I ask as he puts the safety on and places the gun on the table.

"You can try and fight me off but I'll still get you." He leans down and bites my neck before spinning me around to face the patch of trees in the back of his large backyard. "Now run."

I don't hesitate, I run.

When I get into the small forest he has, I search everywhere to find a place to hide. I'm hyper-aware of everything around me.

My breathing comes out ragged and unsteady from the run and the cold air hitting my skin gives me goosebumps.

I look around me, not seeing Slade anywhere. I take that as my cue to run more and find a hiding spot.

If I can't see him, he can't see me.

I start to hear footsteps on fallen leaves behind me making me push myself to sprint faster.

But it does nothing, Slade is much faster than I am.

He grabs my hair and pulls me to him, his front pressing up against my back. I yelp in pain as he threads his fingers through my hair and tugs.

"Got you, *avtor*," he whispers in my ear before pushing me to the floor. Dirt sticks to my clothes as my knees sink into the ground. I try to get up but he gets on top of me. "Where do you think you're going? You thought I was going to give you the chance to let you go?"

He rips my leggings and underwear off. Cool air hits my pussy and I shiver in Slade's hold. "Are you wet, Isabella?"

"Slade," I moan, feeling empty and needing him between my legs.

I take a glance at him behind me and notice he's wearing the black mask.

The same mask he wore when I first met him in the alley.

I never thought I'd be into the kind of stuff Slade makes me do.

I always thought I would want a guy to take care of me with gentle touches and soft kisses.

Slade is the complete opposite. He degrades me and uses my body to chase after his own pleasure. He uses rough hands and dirty words to make me cum.

He knows how to play with my body so well.

Pretty sure he's molding me to be the wife he desires.

Cool metal slides between my legs. "Oh my god, what is that?" I shake while Slade chuckles darkly behind me.

"My favorite toy," he says before rubbing the hard and rigid metal between my legs. Something clicks, the safety, and I realize that Slade is rubbing his gun along my pussy. "You're shaking as if you're scared but you keep moaning, *avtor*." He grabs my shoulder and pushes me down so that I'm in a downward dog position with him behind me still rubbing the gun against me.

Every time he slides it against my opening I want to

scream at him to just start fucking me already. I feel empty and only he can fill me.

I grind my hips against the gun, needing more pressure.

Slade covers my body with his and his lips hover over my ear. "I want you to cover my gun in your cum. So that every time I take someone's life, I can think of you."

"That's psychotic."

"I think the term you're looking for is romantic." He bites my lobe and shoves the gun inside me.

The gun stretches me wide and I scream so loud, I'm pretty sure Slade's neighbors can hear me.

"Fuck, the sounds you make." He pulls out the gun and wraps his other arm around me so that his hand can press against my clit.

I can feel his erection digging into my butt.

His need pressed up against me.

This is so fucked up.

I don't do this.

I can't believe I'm letting him fuck me with a goddamn gun.

"You like that, Isabella? You like being fucked with my gun, huh?" he says as he pushes it back in forcefully.

"Oh, Slade. Please," I beg, feeling my release coming close.

He pinches my clit and I can't stop the cries and screams I let out. I cum around his gun, clenching on the cool metal as he tries to force the gun deeper inside me.

"Such a good girl, my Isabella. Coming all over my gun like a good little slut," he coos on my ear as he slowly thrusts the gun inside me, letting me ride through my orgasm.

"You're crazy," I breathe out, closing my eyes.

Slade rubs his hands over my butt softly and pulls out the gun. "Don't close your eyes, Isabella. I'm not even close to being finished with you."

He throws the gun to the side before thrusting roughly, making me scream.

He gives me no mercy as he fucks and uses my body for his own pleasure. His groans are loud and deep as he hits every spot.

He digs his fingers into my hips as he forcefully pulls me back, hitting my g-spot over and over.

My eyes close and I lean my head to the ground, not able to take it anymore.

My pussy grips tightly onto his dick as he rams inside me hard and fast and rough. My pussy is dripping all over him with need as he shoves me into the ground while pounding into me.

"Slade! Oh my god!" I scream.

He grips my hair with one of his hands and pulls hard. "You respond to me so well, Isabella. Ever since I first sunk inside you."

He fucks me through my second orgasm and black dots appear in my vision.

He doesn't slow down—if anything, he fucks me harder, like he's chasing his own release through the wreckage of mine.

My walls tighten around him repeatedly as my orgasm hits me with full force. Slade tenses inside me as he grunts while cumming.

Slade doesn't stop though, not even when he's done cumming.

He shows me no mercy as he takes control over my body.

40

ISABELLA

Slade said he has a surprise for me tonight.

I don't know what it is but he's been teasing it for the past two days.

I've been telling him how bad I want to go out and just see what it's like outside. I'm scared, don't get me wrong but Slade has been giving me lessons with guns and fighting for a week now and I'm confident enough to go outside.

I feel lonely and sometimes Angel will come over and we'll read books but it still does nothing for me.

I'm bored and a little lonely just being stuck in this house.

Slade knows that so he told me that he has a surprise for me coming today.

I have no clue what he meant by that.

He is cooking lunch for me right now. He's making

me a rice bowl with chicken and other vegetables. He just finished cooking the chicken and now we're waiting on the rice to finish so he can put everything together.

"I need to talk to you about something," Slade says as he leans against the counter.

I hope he tells me what I've been wanting to know, which is what happened the night he left Russia. Every time I try to ask him about it he pushes that conversation to the side and says he'll tell me when he's ready.

I get a little mad at him whenever he doesn't talk about it because he always forces me to talk to him about my issues and problems but never talks about his.

"What is it?"

"In order to catch Georgino we need to use someone as bait," Slade says and I already know where he's going with this. "Because he wants you we need to use you as bait to get to him."

I'm not surprised since he's been training me every single day and talking me through lessons about "what if" scenarios that I knew were true.

I'm still not used to this whole Mafia family business thing with him. I still haven't fully grasped that he was born into this kind of world.

We haven't talked about the important things and that's a huge issue since we are playing house, flirting, having sex, making out, kissing, talking to each other as if we are husband and wife when we literally had our first ever date less than two weeks ago.

"What are you thinking?" He pushes off the counter and leans against the island. "Tell me."

I lick my lips before saying, "This all just feels so weird. I'm not used to it. I had a feeling you were going to use me as bait. It's smart but I can't help but be a little scared of this lifestyle you live, especially since you don't tell me anything."

"The only reason I don't tell you things is because I don't want you to view me as a monster. I want you to trust me."

"How am I supposed to trust you when you don't say or explain anything to me?" I stand up and walk towards him. He keeps his eyes on me the entire time. "I want you to help me understand."

Slade thinks for a minute and sighs. He runs his hands through his hair and his jaw ticks. He opens his mouth as if he's ready to confess something but his phone starts buzzing on the island.

I glance down at the screen and see that Niko's calling him. He picks up the phone and looks at me. "I'm going to go over the plan with you this week for the bait situation," he says before answering the phone. "*Privet*?" Slade and Niko exchange words in Russian. I just watch him as he talks and listens to Niko before hanging up. He pockets his phone and looks up at me. "Your present is here."

I smile softly. "You can't distract me with presents."

His eyebrow lifts in a playful manner. "I think we both know I can distract you in a lot of ways."

I shake my head at him. The doorbell rings and I furrow my eyebrows at him, wondering what he got me.

He motions for me to leave. "Go open the door."

I leave the kitchen and when I get to the front door I unlock it and pull it open.

"Guess who?!" Becky says with her hands in the air.

I don't think as I run into her arms and hug her. "Oh my god, how are you here?" I squeeze her tightly. "Don't you have a book to write?"

"I decided to go on a writing retreat with you." She lets go of me. "Although I wish this retreat was a little warmer."

If only she knew this wasn't a retreat.

"It works." I shrug. "But this is anything but a retreat."

"It can be treated like one but you're not making good use of it." She looks behind me at Slade. "And you, you better be taking care of my Isabella."

I glance at Slade.

His arms are crossed over his chest, muscles bulging from beneath the compression shirt.

"I am and she's my Isabella," he says.

Becky shakes her head. "No, don't start because I've known her longer. You basically stole her from me."

Slade tilts his head. "And I'm not giving her back. So give up," he says before looking at me. "The rice bowls are ready if you guys want to eat and catch up. I'm going to my office to talk with Niko about some things. I'll be there if you need me." He presses his lips against the side of my head.

Once Slade leaves in the direction of his office Becky gives me a smirk. "You have so many things to tell me."

I grab her hand and take her to the library.

Niko is bringing in her bags and is presumably going to put them in the guest room she'll be staying in.

"I know it's been a while."

"Yea, everyone at work is wondering where you are and when you'll be back," Becky says.

"I'll be back soon hopefully. Honestly things aren't as they seem right now. I have a lot of explaining to do."

"Yea, you do. Like when did Slade become rich and why are you even in Russia?" she asks as we walk into the library. "And how could you hide this place from me? I would live here if I could. Imagine how many romance books I could fit in here. It's like a Barnes & Noble." Becky is in complete awe looking at all the walls filled with books.

I take her to the couch Slade put in here and sit down with her. "I haven't been doing much writing honestly. Things have been really crazy."

"Yea. I bet," she says before her eyes go down to my hands.

Her eyes widen and she grabs my hand with the ring Slade gave me. I can't say he's making me wear it because I never take it off unless I'm showering.

Sometimes I'll hesitate to put it back on but I like the fact that Slade has claimed me as his.

It feels wrong but right.

I seriously can't pick whether to be mad at him or not sometimes.

"Since when did you and Slade get married?" Becky asks while admiring the ring.

"When I first got to Russia."

Becky makes me explain everything to her in full detail. Her jaw keeps dropping and she asks many questions, wanting to know more.

I debate whether or not to tell her about what Slade does and who his family is but I just cover it up by saying that he comes from a rich family.

I focus mostly on the stalker and not the things between Slade and I because if he doesn't tell me things for my safety then I probably shouldn't tell Becky.

But my stalker doesn't want anyone but me so she's safe.

"Wow you read and write thriller books but you're literally living in a dark romance book. I'm jealous. I wish Adrian would do those kinds of things to me."

I laugh and shake my head at her. "It's not like the books. It's scary."

"I mean the stalking part is scary but living in this nice house and being married to a Russian nepo baby seems pretty cool."

"I don't even know how I ended up with a ring on my finger." I look down at the sparkling ring

It's perfect.

I find it crazy how Slade knows me so well.

Maybe because he stalked you, my mind says.

"Well good thing I'm here for a week so you can tell me all the gossip. We're going to have so much fun," she squeals while I just laugh.

41

SLADE

I've been having some of my men follow Georgino while he's been in Russia doing god knows what.

Since Isabella has been stuck in the house since the bookstore incident, Georgino has had nothing to do besides get food from some sandwich place across from the hotel he's at.

After that he goes back to his hotel room.

I could have my men or a sniper kill him in his hotel but I want this motherfucker to suffer.

I want to be the one with his blood on my hands.

I want to be the last thing he sees before he dies.

Niko is in my office right now going over the bait plan. We are going over precautions and what to look out for just in case anything happens.

I don't think Isabella is ready.

I don't think she ever will be because I'm starting to realize that I could lose her.

I realize that I have something or someone to lose which means I have a weakness.

I was the type of person to be immune to other people. I was quiet and didn't care about anyone's thoughts or likes or opinions.

But then my eyes settled on hers and everything changed.

I felt the walls that I'd built so high because of my dad, falling and she is the one who fucking brought them down with just a touch of her finger.

I always thought Landon was pussy whipped for his ex but I started falling for Isabella, slowly, deadly, and now I get it.

I fucking get it.

"So when are we thinking about doing this, sir?" Niko asks, writing shit in his notebook.

He writes everything in there.

I have offered to give him a tablet or laptop since it's easier but he would rather write everything down.

"Next week. I want this done as soon as possible to get this shit over with." I lean back in my chair and rub my forehead, feeling exhausted from all of these meetings with my brothers and Niko.

If I'm not in a meeting with these guys, I am with Isabella training or fucking her.

Instead of doing those things, I want to actually spend time with her. I want her to write and me to read books like how we did in the apartment.

I just want a break and to stop constantly worrying.

That's all I do now.

Fucking worry worry worry.

I don't need this shit.

My office door opens and Ryker rushes in. "You know the girls left right? They aren't anywhere in the house."

I stand up and my heart starts pounding but I try to hide my worry. "What?"

"Isabella, Angel, and Isabella's friend aren't here. Boris isn't around either."

"*Yebat*!" I yell and grab my gun from the desk, tucking it into my waistband. "I want Alexei, Ivan, Levi, Ray, and you in a car. Find Isabella's location through the tracker." I tell Niko.

"Yes, sir. Already on it. Looks like she's currently at a club. Has been there for thirty minutes now."

"How did no one know they were gone for almost a fucking hour?!"

I'm fucking fuming and all I want to do is slit someone's throat.

"I'll send you the location, sir," Niko says before leaving Ryker and I in the office.

I'm about to go with him but Ryker grabs my arm and I glare at his hand on my arm. "What?!"

"You need to relax," Ryker says calmly. "You've been like a bomb ever since you came back to Russia and now that you have someone you need to protect and care for, you need to stay focused and calm, now more than ever." He rests his hand on my shoulder. "We'll get her and the rest of them but you need to bring out that old Slade who was in New York. Bring out the cold- blooded killer who I know is still in there."

He's right.

All worrying will lead to is Isabella ending up dead.

And like a switch, it flicks.

I calm down and erase all of the worries in my mind.

I nod before taking his hand off me and rushing out of my office. When I get outside I see the X6M Comp with bullet proof windows leave the driveway with Niko behind the wheel.

I open the garage, and my eyes go to my bike.

After not having it for almost two months, I'm desperate to drive this thing again.

"I'll meet you there," Ryker says as I sprint towards my bike.

I grab the key off the board with all my keys for my cars and my motorcycles.

Ryker gets into his GT3 RS before zooming off, out of the estate.

Two helmets and my backpack are on the bike. After I

put my face covering on, I throw on a helmet and put the other one in the backpack.

I turn the engine on and kick the stand before driving off.

It's a thirty minute drive to the club but I get there in ten minutes.

I ran red lights and cut multiple people off.

I passed Ryker and Niko on the way so I'm the first one to get to the club.

Why the fuck are they at a club anyways?

Are they stupid?

Angel isn't even eighteen yet.

Who in their right mind would fucking-

No, no, no, I need to stop.

I can't be thinking like this.

I need to focus.

I pull into the alleyway between the club and some bar next door. I hide my bike behind a wall that covers the trash bins. I turn the engine off and kick the stand down.

Music is playing from both places and a bunch of people are yelling and screaming.

I take my helmet off, leaving my face covering on, and rest it on the handle bar.

My phone buzzes with a message.

I pull it out and see a message from Ryker telling me to slow down before I eat shit and die.

I pocket my phone and check my gun, making sure it's loaded.

I also have more magazines in my holster that I grabbed on my way downstairs.

I'm not exactly wearing club attire but it'll do. I'm in black jeans and a plain black shirt.

There is a door on the side of the building.

I rush towards the door and turn the handle and thank fuck it's open.

Music blasts and the lights are dimmed. I push past multiple people to get to the part of the club where I can see everything.

I find stairs that take me to the top floor. I shove myself through the crowds and I try my best not to "accidentally" shoot someone's leg to make them move out of the way.

The music in the club makes me feel high.

They are playing Brazilian funk music and some Russian EDM songs. They rarely play English songs in clubs here but a good amount of people in Russia do listen to English music.

Upstairs there are chairs and tables but also a railing that overlooks the entire club.

I rest my arms on the railing as I stare down at all the dancing bodies. My eyes search every single person, trying to find a familiar face.

They go to the bar, the hallway, towards the restroom,

and when I get to the dance floor it's hard to see with the flashing lights and I can't concentrate with the loud music.

"Have you found them?" Ryker yells in my ear, resting his elbows on the railing.

"No, I'm still looking."

He searches with me quietly and after a few more faces I fucking find her.

It's hard to see from here but she is wearing a blue mini dress and her hair is in its naturally wavy state.

She is smiling and laughing and is definitely fucking drunk.

All I feel like doing right now is taking her by her hair and punishing her with a slap to her ass and a hard thrust inside her that just makes her wanna cry. I'm not going to stop until I have her begging.

She has no clue what's coming for her.

The devil in the dark.

42

ISABELLA

Some sort of weird music is playing in the club.

I don't know the lyrics or if they are even singing lyrics.

I just know that I'm dancing as if no one can see me or judge me.

Becky is grinding against me with a small mojito in her hand and Angel is behind me cheering.

She is probably the most drunk, which is ironic since she is not even eighteen yet but drinking age here is eighteen so I guess this is like her being twenty-one in the states.

It was her idea to go to a club tonight and of course Becky, being the party animal she is, agreed and pulled me along.

Slade is going to be pissed but I didn't really care.

I needed a night out and Slade wouldn't let me leave after what happened at the bookstore.

Becky is in town and I want to spend as much time as I can with her.

I feel eyes on me as I dance and I look around but don't see anything. I'm probably just paranoid and need another drink.

"Who wants to come with me to get a drink?" I yell.

"I'm good. I feel like I'm going to throw up," Angel says while groaning.

We probably need to leave soon before she starts vomiting.

Boris is here keeping an eye on us. I knew it would be stupid if we didn't bring anyone to watch us and make sure we don't die.

I leave the girls and stroll towards the bar. "I'll get one more shot of your best vodka!" I yell at the bartender. He nods and leaves to get the shot at the same time a cold wind blows against my face. I get chills everywhere and glance behind, only to see a very familiar face.

Blue eyes and a hood covering his head.

I'm drunk, but not drunk enough to not know that this is the situation I can't be in.

"Little Rossi," he says, smiling at me, creepily.

He looks much older than when I last saw him as a kid.

This was the man that ruined my life and took everything from me for no reason at all.

I suddenly am that little girl again who lost her parents and needs help or someone to save her.

"You," I whisper as my heart starts racing.

I don't feel anxiety or discomfort but extreme fear.

Every hair on my body stands on end. My fight-or-flight kicks in—but I'm frozen.

This night could be my last night.

And it's all my fault because I didn't listen to Slade.

I should have stayed home.

"I'll let you finish your last shot. You'll need it." He motions his head to the glass of vodka the bartender slid next to me. "Drink it, Isabella." I take the glass with shaky hands and throw it back. The liquid burns as it slides down my throat. "Good. Now we can get started." He grabs my hand and pulls me through the crowd of people. "If you scream or ask for help, after I kill you I'm going after your grandma and boyfriend next."

I follow him with weak legs, not knowing what to do.

I need Slade.

I need to find a way to get Slade to come here and save me.

I search the dance floor but don't see the girls anywhere.

Did Georgino take them?

Are they dead?

His hand on my wrist is tight and my hands and my forehead start to build with sweat. I take a deep breath, slowly breathing in and out.

Georgino unlocks a room, with keys he must've stolen, and pushes me inside. I yelp and fall to the floor. While he locks the door I back up until I hit a wall.

"Please, don't-"

He cuts me off with his hand on my throat and pulls me up to stand on my shaky feet. "Do you know why I killed your dad and mom?" He raises a dark eyebrow and takes his hood down. His dark hair is messy and his eyes have that maniac look in them. He looks exactly how he did all the years ago, just a little older in a way because his skin isn't smooth anymore. He has wrinkles and a scruff. "He took everything from me," he says, tightening his grip with every word. "I lost her because of him. She left me because of him!"

"I don't know what you're talking about, please!" I cry in his hold and thrash against him, trying to get him to let me go but it's no use.

He's going to kill me.

"Oh little Rossi, your dad isn't who you think he is. You think he was a good dad and perfect husband but little do you know it was all a lie. It was all a show for him."

I shake my head. "You're a liar. He wouldn't do anything to put someone in harm's way."

"He fucked my wife!" he screams in my face. "He cheated on your mom with my wife and then my wife left me. I have nothing now. She's gone and she's not coming back and it's because of your fucking dad!"

I yelp in pain as he slams my body against the wall.

I shake my head.

No.

No, that can't be.

"Please! Please let me go. I have nothing to do with this!" I cry and beg. "It's not true! It's not true!"

He throws me to the floor and my head slams against the wall making it pound. "It'll be over soon, little Rossi. Your dad is finally going to pay for everything." He raises a knife towards me but before he can take another step a shot rings in the air.

I freeze with my jaw open as blood starts to stain his shirt

Before Georgino can turn around, a gun butts his head and he falls to the ground.

Slade stands at the doorway with dark, voided eyes and a ski mask covering his face. I can only see his eyes and that menacing scar.

His stare reminds me of the time he chased me in the garage.

Like he's capable of anything.

I stay on the floor and wrap my arms around myself.

Slade kneels in front of me and trails his eyes all over

me. "Are you okay? Did he hurt you?" he asks, his voice almost sounding robotic and with forced care.

I nod and go to hug him but he stops me.

My heart cracks a little bit from the rejection. He stands up and backs away from me.

"The one thing I told you not to do, Isabella. The. One. Fucking. Thing!" he yells and walks over to Georgino's unconscious body. "I can't even look at you right now, Isabella. I'm so fucking mad at you right now."

I stand up. "I just wanted-"

He pushes me against the wall. "No! You know everything I've been doing leading to this moment has been to protect you and you just said, fuck it all! Let's go to a club when there is a fucking stalker out to kill me!" Slade yells in my face.

"Don't act like you're all high and mighty. You're just like him!" I cry, without thinking.

I didn't mean it like that.

Regret fills me.

I open my mouth ready to apologize but he shakes his head lightly.

Slade doesn't care to hear explanations.

His eyes twitch and he lets go of me.

He doesn't show that he's hurt but I know he is. His jaw ticks and he nods before backing away from me. "Ryker!" he yells and his brother comes into the room, strolling in and acting nonchalant. "Take him and leave."

Ryker nods and grabs Georgino's heavy body and throws him over his shoulder. "You need anything else?"

Slade keeps his eyes on me. "No, I have to handle something before going back to the house."

I know that something is me.

And I know he isn't going to make it easy on me.

43

ISABELLA

After Ryker left with Georgino's body, Slade grabbed the back of my neck and pushed me out of the room.

He guided me to his bike outside and told me to get on in a demanding tone that made me not want to question him.

Slade put the helmet on me before climbing on the motorcycle and riding out of the alleyway and onto the street. He cut through traffic and the drive felt long as I kept my arms tightly wrapped around him.

Now we are in the middle of a grass field.

He holds his hand out to help me off his bike. The tinted visor doesn't let me see anything, especially since it's dark outside. I take off the helmet and stare at Slade.

With his helmet still on and his visor down, Slade stays on the bike. I can't see his eyes and it makes me anxious.

Why would he bring me out here?

Is he finally going to kill me?

After everything, I knew he could kill me.

Darkness and the need for blood are in his veins.

He craves them.

The chase, the game, the playing with your food before devouring it.

That's why he would always torture before killing because a torturer or any psychopath would love to play with their food.

"Why are we out here?" There is nothing in the distance but miles of green grass and hills. "Slade, take me back to the house." I run up to him and he doesn't answer me.

And it doesn't help that his visor is down because I can't see any reaction from him.

I don't feel drunk anymore, maybe slightly tipsy. What happened in the room with Georgino sobered me up pretty quick.

"I don't want to be here with you, Slade. I want to go back home," I say as if I'm a toddler throwing a tantrum.

Slade throws his helmet off but keeps the face covering on.

Every time he has a face covering on, it reminds me of the time in the alley where we first met. I didn't know he was the guy from the alleyway until he chased me with the face covering. I saw his dark voided eyes and scar and

I immediately knew that I recognized him from that night.

"You fucked up today," he says, his voice full of anger. "What made you think that going to a club in a country you know nothing about while a lunatic is coming after you, was a good idea, Isabella?"

"I just wanted to go out. I knew if I asked you, you would have said no. Becky was here and Angel knew of a place that we could all go to, to have fun. Can't I just have one night where I can feel like I still have control over my life?"

"Not when you have a stalker following you around trying to kill you. What you did tonight was fucking stupid."

"Fuck you, Slade!" I yell as tears build up in my eyes but I don't let them fall. "Fuck you! You're the one who basically took my life away from me. My writing, my job, New York, my grandma, Becky, everything!"

"I wasn't taking it. I was just trying to protect you for a little bit until we dealt with Georgino."

"I don't need protecting. I can handle myself."

Even I don't believe that.

Slade gets off the bike and takes his face covering off, and gets in my face. "What would have happened if I wasn't there tonight? What would have happened if I was five minutes too late? What would have happened if I wasn't tracking you every single second tonight? I would have lost you! I don't give a shit if you think I'm trying to control your life or fucking kidnapping you and never letting you leave, it's better than you being dead," Slade yells, his breath hitting my face. "I started to feel things. I started to fucking fall for you Isabella when that is a foreign concept to me. I don't give girls flowers. I don't go out of my way to plan dates or protect someone like I've been doing with you. I don't fucking kiss or fuck girls because that shit repulses me but with you it made sense. Everything clicked, so I don't care if you get mad at me for doing everything I can to protect you because it better than you being fucking dead."

He's falling for me.

The fucking killer is falling for me.

Slade isn't who I thought he was when I first met him. I didn't think that him helping me with writing my book would lead to this.

How did everything come to this point?

I lick my lips and shake my head. "This isn't how you love someone."

Slade's jaw ticks and he lowers his head, looking defeated.

I fell for Slade too.

Way too fast and easy and that scares me.

After everything he took from me I'm not even mad at him. I can't be mad at him when he's kissing me, planning dates, cooking for me, taking care of my wounds, making me smile and laugh.

Even though he won't let me go back to New York, I still forgive him because I just keep falling.

He nods and motions for me to get on the bike. "Let's go."

"I want to go to the airport," I demand, staying rooted in my spot.

Slade raises an eyebrow. "You're not going anywhere but to the house. Let's go, Isabella. I'm not going to ask again." He struts towards his bike but I don't move, trying to act difficult with him on purpose. He notices that I'm not behind him so he turns his head to look at me. "Isabella, if you don't get on the bike, I won't make it easy on you."

I tilt my head at him, daring him, playing with the devil. His pupils dilate and it makes him look like a devil in a human's body. And who he wants to have is me. "Fine, have it your way. Run."

Gone is the man who was getting me flowers, cooking me food, helping me with my book, and cuddling with me in bed so I don't have nightmares.

A devil is in his place.

I don't think twice before I start running.

I'm stupid.

And a little tipsy.

Maybe that's why I have the need to argue with him.

He wants to come here, I want to go to the house.

He wants to go to the house, I want to go to the airport.

I just want to be able to think freely and not be controlled.

But Slade loves the control.

My lungs feel like they are going to collapse and I don't want to check how far Slade is behind me. He is a fast runner and is definitely close.

I can hear his heavy footsteps and his heavy pants as he gets closer.

His hand grabs the back of my neck and he shoves me to the ground knocking air out of my lungs.

Pain explodes in my chest and I flip over as Slade hovers over me. He pins my hands to the ground as I thrash against him, trying to get out of his hold.

"Let me go! I'm mad at you!"

"And you don't think I'm mad at you?" Slade furrows his eyebrows. "You have no clue how much you pissed me off tonight. All I can think about doing is hurting you right now. Marking you with my blade so no one dares to fuck with you. All I want is to fuck you and edge you and chase after my own pleasure but give you nothing. I want you to fucking cry and beg for me all night so you know how I feel."

I scream and try to knee him but he leans down and presses his lips against mine, biting my bottom lip. Blood oozes from my mouth and Slade swallows it as he kisses me.

Slade comes from a darkness that I'm just learning about.

And he's trying to take me down with him.

I stop struggling as Slade ravishes my mouth and grinds into me. When he feels me submitting he lets go of my wrists and trails one hand down my body to where the hem of my dress is. I wrap my arms around him, drunk off of the lust instead of the alcohol.

He reaches beneath my dress and his fingers press against my underwear-covered pussy.

"You love this shit. You're just as dark and fucked up as I am," he says against my lips.

"Fuck you," I yell, feeling the need to fight back.

Slade moves my underwear to the side and runs his finger over my clit. "I shouldn't even be fucking touching you right now. I shouldn't be giving you anything."

"Then don't. I don't need you," I spit out.

He thrusts two digits inside me and I moan loudly at the sudden intrusion. "You don't need me, huh? Your pussy is clenching onto my fingers pretty tightly for someone who doesn't need me."

I ignore the pleasure coursing through my body as he fingers me with slow thrusts. My hand claws at his chest and I attempt to push him off despite how good he's making me feel.

I attempt to close my legs but he doesn't let me. He forces his fingers in and out of me, going fast and hard.

I moan and scream against him while he leans down and sucks my neck.

When Slade presses his thumb against my clit, my whole body tenses as my orgasm rushes through me.

"Ahhh! Oh god! Slade!" I moan loudly as he milks my orgasm out of me.

He pants against my neck and I realize this is the perfect time to run.

I don't waste any time to knee him in the dick and shove him off of me.

I run as my dress falls back down and covers my butt and hips. My underwear is still pushed to the side, my pussy exposed, but it's fine. I'll fix it when I can.

I get to Slade's bike and search for the key.

I don't know how to ride a motorcycle but I can learn.

It should be easy.

Like riding a regular bike, right?

Right when I touch the handle of the bike, Slade shoves me against the bike and holds the back of my neck. *"Ty vedesh' sebya kak plokhaya devochka, avtor,"* he whispers in my ear. *"Mne nuzhno vybit' iz tebya takoye povedeniye, ne tak li?"*

"Yes," I moan even though I don't know what he just said.

Adrenaline pumps through my veins and suddenly I'm ready for whatever he has for me.

He pants against me, his chest rising and falling with every breath. His hardness nudges my butt and I can't help but grind into him. "Oh now you want my dick, *avtor*?" He grabs a fistful of my hair and pulls, making me scream. "*Otvet'te mne,*" he barks.

"Ahhh. Yes," I say in pain, unsure of what I'm agreeing to.

Slade turns me around and he shoves me to my knees. He unbuckles his pants and pulls his hard dick out. Precum is leaking from the tip and he squeezes the length in his hand. "Open your mouth." Just because I feel like being a brat, I keep my mouth shut and raise an eyebrow at him. He grabs my hair and presses his dick against my lips. "Open that fucking mouth before I decide to stick my dick somewhere else. I'll give you a hint, it won't be your pussy."

My mouth parts and he takes that opportunity to shove his dick all the way down my throat.

Tears form in my eyes and I gag on his cock.

He thrusts in and out of my mouth with his hand in my hair. He doesn't give me any mercy. I whimper but he doesn't stop or go any slower. He fucks my mouth rapidly, pounding into me as if it was my pussy.

My core tightens on nothing.

I need him inside me.

From his fingering, I feel needy and empty and only he can fill me.

"Your fucking mouth, Isabella. This is my mouth," he groans.

I look up at him and see his chest rising and falling. Lust fills his dark eyes as they lock on mine.

Slade is a depraved monster and I'm sure whatever he went through that has to do with sex or anything of the sort made him feel possibly uncomfortable being intimate with someone. But he's kept that dark and sadistic side in the shadows before me.

And now that I'm here he wants to inflict all of his pain and suffering on me.

I'm taking it with open legs and an open heart.

I rest my hands on his thighs, needing something to hold onto as he fucks me rough and hard.

I never thought I'd like to be used like this. It's like I'm depraved and want more.

I want him to break me and use me and fuck me until I'm a broken mess.

His broken mess.

Slade pulls out of my mouth, my saliva connecting with his dick. He pants heavily and motions me to stand up.

"Stand up and bend over the bike."

I do as he says, the seat pressing into my skin. Slade

presses up against me, grinding his hips into mine. He shoves my dress over my hips and rips my underwear off.

I turn my head and glare at him. "I don't have a lot of underwear left because of you-"

He cuts me off with a rough thrust inside me. I choke as if his dick was inside my throat.

"Fuck, Isabella. I'll buy you more." He pulls out and slams in an animalistic way.

He plunges his dick into me so violently that I cry and whimper with every shove. I hold onto the bike while Slade has one hand on the back of my neck and the other on my hip.

It hurts.

It all feels so good.

I'm so wet and my need drips down my leg for him.

The pleasure is building and building and Slade's punishing grips make it too much.

His dick is hard like stone and I can feel his veins pumping.

"Oh my god. Slade!"

"That's right. It's me fucking you. It's always going to be me."

"Fuck you!" I moan. "I hate you!" I yell, trying to hurt him like he's hurting me.

He lets go of my hip and brings that same hand down to my ass. I whimper, lowering my head against the bike.

"I'm not playing that game with you Isabella. Either

keep your mouth shut or keep moaning my name or else I'll cum and leave you dripping with need." He grunts and puts his hand back on my hip, fucking me hard and fast.

I'm scared of the bike falling over but I hold myself steady as he rams inside me. He drives his dick into me with force and need.

I can't get enough.

My body is on fire and my moan echo in the distance.

I never thought that Slade would be like this.

An animal after his own pleasure, not caring about the consequences or people in his way.

Slade was a force I never saw coming. I wasn't prepared for the damage he would do or the control he would have over me.

He wants only one thing and that's me.

"Fuck you're so wet." He groans and leans down, pressing light kisses to the back of my neck and my ear. I arch against him, feeling my release sneaking on me. "Your fucking pussy is mine, Isabella. You say you hate me but your body tells me a different story."

He turns my face so that he can press my lips onto his. His grip on my neck is tight as he forces his tongue inside my mouth. Slade groans with every thrusts and black spots appear in my vision as I come closer to the edge.

His movements become rapid and out of control before he stills and his seed spills inside me. My walls clench around him as everything goes black and stars appear in my vision.

I shake through my orgasm and he slows his thrusts.

Our lips disconnect and I rest my head on the bike, closing my eyes.

I am spent and tired, like my whole body is sensitive and numb.

Slade runs his hand down my back and slowly pulls out of me. He still feels hard but instead of going for another round he says, "Come on. Let's go home."

44

I toss and turn in the bed as I slowly start to wake up.

The spot between my legs feels empty and sore from the punishment that Slade put me through, although I can't really say it was a punishment.

I open my eyes and notice that I'm in our bedroom.

Silk sheets cover me and the curtains are closed but some of the daylight is shining through.

Light filters under the bathroom door and I hear water splash in the sink.

Last night after Slade finished fucking me he tucked his dick back in his pants and helped me look put together again. He shoved the helmet on with firm hands, then clipped it tight like he was claiming me, without saying anything, and then he drove us back to the house.

By the time he parked his bike, I could barely move my

legs from how sore they were so Slade picked me up. I passed out in his arms as he carried me into the house.

I don't remember much after that.

A few seconds pass before Slade walks out of the bathroom in a white t-shirt and black pants. His hair is wet, like he just washed it.

I sit up in the bed as he walks over and sits on the side of the bed next to me. "How are you feeling?" he asks.

He seems different.

Distant.

I can't help but wonder if that has to do with everything that happened last night.

I remember being tipsy after what happened with Georgino.

Every word I threw at Slade was sharp-edged, soaked in pain. I didn't just want him to hear me.

I wanted him to feel it.

"Fine. A little groggy but I think I just need some water and food." Slade grabs the water from the side table and hands it to me. "Thank you." My eyes go to his fists as he rests them on his thighs. He has marks on his fists that I don't remember being there last night. I reach for his hand but he pulls away. "What happened?"

He shakes his head. "I need you to do something for me."

I meet his gaze. "What is it?"

"I need you to identify Georgino. I need you to make sure he's the one who's been trying to kill you."

"Why? Don't you know what he looks like?"

"Yes, but I need you to identify him," he demands, giving me no room to argue.

"What are you going to do with him?" I ask even though I already know the answer.

He raises an eyebrow at me. "What do you think, Isabella?"

He is going to kill him.

He is going to do what he did to other people, to Georgino.

"Was what he said true? My dad being a bad person and cheating on my mother? Is it true?"

I hope it's not.

Every time I think of my dad I think of all the good memories we had.

I was his little princess and he wouldn't let anyone hurt me.

He would always say how much he loved his girls, meaning me and mom.

But was it all a lie?

Slade doesn't say anything, and I swear I feel my heart crack.

Another thing he hasn't told me.

Slade slides his hand on my thigh, but I push it away.

"Why didn't you tell me? You knew and you kept this from me?"

"Because when I found out, I didn't connect the dots between the stalker and what happened with your father. I also didn't want to ruin whatever memories or opinions you had of your dad." He slides a hand on my shoulder and scoots closer to me. "Whatever that cunt in there says, don't believe it. He's crazy and not right in the head. We don't know for sure if your dad did whatever he is saying. It's his words against your father's. And even if he did, it doesn't give Georgino the right to kill your family or you." Tears fall down my cheek but I nod. Slade slides his hand to my jaw and strokes my cheek. "Now I need you to look at him for me. After that, this mess will be done and you'll be safe."

Slade lets go of me and stands up so that I can get out of the bed.

We leave the bedroom, head downstairs, and pass everyone in the living room. Ryker, Angel, and Becky are sitting in the living room just talking.

When we go into Slade's office I don't see Georgino anywhere. I'm confused until Slade walks towards his large bookshelf on the other side of his office. He pulls down a book, which I realize is actually a lever, and pushes the wall.

I furrow my eyebrows, watching him push the bookshelf to the side. He glances back at me and holds his hand out for me.

Despite everything, I take it.

He pulls me through the opening and Georgino is sitting with chains on his hands that are cemented to the floor.

The walls are covered with all sorts of weapons.

Guns, ropes, knives, pillars, and other tools that can inflict damage on someone.

This is Slade's version of the red room.

Georgino is sweating on the floor with a bullet wound that is untreated, bruises and bloodied marks on his face, and a small slit on the side of his neck.

It looks like Slade already got started on some of his work.

Slade probably wants me to see Georgino one last time before he finishes off the job.

Slade lets go of me and walks towards Georgino. "You know this girl?" Slade grabs his hair and makes Georgino glance up at me instead of the ground.

Georgino winces as his eyes connect with mine. "Yes."

"Who is she?"

"Little Rossi," he says slowly before smiling at me.

Slade pulls his hair and Georgino cries in pain. "Say her name."

"Isabella Rossi."

Slade grabs a knife from his pocket and he points it right in front of Georgino's eye.

I force myself to watch Slade as he stabs Georgino in one eye.

The blade sinks in with a wet crunch, and a sound rips from Georgino's throat that I'll never forget. My hand flies to my mouth. I think I'm going to be sick.

Slade doesn't even hesitate. He goes for the other eye like he's flipping a switch, like Georgino isn't even human anymore. Another stab. Another scream. And I'm shaking —violently. My breath comes in broken gasps, my vision blurring with tears I didn't realize I was crying.

I can't tell if I'm horrified by what Slade just did or by the part of me that understands why.

I force myself to watch as Georgino cries in pain and thrashes against Slade's hold on his hair. Slade leaves the knife in one eye and looks up at me. "He is the one who killed your parents?"

I look away from Slade and back at Georgino who is crying and begging for help.

Georgino thrashes against the chains as he tries to break free.

He leans down and his breath hits my face.

He smells of death and cigarettes. "Be careful Isabella, because I might not come for you right now. But one of these days, when I find you again, I'm going to stop at nothing to destroy Richard Rossi's life," he says, gripping my arm harshly, making me let out another cry. "And the final reward is going to be you, Isabella."

He tilts his head down giving me a sinister look before his lips form a creepy smile.

"Please," I whimper, shaking my head and shutting my eyes so he can't see me.

If I can't see him then he can't see me.

"Be ready, Isabella."

Tears fall as I remember the moment he killed my parents.

"Yes," I say, basically signing someone's life away.

Slade nods and lets go of Georgino's hair. "You can go," he says but my feet don't want to move. I'm curious about what Slade is going to do. I want to see what he told me to write in the books. That must be the depraved part of me talking. "I said you can go. I don't want you to see this shit."

"I want to see."

Something passes over Slade's eyes and I'm pretty sure if Georgino wasn't here, he'd pin me against the wall and have his way with me.

Slade nods and walks over to his wall of weapons. He stares for a minute before deciding on a hammer.

He strides back over to Georgino. He pauses in front of him and looks at me. "Last chance. You already think of me as a monster. I don't want you to think of me as a demon or worse."

"I know why you're doing this Slade."

I think I've accepted the fact that he kills.

The thing that makes me mad is that he tries to control me and doesn't let me leave. He keeps things from me which makes me feel unsafe.

I want the Slade who tells me everything and lets me in.

He still hasn't even told me about this dad.

Slade raises the hammer and brings it down on Georgino's shoulder.

Not once, but twice.

Georgino tries to move away from Slade's wrath while screaming in pain.

Slade pulls out his knife from Georgino's eye and starts slicing his body after throwing the hammer to the side.

It feels surreal to watch him cut Georgino's body as Georgino calls for help. I'm watching my book come to life as Slade destroys his body.

My book feels much more tame than seeing everything in real life play out.

"You fucked with the wrong girl," Slade says before pulling on his hair. "She's mine. You touched what's mine and I don't like it when people touch my things."

Slade's sharp knife scalps Georgino, removing the skin from the top of his head. Vomit builds in my throat.

But he deserved it.

He was going to kill me.

I feel like I'm going to throw up when Slade tosses the piece of skin that he cut off to the side. The skin hits the ground, almost sounding like a slap.

Georgino's face is covered in blood as it pours from the top of his head.

You can see his skull through the blood.

I can't believe he is still breathing.

Slade looks at me with dark voided eyes, the darkness in him settling in. "Leave. I don't want you to see what's next."

"I can handle it-"

"Leave Isabella! I won't ask again! Get the fuck out of here!" Slade yells.

For once I listen to him, running out of the room and office, slamming the door behind me.

I swear I can still hear Georgino's screams and cries for help as I stand outside Slade's office door.

45

SLADE

Georgino's body has been cut up into so many different pieces.

His head is the only thing that you can tell, out of all of these pieces of his body, was from a human. If I were to take his head and leave this mess here, people would assume that it's just regular meat that someone would pick up from the store.

The room smells like shit. I'm fucking exhausted and want to go to bed, and I need a shower to get this smell and blood off of me.

And then there's Isabella.

I know she's waiting upstairs. Ryker came down here to check on me and see what I was doing. He told me that Isabella locked herself in the room and I told him that I'll deal with her later and to leave.

He didn't look scared when he saw the mess I made because he knows better.

He knows me and what I am capable of. That's why I made Isabella leave because I didn't want her to see the real me.

The monster.

The devil that my dad said I am.

I leave my torture room and make my way upstairs.

I already told Niko to have someone clean that mess up after I leave.

My team is used to what I do.

They understand what to expect when they work for me. I pay them a good amount and make them sign an NDA so they'll keep their mouths shut while doing any job I request of them.

I probably pay my team more for one job than what Isabella gets paid per month

When I walk inside the bedroom, Isabella is thankfully sleeping.

It's nine at night.

I've been in that room for almost the whole day.

I strip off my clothes and put them in a bin where they will be either thrown away or dry cleaned. I turn the shower on and jump in, immediately closing my eyes and relaxing.

Most of the time I was torturing him and playing with him a little bit, making him regret his decision of targeting

Isabella. And the rest of the time spent there was me just thinking.

I was thinking about Isabella, my mom and dad, that night, my siblings, myself, everything.

I haven't killed or tortured someone in so long and I realized how good it feels to have someone's blood on my hands.

The pure adrenaline from the kill rather than the intensified high I would get from snorting coke.

After I wash my hair and my entire body, I turn off the water and get out of the shower.

I wrap a towel around my waist and walk up to the mirror.

I'm Satan's spawn.

A devil in disguise.

My dad created me this way.

He made me look the role with the scar on my eye and act the role with the coke lines he'd made me take for missions when I was still a minor.

He molded me into what he wanted me to be.

"Slade?" Isabella says from the bedroom, probably just now waking up. I walk away from the mirror and go into the room, opening my drawer to get sweatpants out. "Is everything okay?"

"Everything's fine. Go back to bed." I close the drawer and drop my towel to put my sweatpants on.

"Is he..." She trails off but I know exactly what she is trying to ask.

"Yes. He's dead," I answer her. "Why? You're wondering if I actually went through with finishing the job or not?"

"No, I knew you would." She looks sad and almost defeated. Isabella sighs before saying, "We need to talk, Slade."

My whole body tenses and I already know where she is going to go with this "talk". She wants to leave.

She's been begging to go back to New York since we first got here.

"There is nothing to talk about Isabella."

I'm fucking tired.

All I want to do is sleep but then you have Isabella here going against every little thing I say.

My eyes feel like they are going to close and I'm going to fall asleep any second.

"Now that Georgino's gone, you can't keep me here. I'm leaving with Becky this Sunday."

I chuckle and shake my head lightly. "I don't know who you think you are, Isabella, but you don't make the rules. You aren't going anywhere. You're staying here by my side as my wife."

Isabella gets out of bed and she holds up her hand that has my ring on it. "This is fake! You forced me into this for god knows what reason. This isn't how a relationship works, Slade. We just met not even six months ago and you dragged me to Russia."

"I have already explained to you more than ten times why I dragged you here with me. You were in danger. I wanted to protect you."

"And the marriage?" She raises an eyebrow at me.

That, she can never know.

I did want to marry Isabella but she can't know why I had to marry her so quickly.

I could have taken the long route and done things the right way but I needed to get this shit over with.

I didn't want to think about my father's dying wish for me anymore.

"To protect you. You're under the Rykov name so no one would dare touch you." I walk up to her. "I have enemies, Isabella. A lot of them. But I also have allies too that would help my family if they needed it. You're a part of my family. You're a part of me so that's why I made you marry me."

Isabella's eyes start to water. "I want to go home. I want to go back to New York."

"Not gonna happen Isabella. So stop fucking asking."

I reach the door, ready for this conversation to be over but then she says, "I wish I never met you! I hate you!" Tears fall down her cheeks.

I stride back up to her and get in her face. My hand makes its way to her throat and she gasps.

"I have done so much for you. I literally confessed my love to you last night, killed a guy who was making your life hell, have given you everything I didn't even have to offer, Isabella. You're saying you hate me because I fucking fell for you?" I ask but she keeps quiet and glares at me with watery eyes. "Even though you hate me, baby, I'm going to keep falling for you because I can't help it. You're in my blood Isabella and I can't get you out. No matter how much you hate me, you're staying there."

Isabella shakes her head. "I just want to go back to my life."

"Your life is here now." I let go of her and walk out of the room, slamming the door behind me.

I can hear her crying from outside the door, screaming how much she hates me.

She'll get used to it.

She'll learn to love me.

46

SLADE

It's Saturday and Becky leaves tomorrow.

It's been three days since Isabella and I had our argument.

Three days since I killed that fucking bastard.

Three days since Isabella last talked to me.

I'm trying.

I'm trying to reason with her and explain to her and be there for her but every single time she ignores me.

At night when I get into bed and she's awake, she rolls over to face away from me and falls asleep.

When I know that she is in a deep sleep I'll pull her next to me just so I can feel her and then I leave right before she wakes up. Whenever I'm in the kitchen she'll avoid eye contact with me. If I ask her a question, she straight out ignores me.

I've tried flirting with her over text but that doesn't do anything either.

> Keep ignoring me and I'll chase you down and edge you until you're begging, avtor.

> I'm starting to get annoyed with the attitude. Drop it.

> You know, I never thought that you would start acting like a child. Not very mature, Isabella.

> You won't be so silent when you're bouncing on my dick as I make you cum.

> Can you please just talk to me?

Isabella doesn't get it.

She doesn't understand my world and how we do things here.

"What are you thinking so hard about, *mladshiy brat*?" Landon asks.

Ryker left on a work trip a little bit ago. He told us that he was going away for an assignment and not to expect him anytime soon. So I'm stuck with my fuckwit brother, Landon. He has nothing better to do in this country so that's why he's at my house bothering me. I'm surprised he's not back in New York stalking a certain brunette.

"None of your business," I mutter, as I scroll through photos on my phone.

They are all pictures of Isabella.

I'm acting like a high schooler who just got dumped by his girlfriend.

It's pathetic.

"Your face looks very similar to how I used to look."

I furrow my eyebrows. "What do you mean?"

Landon smirks. "You look like I did when she broke my heart."

My jaw ticks and I glare at him.

"It can't be broken if there is nothing to break," I say.

"I thought the same thing. Until she actually broke my heart."

I run my hand over my face. "I'm not doing this shit with you, Landon."

"What? You don't want a brother bonding moment?" he playfully teases.

Landon will never get over his first love. He still checks up on her seven years later.

I don't know what his plan is but I know he is going to get her back. The how and when is the question.

"No. Your advice sucks." I glance back down at my phone and read emails instead of staring at pictures.

Most of the emails I have are about kills or people who want to be allies. I really only respond to the emails about the kills because those interest me. Making allies and building a huge empire myself are a bore since the business side has never had my attention.

It was all about the killing and the action.

Ryker is good with the business side of things.

He never likes getting his hands dirty.

So it's surprising he is going on a long trip for a mission.

I'm good with killing, better than my brothers.

My dad trained me to be the way I am while he left Landon off to the side since he's the middle child and then Ryker, he taught all of the important stuff like tactics when it comes to business, how to be sneaky, which organizations to look out for.

Landon surprisingly is good with killing and business even though he wasn't taught anything by our dad. So, I guess my dad not focusing on Landon benefited Landon.

Landon is smart but he's also fucking annoying.

"Let her go, Slade."

I look up at Landon, glaring daggers at him. If looks could kill, he'd be at the bottom of the ocean. "What did you just say to me?"

"Let. Her. Go," he says slowly, making sure I hear every word. "Let her go. Give her the time away from you that she wants. Give her space."

I stand from my desk as I pull my gun out of my waistband. I aim it at him, but Landon doesn't look affected.

He has a blank face as if this is just another tantrum I'm pulling.

"Leave before I fucking shoot you for suggesting that."

"You forget that I had to let the love of my life go." Landon tilts his head. "I had to let her go because if I didn't she would have hated me. I would have had no chance of winning her. You're playing at this all wrong." Landon walks towards me, grabs the gun, and sets it down on the desk. "You want her to love you? Want her to want you? Then let her go, Slade."

My jaw clenches and my entire body feels like it's going to erupt.

I don't want to fucking let her go.

I found the one person I actually care about and fell for her and now Landon is telling me to let her go.

I nip my bottom lip, thinking.

"If you keep her here, she'll hate you. Trust me. Look at what happened with mom and dad."

Out of us three brothers, Landon would know since he is the only one who has had a serious relationship.

I want to trust him.

I'm thinking about the possibilities but then also the consequences of me doing that.

"And if I let her go, what if I don't get her back?"

"You'll get her back. You just need to give her the time she's asking for. This is what love is about, compromise."

I shake my head at him.

He lost the only girl he loved and he's doing nothing to get her back

He hasn't been in a relationship in like seven years.

"Are you still going after her?" I ask,

Landon smirks. "It's her or no one. I'm getting the girl back, Slade. I'm just taking the long way to do it."

Difference between Landon and me is that I have no fucking patience.

—

I already had Niko make flight arrangements for Isabella.

Her clothes are packed and her shit is in the car.

I'm having Becky and her take my jet back to New York.

I told Becky about Isabella leaving with her and she got really happy before asking me why I was doing all of this.

I told her it didn't matter and to be ready for the car to leave as soon as Niko gets here.

I'm giving Niko the heads up right now because as soon as I tell Isabella, I want her fucking gone before I change my mind and keep her locked up here.

She's in the library, reading when I walk in.

Isabella's eyes lift to me before going back to reading her book.

I stride over to her and sit down on the couch.

She places the book mark on the page and closes her book, about to get up before I stop her.

"I need you to listen to me very carefully," I say, calmly. I know she's probably freaking out over my changed tone rather than how I usually am, desperately trying to flirt with her and get her attention. "The car Becky is taking to the airport leaves in ten minutes. I want you to get in the car and leave."

Isabella furrows her eyebrows at me and finally fucking talks after not talking to me for almost four days now. "What?"

"I want you to get in the car and leave for the airport with Becky. Your bags are packed, and I'll have a car waiting for you outside of JFK to take you to the apartment."

"You're letting me leave?" She stands up, still keeping her eyes on me.

I stare up at her from my spot on the couch. "Yes. You now have eight minutes. If you don't leave now Isabella, I will keep you here and I won't let you go."

"Why are you letting me leave?" Isabella asks, sounding shocked and almost hesitant.

"Why are you questioning it? This is what you wanted?" I glare up at her.

"But why? Why the change of heart?"

"Why does it matter?" I ask, getting pissed off. If she doesn't leave in the next two minutes I'm keeping her. Fuck Landon's advice. "The car leaves in seven minutes. You need to put on your shoes and get the fuck out." She doesn't move. She stays staring at me probably thinking it's a trap. I stand up and grab her arms. "*Chert voz'mi,* Isabella. Fucking get out of here before I make you stay. I'll fucking lock you up and never let you see the outside world."

I push her towards the door of the library but before she leaves she turns around and launches at me, wrapping her arms around my neck, and pulls me in for a kiss.

I freeze as she kisses me with longing and need.

I almost kiss her back.

Almost.

But I know if I do I won't let her go.

I push her away and she looks hurt by it, her eyes watery but she doesn't cry. Her lip trembles as she takes a deep breath and shakes herself out of it.

"I'll come back for you, Isabella. I might be letting you go now but that doesn't mean you're not mine. If I find out anyone touched my wife while I'm not there, consider them fucking dead."

She licks her bottom lip. "Thank you, Slade."

I motion her to leave with my head. "Go."

She hesitates for a few seconds before turning around and rushing out the door.

With my heart in her hands.

47

ISABELLA

"We're glad to have you back, Isabella," Bentley says with a sincere smile on his face.

When I left, Slade sent a long email to him explaining my whereabouts and how I needed time away from work to refresh and start a new book.

I explained to Bentley that I was going through some personal issues so I wasn't writing, I just needed a mental break away from work.

But now I'm back and ready to write.

Or at least I kind of am.

I tried to write last night but I couldn't think about anything other than leaving Slade and his last words to me.

I shake my head lightly, trying not to think about it.

Instead I focus on Bentley and my agent Coraline. "I'm glad I'm back too. Honestly the break was getting a little too long. I've missed working and I'm happy to be back."

Bentley and Coraline both smile at me. "Well I know it's too soon but do you have your next book in mind? I know you were talking about writing a second book on Long Lost Love. Is that still going to be in the works or are you thinking about something else?"

I nod. "That's still in the works. I saw all the marketing for Long Lost Love and it seems like people are really excited for it. I'm sure the next book will be more in demand since the first book ends on a cliffhanger."

"Exactly. We're glad you agree and are continuing the duet." Coraline smiles. "Keep it up, Isabella. You're doing great."

"She's right," Bentley says. "You should think about writing more books like this. You and Becky could possibly co-write a book together in the near future. Who knows?"

I know he is really happy I'm back because he always said that I was one of his favorite authors he took in here.

"Yea, I wouldn't be opposed to it. It could be fun," I say.

"Also, I just want to apologize on Miranda and Matthew's behalf about the whole issue that's going on in the news and what you wrote. I think they were just a little paranoid. I hope you don't take any offense to it," Bentley apologizes and I shake my head at him.

I know that Georgino was the one who reported me but Miranda and Matthew were the ones who brought it to Bentley's attention.

"No, no no, it's fine, Bentley. They were just voicing their concerns." I brush it off, making him smile.

Bentley concludes the meeting, letting me know that Miranda and Matthew are finishing off the edits. I leave and go back to my office so that I can start writing the second book.

Instead I end up sitting at my computer doing nothing but thinking of all the words and scenes I want to write but can't. The cover for Long Lost Love is done and I'll get to reveal it soon.

Things are moving along as if I never left.

Niko told me that he handled the police and everything with the book scenes. I guess Slade made it seem like these killings were connected to another murderer, not Slade.

So I'm back in New York as if nothing even happened.

As if I'm not married or I didn't get stalked or chased around by some maniac who killed my parents.

I look down at my engagement ring while thinking about Slade.

It's been a week since I left Russia with Becky. I gave myself a break before going into work just so I could digest what happened while I was gone.

I've cried maybe three times out of the week because I

felt lonely in the aparment and not having Slade around is weird.

Him not bugging me or checking up on me feels so foreign because I've gotten used to him and his company.

The way he would hold me and care for me.

Even though I wanted to leave, I never wanted to leave him.

I wanted to leave Russia and have my life here in New York.

Finish my career, not get married.

I just wanted normal but Slade isn't normal.

Stop.

I shake my head and rest my face in my hands.

I need to stop.

I place my hands on the keyboard and breathe.

There are too many thoughts in my head and I can't think straight.

This is the worst thing about not being able to write. There are so many amazing stories and ideas I have but when I have my fingers ready on the keyboard, I suddenly forget how to write.

It's terrible since I like writing and it makes me happy.

It's a way for me to express my feelings and thoughts and because I can't do that, all of my emotions and thoughts are just stuck in my head.

Slade hasn't bothered to reach out but neither have I.

"I'll come back for you, Isabella. I might be letting you

go now but that doesn't mean you're not mine. If I find out anyone touched my wife while I'm not there, consider them fucking dead."

Chills go down my spine and I get goose bumps all over my body.

I look at the title of my second book on my computer screen.

I just need to start writing.

I take a deep breath and rest my hands on the keyboard trying to think of the right words when all I can see is Slade in my mind.

48

ISABELLA

I'm at my Grams' house this weekend.

It's the first time I've seen her since I got kidnapped by Slade and taken to Russia.

Grams was wondering where I've been and what I've been up to since I haven't spoken to her much.

Things are slowly going back to how they were before Slade entered my life.

I haven't heard from him, which surprises me because I thought he would start blowing up my phone to demand that I go back to Russia with him.

Grams comes back to the living room with two cups of tea. I don't usually like tea but Grams always makes the best tea with the best spices and her special honey sauce.

"I'm so happy you're here. I've missed you so much, Bella." She puts her hand on my cheek and smiles at me.

I didn't realize how much I missed Grams until she opened the front door.

I started crying when she hugged me. I missed her scent and her tight hold.

She is the only person in this world who I can talk to about my mom.

And being in this house reminds me of all the good memories of my childhood. I grew up in a really good family unlike Slade and every time Slade mentions how horrible his dad was, I feel grateful for my family.

Sure I was disciplined like every kid but my parents always supported me and made me smile. They gave me gifts and sometimes gave me life lessons even when I was young.

Grams always made sure I was taken care of and never sick.

I would never complain about my family.

"I missed you too, Grams."

"You have to tell me what's been going on with you. How's work going?" she asks as she settles into the couch.

"Work is good. I just returned after my little getaway. They finished the cover and the release is going to be happening soon. I'll have a few signings around New York and a few other states. I'll make sure that there is a signing somewhere close so that you can come."

"I would love to." She rests her light hand on my knee.

"And then the roommate? What's going on with him, mmm?"

I can't help but blush just thinking about Slade.

But these are the way things have to be.

We're so different and although I wish he would come and live his life with me here, he is too different from me.

We don't belong together.

He kills people for a living while I write and read books.

"He's good. He actually moved out of the apartment so it's just me now."

"Why? What happened?" She furrows her eyebrows.

I have told Grams some things about Slade and I.

Like how he got me roses for my birthday and Grams always thought he had a huge crush on me.

Which he did, she just didn't know the extent of that.

"He wasn't a good person, Grams. He did bad things."

Grams nods slowly, looking skeptical. "Did you love him?"

"Did you love him?" she repeats.

I open my mouth, about to say 'no' but then I close it.

I felt something for Slade.

I liked him a lot, more than I should have. He made me feel things I didn't think I could feel.

He painted the world a pretty picture for me before it all crumbled down and burned. When I was with him I thought anything would be possible. I saw my life with him even though we'd just met.

He was everything a girl could want from a man.

So yea, maybe I did.

But I love and care about myself more.

"I know the look of love, Isabella." Grams smiles. "Was he bad to you?"

I shake my head, not able to speak all of a sudden.

"Then what happened between the two of you?"

"We just weren't good together. We're too different and have incompatible lifestyles."

She nods, understanding. "Were you with him during your break?"

"Yes."

"You were gone for a long time. You don't tell me anything anymore."

"That's just because it's too much. I don't want to bother you with all that bullshit."

"You will never bother me, my Bella." She scoots closer to me and wraps her arm around my shoulder. "You're my family, the only one I have left. I beg you to bother me."

I hug her and just stay in her hold for a while.

I pretend it's my mom hugging me and reassuring me that everything happens for a reason. There is a plan and I should just trust it.

And if Slade isn't in that plan then it wasn't meant to be.

49

ISABELLA

Becky and I are having drinks right now at a bar called Stag.

She said we should go because I've been moping around for the past three months but it's hard not to mope when all I've been thinking about is Slade.

I haven't written as much as I would like to due to all of the stress and overthinking I've been doing.

Long Lost Love was released two months ago and it's been getting a lot of love from readers, old and new.

I'm doing a signing in a couple of weeks with Becky by my side since she released her book last week.

We celebrated at her house with drinks instead of going out.

Becky ended up dragging me out of the house anyway

tonight since she is getting restless from staying in and not doing anything.

"A mojito please," Becky says, smiling at the bartender.

He nods and then looks at me. "And for you?"

"I'll get an espresso martini," I say. He leaves to get the drinks and I focus my attention on Becky. "How's writing for you?"

"It's going good. I'm like three chapters away from the ending. I should be done tomorrow. So we'll have to go out for drinks again to celebrate."

I roll my eyes at her and shake my head. She's for sure an alcoholic.

"How's the book going for you? Are you still having trouble?"

I shrug as if it's no big deal. "Yea, but I'm fine. I'm just having a hard time starting the chapters but after I get the first three hundred words written, it's pretty easy."

"What's the second book about?" Becky asks. "You never told me."

"So you know already that he saves her from the end of the first book, so the second book is just about them taking down the entire organization while they are being targeted," I explain to Becky and she nods.

The bartender comes back with our drinks.

We talk about drama at work, like how apparently

Matthew and Miranda have been hooking up which is no surprise because they always seemed close.

Bentley is changing some things around in the office so who knows what is going to be happening towards the end of the year.

I've been visiting Grams a lot more because after everything that happened in Russia, I'm realizing that we don't have forever and she's only getting older.

I usually stay at her house over the weekends to keep her company and so that I don't feel alone.

The apartment is so quiet and lonely without anyone there.

When I got back to New York three months ago, Niko told me that I don't have to worry about paying for the apartment since Slade directly deposits the rent every month.

Even though I told Slade that I still want to pay rent and that his money isn't my money, Niko said that I shouldn't worry and if I try to pay, Slade will just keep it in a safe and save it for me.

"Have you heard from him?" Becky asks, like I knew she would.

She hasn't asked me about him in a while. She usually asks me once every month.

I haven't gotten any messages or anything, period, since he made me leave.

I've seen Niko around a few times. He seemed to be

checking to see how I was doing. I know he probably reports back to Slade about me.

I asked him once how Slade was doing and he said he was fine but that's it. After that I didn't bother asking him about Slade anymore since I know he won't give me any information.

Sometimes I think about reaching out to Slade but I always end up talking myself out of it, thinking it isn't a good idea to bother him or reach out after everything we both said to each other.

I miss him but I know it wouldn't be smart to get involved with him.

"No. I haven't heard anything from him. Pretty sure whatever that was, is done," I say while twirling the engagement ring around my finger.

I still wear it.

And sometimes I sleep in his bed.

But no one has to know.

"Still? Have you reached out to him?" she asks.

I shake my head.

"Who knows. Maybe this is for the best. I mean he wasn't a good guy right?"

"Yea, you're right."

Becky and I swallow down two shots before we decide to get the check and leave.

I'm a little tipsy and am slowly starting to feel the

drinks in my system. Becky is laughing more than usual and I know she is for sure close to being drunk.

I call us an Uber to get us to her house since it's pretty late and walking through the city or taking the subway isn't safe.

When I get to her apartment her boyfriend, Adrian, asks me if I need a ride home or if I'm okay to get home by myself.

I told him I was fine and that I already have that same Uber waiting for me downstairs.

The drive from Becky's apartment to mine isn't long. It takes about eight minutes because there isn't any traffic.

I tip the Uber before getting out and slowly making my way to the front doors of the building.

It's close to eleven so the lobby is pretty much empty except for the doorman. They always have a doorman on site.

"Long night, Miss?" Trevor, my favorite doorman, asks.

"A little too long. I think I'm ready for bed," I say before groaning.

All I want to do is close my eyes and go to sleep.

Trevor presses the elevator button for me. "Well good thing you're not far from your room," he says as the elevator doors open. "Have a good night Miss." He nods and I smile before walking inside the elevator.

I check my phone as the elevator slowly goes up.

When the doors open, I head towards the apartment.

I stumble as the wave of the last drinks hits me.

I unlock the apartment door, push it open, get inside, and close it behind me.

It's dark so I turn on the lights and rest my things on the island.

There's a shadow on the couch.

I flinch away before I recognize the person sitting there.

Slade stands up and smirks. "Hey, *malen'kiy avtor.*" He tilts his head to the side. "I told you I'd come back right?"

50

SLADE

"W-what? What are you doing here?" Isabella stutters, looking scared as she backs up into the front door.

I walk towards her with slow steps, not wanting to scare her. "I told you I'd come back. Landon said to wait for years but I don't want to waste time. I know what I want and I told you, Isabella, I always get what I want."

I didn't know how she was going to react when she saw me.

I thought that a lot of different things could happen, the first one being her running away. She hasn't reached out to me and I knew she wouldn't because she was probably scared I would take her back to Russia.

Which I won't.

I'll be patient with her if it means I get to keep her forever.

"Are you here to force me to go back to Russia?"

I shake my head. "No, I'll play this game with you. But eventually, yes, I will want you to move there with me. I'll let you finish out your career and life here but the only condition is that I want to be a part of it."

She shakes her head softly. "How can you be a part of it when you have your own life that's so different from mine?"

"Does it matter?" I hold her face in my hands. "I can still take over the world and kill the devils in the dark from New York."

"You hide things from me," she says, ready to probably list off more reasons why me being here with her isn't a good idea.

"I can tell you if you give me a chance."

"You're a killer. You'll be killing and torturing people. What if the police ask me about you?" She raises an eyebrow.

"They won't. I'm pretty sure you know that I'm powerful enough to get away with anything. I have the police here in my pocket." I lean closer to her. "Stop trying to fight this. I know you want me."

"That's a cocky thing to say."

I pull her closer to me and grind my hips against her. "I can give you something cocky to choke on." I smirk down at her. Isabella's lips part and I don't think twice before kissing her so she can't say anything else. She rests her hands on my chest, as if to push me away but instead she grips onto my shirt and kisses me back. "When you left, I was so fucking pissed at you," I mumble against her lips. "You've been making me run around in circles since I met you."

"You deserve it for forcing me into a marriage and taking me to Russia." She wraps her arms around my neck.

I pick her up and wrap her legs around my waist as I walk us towards my bedroom down the hall.

"Don't act like you didn't like it." I kick open my door. When I get to the bed, I sit at the end with Isabella still wrapped around me. "You like that I forced you to do things. I make you not have to think."

Isabella doesn't respond, she just keeps kissing me as if she can't get enough.

Her hands run through my hair and I swear it feels like the best thing in the world.

I'm happy I didn't shave my head while she was gone because if I did, I wouldn't feel her soft hands through my hair.

"I hate how much I love you," she says in a breathless tone.

I grab her throat and pull away from the kiss. "Say that again."

"I hate that I love you." She narrows her eyes as I squeeze her neck tightly.

"The last part only."

She smiles. "I love you, Slade," she reveals. "Even when I hated you, even after all these months, I fell so hard for you I couldn't stop."

Fucking finally she said it back.

I lean forward to kiss her again. *"YA tebya lyublyu,"* I mumble against her lips before moving my kiss down her neck. Her hands trail to my belt, undoing it. "What do you want?"

She unzips my pants and she pushes her hand inside, grabbing my dick immediately.

My eyes roll when she grazes the tip.

This girl's fucking touch undoes me.

"I want your mouth." She ghosts her lips over mine and I give her what she wants.

She grinds against my lap while also stroking my dick, her thumb playing with the tip. My lips take hers into my mouth and I claim her like she's mine, like I'm starving.

Holy fucking shit.

I thrust my tongue into her hot mouth and groan.

Isabella grinds on me hard and tightens her hand around my dick.

I can't.

I need to be inside her.

"What?" she asks when I move her hand and lift her off of me.

I shove my pants down and pull her towards me by the

waist. I raise her dress around her hips, move her underwear to the side and finally fill her completely.

We both gasp loudly as she wraps around me.

Isabella screams and holds onto me as she grinds down on my dick. "Oh my god. That feels so good," she moans as she digs her nails into my shoulder.

Isabella and I are connected in ways so many people wouldn't understand. It's like she is the missing puzzle piece for me. She is the only one who fits me and fits into my world.

That's why when I say I can't have anyone but her, I fucking mean it.

I rest my hands on her waist and guide her against me. Isabella rides me, rising from my dick and then sinking down with a loud moan. Her hand trails from my hair to my shoulder, leaving scratches.

"Tell me how good I'm making you feel. Tell me what I'm doing to you," I say while my hand wraps around her hair.

"You're fucking me," she moans. I tug her strands. "It feels so good, Slade. I'm going to cum."

I chuckle at her. "Of course, *avtor*. You're a fucking slut for my dick." I grip her hips and pound into her rough and hard. I take her lips in mine and she holds on tight, grinding into me. "Fuck, I can't fucking get enough of you, Isabella. You're like a drug," I say between kisses.

Her walls clench around me and my orgasm slowly starts creeping in with every thrust.

My rage comes out and I feel like hurting her. I flip us around so that she is on her back. I pin her arms above her head and ram inside her fast.

She chokes with every moan and screams with every thrust. "You're gonna cum?"

"Yea," she cries and closes her eyes and arches herself into me. "Yes, oh my god, Slade!"

"Cum for me, *avtor*. Cum with me," I pant before I feel my balls tighten and I release inside her.

She clenches, her walls hugging me tightly as I slowly thrust into her, getting my release out. She relaxes in my hold and a smile slowly appears on her face.

I can't help but smile at her. I lean down and press my lips onto her. I let go of her arms and rest my body on her with my dick still inside her.

She wraps her arms around me and hugs me tightly against her.

"I missed you," she mumbles in between kisses.

"I missed you too, *avtor*."

51

ISABELLA

Slade's arms are wrapped around me when I wake up.

Like he doesn't want to let me go or let anyone take me.

His head is pressed against my chest and he is breathing steadily.

He looks so calm and relaxed sleeping.

Like nothing will touch him or hurt him.

Last night he fucked me five times. He said, "I have to make up for the time that I lost," before he went down on me and made me scream his name for all of New York to hear.

I was chased around the apartment with Slade hot on my tail and when he caught me he started fucking me from behind.

Slade doesn't just take, he devours. Like my body is a

hunger he'll never fully satisfy. With him, enough doesn't exist. Every touch just fuels the next.

It's like he always needs more.

Just thinking about it makes me want him again.

I didn't realize how much I missed him after not seeing him for three months.

I mean I did subconsciously wait for his calls or a text or just something from him.

I would complain to Becky and my Grandma about Slade but then when I saw him, all I wanted to do was hug him instead of push him away.

But there is still so much we need to talk about.

I play with Slade's hair until he finally wakes up.

He looks tired as he opens his eyes even though we slept in until the middle of the day. *"Ty vyglyadish' takoy krasivoy,"* he says, putting his hand on my face and stroking my cheek.

I can't help but blush and tilt my head. "What?"

"I said you're beautiful." He stares down at my lips. He leans up to try and kiss me but I cover my mouth. He glares and tries to pull my hand away. "Stop covering your lips. They belong to me."

"No, you distracted me last night. I'm still not happy with you."

Slade rolls his eyes and rests his head on the bed. "Why?"

"Because you came here uninvited, you never told me

about your dad, you still kidnapped me and took me to Russia, you lied to me about who you are, should I go on?" I raise my eyebrows at him.

He shakes his head lightly. "Dramatic." He sighs. "I have a key here. I pay the rent so I can come and go as I please. My dad is a sore subject. I don't like talking about him. But if you must know I'll tell you. I kidnapped you to save you. I didn't lie, I just never told you. Two completely different things."

"If we do this you need to do this the right way," I scold.

"There is no right way to have a relationship. Plus I'm too fucked up for that." Slade shrugs as if it's nothing but he shouldn't say that or feel that way.

Slade isn't a good person but I can tell he tries to be one with me even though all he's ever known is darkness.

"You're not. You've just never been in a real relationship." I stroke a strand of his hair.

"Yea, my dad fucked that up for me," he mumbles.

"Tell me."

Slade shakes his head softly. "It's not even that deep. He just made me lose my virginity in a fucked up way. He hurt my mom and that's the end of it," he explains.

"How did he hurt your mom?" I ask.

Slade bites his bottom lip before saying, "He raped her in front of me to show me how a man handles a woman." My jaw drops and my heart breaks for Slade and his mom.

No one ever deserves that. "My dad died that day and I felt such a relief when he died, Isabella. I felt like I could finally breathe and think."

I hesitantly ask, "How did he die?"

Slade's body tenses against mine. "I killed him."

Why am I not surprised?

From everything Slade has told me, he had it bad as a child. I don't know what his brothers went through, but from what I know, Slade was broken beyond repair. I understand why he would want to kill him because in a way, what Slade experienced was torture and torment. God knows what else that man did to Slade that he isn't telling me.

My eyes go to the scar near his eye. "And that? You said he did that? Why?"

"After he raped mom I came up to him to push him off and he used his knife to try to get me off. His blade slashed my eye but I didn't stop. I grabbed that same knife and stabbed him twenty-seven times," he says with a straight face, his jaw ticking. "He ruined my life, Isabella, and that's why I don't like talking about him. I don't want to give him the satisfaction that I was his victim."

"You're not. He's dead because of you." I run my hands up and down his chest trying to give him some comfort. "Do your brothers know?"

He shakes his head 'no' and continues to run his hand through my hair. "They can never know. The only people who know are my mom and now you. You can't tell anyone because if you do then his allies will retaliate by going after me."

"But don't his allies work for you since he's dead?"

"Me and my brothers are in the process of getting the Pakhan title. We have a certain deadline to finish our tasks." He pauses trying to think of the right words and I can tell that he isn't telling me something. "I already kind of told you about it. But during this period where there is no Pakhan, my brothers and I take over his role while being under close watch by his allies and other people involved with his business."

God who did I get myself involved with?

Slade's life is dangerous.

I keep thinking that every time he tells me more things about his life.

"Out of everyone you killed, your dad deserved it the most. He is the one person I don't disagree with you killing."

Slade licks his lips. "I'm going to keep killing, Isabella. It's what I was trained for. I will keep leaving corpses until I can't anymore. But all you have to know is that I will never hurt you. You are the one person I will always protect no matter what. I'll literally start an entire war if you ask." Slade grabs me by my waist and pulls me on his lap. "I've never done this before. I've never felt this way before so this is all new to me. All I'm gonna ask is that you be patient with me. We'll both learn from each other."

I poke his chest. "Then you need to go slow and take your time with me. You marrying me a week after I got to Russia isn't slow."

Slade smiles and his eyes drift to the ring on my finger. He grabs my hand and presses his lips to the ring. "Why do you still wear it?"

I shrug. "I don't know. I missed you and the ring made me feel close to you."

"I like seeing my ring on your finger. You belong to me."

I roll my eyes. "You're too possessive."

He digs his fingers into my skin and he thrusts his hips up to meet mine. "You're mine. I like making sure people don't touch things that are mine." He grabs my neck and pulls me down so that my lips attach to his.

EPILOGUE
SLADE

FIVE YEARS LATER

"**O**h, Slade! Slade! Oh my god!" Isabella yells from above me.

My cock grows as I lick and suck her pussy.

She tastes so fucking tempting, better than ever before.

My hold on her thighs is tight while I keep her from moving although she is trying to grind against my face, my nose nudging her clit every single time.

Her hands are in my hair, pulling and gripping me to try and shove more of my tongue deep inside her pussy.

I keep my eyes on her as she throws her head back and arches her back. Her stomach is swelling with our second child.

Isabella thrusts into my face as she gets closer to her release, craving it. I move my hand from her thigh to her pussy and thrust a long finger inside her.

She starts screaming and I'm pretty sure Ryland will think his mom is getting fucking murdered.

I pump my finger into her hard while flicking my tongue against her clit and it's not long before she cums on my face.

Her cunt's need is dripping down my chin and my cock is fucking aching for a release.

Her moans echo off the walls as I suck her through it, tongue relentless, drawing out every pulse of her release. Her hands let go of my hair and instead just softly play with the strands.

"Slade, oh my god," she whimpers, shaking.

When she opens her eyes I keep mine pinned on her as I take a long lick of her entire pussy. She shivers in my hold and I already know she's ready for my dick.

"Get down. I need to be inside of you," I demand, moving her so that she is sitting on my lap facing me.

Soon we won't be able to do this position since her stomach is slowly getting bigger everyday.

My dick is between her legs and she moans again when my tip thrusts against her entrance.

But of course, of fucking course, like clockwork, our son Ryland bangs on our bedroom door.

"Mommy! Mommy! I'm hungry!" he yells.

I shove my dick inside her and cover her mouth as she moans. "Too bad, Mommy's busy taking care of Daddy," I whisper in her ear.

She mumbles against my hand and moves her head away. "You do this to him all the time," she says out of breath.

"He needs to learn how to make his own food." I groan, thrusting into her a little.

She shakes her head and laughs.

"He's only three." Isabella leans forward and hovers her lips over mine. "You can do whatever you want to me when we put him down." Her lips press to mine before getting off of me, my dick sliding out of her pussy. "I'm coming, baby," she yells as he tries to open the locked door. She puts on some flimsy black pants and a white tank top that shows the dark spots of her nipples.

She's a fucking tease.

Isabella looks at my hard as fuck dick that's still standing. She smiles before unlocking the door and leaving with Ryland.

Oh she's for sure going to get it tonight.

I roll out of bed after contemplating whether I should just stroke my dick like a fucking teenager. Instead I take a shower and change into a pair of black jeans and a plain black shirt.

When I get downstairs, Isabella is cooking while Ryland is sitting at the kitchen island, eating.

I walk over to Ryland and mess up his black hair. "How'd you sleep, *malysh*?"

"Good, I dreamed of me driving a race car," he smiles up at me.

He is a carbon copy of me, as Isabella likes to say.

Same hair, eyes, and facial features as me.

Even the kid has the same obsession as me, his mother.

We're both fighting over her and the little shit is always cheating.

He's always crying for her and showing her his cool drawings. He always wants her to read a bedtime story or sometimes he'll distract me away from her and ask me to give him a bath.

He knows what he's fucking doing because sometimes he'll give me a sneaky smile before stealing her.

But I love him.

He's cool.

"I have a doctor's appointment today. Did you want to come?" Isabella asks me while she puts eggs on two plates that already have bacon and potatoes on them.

I nod. "Yes, I'm coming to every single one."

Isabella first ended up pregnant in New York a year after we reconnected.

After a lot of convincing, I brought her to Russia with me.

I told her that my sister would be around to help as well as my mom. My work is here, I'll be able to provide for her and the baby with everything, and she won't have to work and if she wants to, she can write whenever she is free.

She didn't have to work in the office.

Yea, Becky and her grandma are in the U.S. but it's not like Isabella can't ever visit them. We visit them a few times out of the year or I have a plane come and pick Becky up.

Isabella's grandma can't really travel much since she is getting old.

Isabella is happy over here though and I renovated the house that I built when I was eighteen to make it more child and family friendly.

Things between Isabella and I have been good.

I take every single moment with her that I can get.

"Can I come too, mommy? I wanna see my sister."

"Of course, baby. We'll spend today together as a family." She grabs the two plates and places one in front of me and the other in her spot, which is next to me. I don't let Ryland sit next to her because he gets her most of the day with her while I'm working. He can deal with not sitting beside her for meals. "We'll go to my appointment first, get lunch, go to the library or the park, and then have dinner with *babushka*?"

"Yes! I want to see *babushka*!" Ryland cheers before stuffing pancakes in his mouth.

Isabella smiles before she starts eating her food.

I place my hand on her thigh. "How are you feeling, *avtor*?"

Her morning sickness has gone away but now she is starting to have mood swings and is feeling tired.

When she had Ryland her hormones were out of control but what I love about her being pregnant is how horny she gets.

I swear I could be touching her thigh innocently and she'd want to take my clothes off.

"I'm feeling good," she assures me. "It'll be nice to spend time with you and Ry today."

Usually I'm working with Ryker or trying to help Landon stay out of prison.

He is on house arrest due to him killing members of the FBI. It's an ongoing investigation but at least he is out on bail.

But that's a story for another time.

Even though I'm pretty sure I did my task first for my dad's dying wish, we still haven't heard anything about who's going to be Pakhan.

But at the end of the day if I don't get it, I don't care.

I have everything I need right here.

Sounds cheesy but it's true.

All I wanted was Isabella to be mine and she is.

We have one kid, another on the way, and many more to come. She's living with me and she's happy and healthy.

"YA tebya lyublyu, avtor," I say before kissing her cheek.

"I love you." She blushes before looking at Ryland and me and smiling widely.

Our messy love turned out to have a happy ending.

I couldn't be more content and at peace.

I finally found the person who makes me feel complete.

She makes the darkness in me fade away and shines light through the cracked parts of my heart.

Who knew the girl with her nose stuck in a book would fall in love with the devil of the dark?

The End . . .

To this story at least.

If you enjoyed this book please feel free to leave a review as it would mean a lot to me.

I always enjoy reading good reviews and I always love reading reviews that have criticism in them. Criticism makes me a better author and I always love knowing what I can work on as a writer.

A simple, "Great Book" would be amazing.

Appreciate your love and support so so much!

ACKNOWLEDGMENTS

This book was so much fun to write. I've had this idea in my mind for about two or three years. I've been waiting to write this book since then because I loved the idea of a serial killer roommate and book nerd falling in love. I love Slade and Isabella's character as I was writing them.

If Ash, from Broken Beauty, and Killian, from Killian De Luca, had a baby then Slade would be it. He fits with Isabella so perfectly and I'm glad I was about to write this story perfectly for them.

It took me a minute to write this book because I had a writers block for a little bit. I forgot how to write and it was one of the worst things in the world. But after writing this hook I had so much motivation to write and couldn't stop. It took me two weeks to write this book, the second fastest book I've ever written.

I really hope you all loved this book as much as I love writing it.

I want to say thank you to firstly Ama. She created this beautiful cover as well as a few of my other covers. She's not only been a great cover designer but also a great friend. We work so well together and we are such a great team. I'm lucky to be able to call her my friend and work with her.

Antonia, we've been working together since my first published book, Ace De Luca. I can't express how happy I am that I have you to help me with my grammar errors and mistakes. Because of you, I have been able to publish books and work towards my dream, so thank you.

Katrina, you've been such an amazing friend to me for the past few months. I'm lucky to be able to have a friend like you by my side, talking to me and reassuring me every step of the way. I can't wait to see what publish in the future and see how far you go.

Britney, thank you for being so helpful with me and teaching me new things about writing and editing. I'm happy that I was able to find you and work with you. Can't wait to see what else we come up with in the future.

And lastly, my readers. This year has been a hard one for my writing since I've been so busy with real life stuff but you guys always understood and were kind and so supportive of me. I'm grateful and so beyond bless that I have you guys in my corner. So thank you endlessly for you'r constant love and support.

ABOUT THE AUTHOR

Jaclin Marie is a Self Published Author who lives in Southern California. When she isn't writing a compelling story or reading, she either spends her time at the gym or watching Disney Animation movies.

Jaclin started writing at the age of sixteen but she has always been a book lover. She started writing on this writing platform called Wattpad before she decided to publish her debut, Ace De Luca. Although that was her first published book, it wasn't the only book she has written. Since she started writing, she couldn't seem to stop and just like she found her passion.

Darkness evades Jaclin's mind and it demands to be heard. Writing darkness down on paper is something she loves doing. She makes her readers not only think about her plots but completely sob over them.

Her current works published are just a taste of what goes on inside her head.